A MOMENT PLEASE...

This book is written in British English, with the odd Kiwi idiom—if I can sneak them in without my wonderful editor noticing!

You cannot offer me enough coffee to prise that extra 'u' or 'l' from me. Nor will jam & cream scones served the correct way (jam first) persuade me to insert a 'z' when 's' does an entirely satisfactory job.

These books are based in England, Scotland, or New Zealand—where we speak British English. As the old saying goes... *when in Rome....*

LEAF & SCALE

2

THE TATTLING WHISPERWOODS

TILLY WALLACE

CHAPTER 1

Nemython House, Drake's Bend, England.
  Late Spring

THE SCREECH PIERCED Fern Oakby's skull as effectively as an iron pin thrust through her ear. She tumbled out of bed, landing on the floor in a heap of bedding as she uttered colourful curses taught to her by local lads. While her brain caught up with her body, she scrabbled on her hands and knees to grab her dressing gown. Then she jumped to her feet, shoving her arms in the sleeves of the green floral robe as she lunged for the door.

"Millie!" Fern called out, yanking on the latch.

Fear slid through her. Had her new friend's horrid brother snuck into the house to kidnap her and spirit her away to Bedlam?

Out in the hall, George took long strides towards their guest's door, his hands curled into fists and clad in only a hastily donned shirt. Fern uttered a silent prayer that the garment was cut with sufficient length that it covered his rear end, and her confuddled brain only had to deal with his exposed hairy *legs*.

Ambrose hurried behind in his patterned yellow silk banyan, clutching a cavalry sword. He had, briefly, enlisted. Until he discovered that while, yes, he did look incredibly dashing in the uniform, army life wasn't anywhere near as romantic as he thought. George had rescued him by pulling the last string that connected him to his noble family.

The three of them converged on the door to the guest room, ready to burst in and confront whatever villainy was being committed behind the solid wood. Before George could reach for the handle, Mrs Millicent Carlisle flung open the door. The young woman was clad only in a fine lawn gown with a delicate lace edge, her dark hair in disarray, and her eyes wild.

"He's alive!" she shouted and thrust out her hands.

Fern gasped at what the other woman held.

Squib, the little origami dragon, reared up on his hind legs and flapped his wings. He trumpeted a cheerful tune. Paper had been made flesh once more by the previous night's storm. He wasn't identical to his previous form. Fern thought he looked a little taller and his wing span a bit broader. The letters written with love over the paper formed scalloped purple scales that gave him a distinctive regal air.

"Squib! We are pleased to see you again, little fellow," Ambrose said, and he stroked under the dragon's chin.

"It worked, just like you said." Tears shimmered in

Millie's eyes, and passing her small companion over to Ambrose, she flung her arms around Fern's neck.

Fern hugged her back. "I am so glad."

She should probably tell the horrid Lord Drakeman that he had been right. But before she visited the reclusive alchemist, she would call on the Moray sisters. Fern needed to thank Morda for telling her that another magical storm would pass through their village. Without the rare clash of elements, Squib might have remained inanimate paper for another thirty years.

"Good," George huffed, then he turned and walked away.

"Coffee and trousers are called for, I think," Ambrose said as he watched his partner's naked behind returning to their room. He raised his hand to Millie's shoulder so the pixie dragon could return to his mistress. "George will be intolerable if we don't placate him with coffee and bacon."

"I am ever so sorry for screaming, Mr Reid, and disturbing you all. I simply couldn't contain my excitement when Squib blew warm air over my face." Worry tugged at Millie's expressive eyes, and she sucked her lips together as though she were trying to call back the screech that had so rudely awoken the household.

Ambrose patted her arm. "Perfectly understandable, my dear. We all have moments in our lives when we scream from sheer delight. Why don't you get dressed, and we'll all meet in the kitchen to marvel at the return of Squib?"

"It was a rather effective wake-up alarm." Fern crooked her finger and stroked the tiny dragon's face. "I am so sorry for what I had to do to you, Squib. It was the only way to destroy the vine without also destroying you entirely. I hope you can forgive me."

The little dragon stretched out his neck and narrowed his gaze at her. Then he folded his wings against his sides in a gesture that reminded Fern of someone crossing their arms. She had the distinct impression he was considering whether or not to hold a grudge.

"I would have simply *died* if you had been slashed to tiny pieces and burned up with that horrid plant!" Millie rubbed her cheek against his soft hide.

His mistress's distress settled the internal debate for the pixie dragon. He blinked and huffed warm air towards Fern. With each puff, some of the guilt she carried at having to erase the magical words from his hide vanished.

"Thank you, Squib," she said and placed a kiss on the top of his head. "I shall see you both downstairs shortly."

Fern returned to her room to dress and splash cold water over her face (her brain and body were still shaking off the vestiges of deep sleep), and then she headed down to the kitchen.

Mrs Bentley stood in the doorway, her favourite knife clutched in her hand. "What was that terrible scream? Is Mrs Carlisle unharmed?"

"Everyone is fine. It was a scream of excitement, not one of alarm. Sorry to worry you, Mrs Bentley." Fern had forgotten that the housekeeper might already be in the house, preparing breakfast.

"Mr Hawkins will need extra coffee this morning." The housekeeper's gaze turned upwards for a moment as though she could sense George stomping along the hall.

"I think we will all need something a bit extra this morning. Like a stronger brew of tea for Ambrose and Millie." Fern opened the cupboard and fetched the small wooden tea caddy containing an expensive brew that Ambrose reserved for special occasions. After swirling a splash of hot water into the pot to warm the porcelain, Fern measured out the fragrant leaves.

Soon, everyone was assembled. George hunkered over his tankard of coffee and held his silence. Ambrose sipped his tea and sighed with pleasure. Millie sat beside Fern, a mix of excitement and relief lighting her eyes.

Squib marched up and down the table, showing off his purple scales and flapping his wings as he glided from the candelabra (thankfully unlit, so he didn't scorch his hide) to the milk jug.

"It is quite marvellous how he has returned to you, Millie. An act of magic, wouldn't you say, George?" Ambrose teased his partner.

George huffed and drank his coffee. He preferred rational and scientific explanations for how things worked.

Fern kept her silence. There was no point in prodding the bear.

"I think his new form is more magnificent than his previous one," she said. In their short association, she realised the pixie dragon approved of compliments. Besides, she still needed to make amends for *erasing* him and turning him back into an origami figure.

"Oh, yes. He was marvellous before, but now he is simply perfect. I believe it is because I wrote a story just for us and poured all my hope and longing into the words," Millie said as she nibbled her buttered crumpet.

Story. The word bounced around in Fern's head. Another sip of coffee and cold dread trickled down her spine, and she nearly dropped her cup to the table's surface.

"Millie, what sort of story, *exactly*, did you write?" Fern half-rose to stare out the window at her garden. She needed to inspect for storm damage, but would she also need to arm herself in case a man-eating monster was clinging to the wall? A *Helix mortifera* better not have taken over her lunanavis!

"Oh, nothing like that! As a writer, I could see that my previous story had gone in an unexpected direction. This time, I considered every word most carefully before it was inscribed onto my dear friend." Millie beamed at Squib, who twisted and turned to examine the writing that covered every part of him.

That didn't reassure Fern. The Stormborne Serum had distorted the previous story to create a monstrosity. How could Millie be sure it hadn't happened again?

The heart of this story is different, she reassured herself. Millie no longer sought escape but a place to belong. The gothic novel had turned into something cosier. Hopefully.

"Perhaps you could tell us about the story, dear? So we know what to look for in case anything else came to life besides Squib." Ambrose poured more tea into his cup.

Millie blushed and cast her gaze downwards, her attention swirling within her teacup.

Fern reached out and gently squeezed her hand. "You are among friends. No one here will ever call your stories silly. In fact, I was going to suggest that Ambrose ask his editor to serialise one of them. I think you would find your audience among the readers of the *Midnight Chronicle*."

Millie sucked in a breath, and when she looked up, her eyes were wide with wonder. "Truly?" She glanced at Ambrose.

"Oh, yes. I intend to write to him today if you have the first few pages of a story I could include as a teaser?" He winked at Millie.

She closed her eyes, drew a deep breath, and her fingers tightened on Fern's hand as though anchoring herself before she spoke. "I wrote of a lonely woman and her pixie dragon companion who settle in a quiet and welcoming village. There, she opens a bookstore and spends her day writing stories that, sometimes, become the books she sells to the villagers."

Fern hunted for the hidden monster in the few details Millie gave them. It sounded...peaceful. Perhaps the bookstore shelves reached out and devoured customers who folded down pages or bent spines? "So we're looking for a bookstore? But Drake's Bend doesn't have one."

"Could it be in another village?" Ambrose suggested.

"I don't know if the magical ink works like that. The vine was transformed close to Millie, so the magical bookstore should be nearby too. After I have fed Eurydice, we could take a walk to the village. I need to stop and see the Moray sisters, and I am sure they would love to meet you, Millie, and see that Squib has been restored." Fern's thoughts turned to the other dragon, who struggled to thrive out in the stables.

The dragonet had shown some improvement since Fern followed the advice found in the journals at Wyndham Hall.

Or had it been the metal-like kelmsgale seeds she ate? Fern shook her head. Those would have passed through the creature's body intact. It had to be the fish broth that wrought the change in the sickly and lethargic dragon.

Ambrose chortled as he read the newspaper. "The season of scandal continues in London. Now they are all gossiping about Lady F and the revelation that she gave away a child to be raised by another family two years ago, and her noble husband was told the baby never drew breath."

"An odd thing to do, but surely she had her reasons?" Fern had given up trying to understand why nobles did anything. Much of it made no sense.

"Here is the rather salacious bit. Apparently, the babe bears no resemblance to Lord F, who is described as pale and reedy. But has a startling resemblance to the family's major-domo, a tall and robust fellow who hails from the West Indies." Ambrose dropped the paper on the table and picked up his cup of tea.

"If Lord F is Frampton, I don't blame his wife," George said before returning to his breakfast.

Fern kept her silence. London society existed on scandal and gossip as much as tea and cake. There was always someone being vilified for their behaviour or held up as an object of ridicule.

Mrs Bentley placed a bowl at Fern's elbow. It contained chunks of fish and root vegetables in a thick broth. "That's breakfast for our young miss."

Fern swallowed the dregs of her coffee and finished the last spoonful of her porridge. "Why don't you come out to the stables when you are ready, Millie?"

Before she headed in that direction, Fern cast a quick glance around the walled garden and her greenhouse. Fortunately, the fierce storm hadn't caused any serious damage. She would need to prune a few ruffled shrubs and sweep up all the fallen leaves and twigs, but that could wait until after her walk with Millie.

Satisfied that her beloved plants had not been unduly harmed by the weather, nor did there appear to be any new carnivorous vines to worry about, she headed across the yard to the stables.

Eurydice was awake and rose from her bed to greet Fern. The dragonet made a trilling noise as she butted against Fern's knees.

"Good morning, Eurydice. I thought that now we are better acquainted, I might start calling you Riddy, if that is acceptable?" Fern knelt in the straw to wrap her arms around the dragon's neck, and Eurydice nuzzled her face against Fern's like Squib had done to Millie. She took that as approval of the shortened version of her name.

The dragon was still horribly skinny, and it would take time to slowly put condition back on her body. But already, a slight sheen returned to her scales. Rather than a dull grey, a mossy-green shimmer bloomed at the edges. Time and health restored her hide, like polishing a blackened piece of silver to reveal the hidden glint of metal beneath.

While the dragon nosily ate her breakfast, Fern fetched fresh water, mucked out the dirty straw, and replaced it with new. By the time the stall was cleaned and Eurydice was full, Millie and Squib appeared in the aisle.

Millie wore a long, bright-blue, woollen redingote. She

bent down to stroke Eurydice's head. "I am gladdened to see you on the road to recovery."

Squib flew down to sit on Eurydice's back. The larger dragon turned to gaze quizzically at the pixie subspecies.

"Do you remember how Squib curled up next to you when you were terribly ill?" Fern asked.

Eurydice butted her face against Squib's side and made a noise that sounded much like a cat's contented purr.

"She remembers, and it appears they are friends." Millie laughed as Squib nearly fell off the side of Eurydice's back from her attentions, and the dragon caught him with her wing and eased him back onto her.

Fern shook out the blankets and re-formed the nest for the young dragon. "Perhaps this afternoon you could help me in the garden, Riddy? I promise there are no barking dogs or broken fountains in my garden, and you might like the warmth of the sun after so long in the stables."

The dragon trilled and then padded on the blankets. She settled down and stared at Fern with a wide-eyed look, which Fern was learning meant she wanted covering up for a nap. Squib flapped over to Millie as Fern tucked a blanket in over Eurydice.

Content, Eurydice nestled her head between her front paws and closed her eyes.

"Now, let's see if we can find what the storm might have created." Fern linked arms with Millie.

There was a chance that nothing had sprung into life during the magic-laden event. Millie's story might have found its happy ending in her relocation to Drake's Bend. But those were questions she could discreetly ask of the trio of witches.

Millie and Fern chatted as they strolled along the road. The two young women fell into step in more ways than one as tendrils of friendship wove between them.

"Is it true that the whisperwoods can talk?" Millie asked in wonder, referring to an ancient grove not far from Drake's Bend.

Fern thought of her visits to the old trees, who took confessions and secrets from troubled people. "It's not like a conversation, and you can't ask them questions. You unburden yourself, and they whisper gentle advice back to you."

"Gosh. Trees that can whisper, though. I've never been, but I wonder at the secrets they have heard over the centuries." Millie's writing brain never ceased to seek out stories.

"Secrets are sacred; they are never shared." Fern nudged her new friend as they walked up the path to the quaint cottages where the Moray sisters lived.

The door to the larger cottage swung open at their approach, and Decima welcomed them inside. Millie fell silent and lingered on the threshold.

"Come in, scribe, we are all sisters here," Morda called out. "You cast spells with words with as much skill as we do with golden motes."

Millie glanced at Fern. "What Morda means is that all women are witches in one way or another. We are bound together in ways men do not understand."

"But other women are not as...welcoming of me," Millie said in a quiet voice.

Nona scoffed. "That is their loss. Like our Fern, the Fates

set you on a path to find your true sisters. Come. We see the storm has restored your little friend."

Fern dropped to her favourite cushion at Morda's feet and reached up to take the old woman's hand. "Thank you, Morda. Without your urging, I wouldn't have put the quill in Millie's hand and made her write a new story on Squib."

The old witch cackled. "I might be blind, but I see clearly."

CHAPTER 2

Squib basked in the sisters' adoration as he was passed from hand to hand. Each woman exclaimed over the marvellous changes to his previous form and how much the lilac-edged scales (with a faint shimmer) suited him more than the near black-purple of his previous incarnation.

Decima poured fragrant tea into mugs and handed them around. Overcoming her initial reserve, Millie settled on a purple floor cushion beside Fern. She sipped her tea and held her silence, but her eyes were wide with curiosity as she studied both the old women and the eclectic interior of their cottage. Bundles of herbs were bound with string and hung from the ceiling to dry, reminiscent of dangling mistletoe at Christmas time. But there were no kisses under these flowers, only murmured wisdom.

After a pleasant hour filled with laughter, Fern and Millie waved goodbye to the old women and carried on along the road. They walked the eastern side of the village, where the road followed the curve of the river. Fern called out greetings to the locals they passed. The water burbled beside them as they approached the old stone bridge that crossed to the tavern and village green. A group of villagers gathered nearby, chattering away like roosting birds.

Millie halted and pointed to a two-storeyed cottage nestled in the sweep of lawn at the foot of the old bridge. "That's it," she said. "The cottage that welcomed the lonely writer."

"It can't be. That's..." Fern's voice trailed off. She had been about to say *that's George's cottage*, but the place she had known for most of her life was no longer the building she remembered.

Now she understood why the villagers were gathered on the road. Pointing. Others stood at the halfway point on the bridge, their elbows leaning on the weathered stones as they gazed at the cottage.

Fern looped her arm through Millie's and hurried her along. Built of pale-cream stone and two storeys tall, like Squib and the Boston ivy, the cottage was now transformed into something different. A bay window jutted out, and behind the mullioned glass were visible piles of books. Between the solid door and window, a sign dangled from an ornate metal limb. The purple words (that held the faintest sparkle in the morning light) declared the place to be *"Scribbles."*

Millie clapped in delight. "It's my bookstore!"

The assembled people moved apart to allow her through. Fern walked more cautiously behind. All the while, hoping the cottage didn't turn out to be a portal to Hell or something as horrible as the vine that had eaten a gardener and set its sights on Millie's brother as its next meal.

"It didn't look like this last night," one gentleman said to murmured agreement from the others.

"It was the storm. The Moray sisters said it had the power to transform things if somebody wished hard enough," Fern said by way of explanation. No need to go into the finer details of an ancient and arcane magical ink and a passionate writer's ability to bring words to life.

"I wish I had known last night. I would have wished you were handsome, Mr Alder!" Mrs Alder said to the raucous laughter of everyone else.

Millie stared up at the sign and turned to Fern with a grin. "Can we go inside? Please?"

"It will be locked. We will have to get the key off George or Ambrose." Even as Fern said the words, Millie reached out and grabbed the brass handle.

The door gave way under the other woman's touch, and she pushed it open. With a backwards glance, she stepped over the threshold and gasped.

Fern followed behind and likewise halted and stared. Twenty years ago, George had purchased the cottage for him and Ambrose to live in after they had moved to Drake's Bend. The downstairs had been their parlour, study, and kitchen. Now, the front half of the space had been transformed into a bookstore. Shelves lined the walls, and stacks marched across the floor. Wooden ladders with brass wheels waited to zoom along the rail as readers hunted for their next book to read. Bright light shone across the floor from one side and beckoned Fern closer. She crept between the stacks, expecting to find a large window.

What she found was the side of the cottage opening out into a small conservatory. A sun-filled space that had not existed in its previous form. The glass room took full advantage of facing south. Two comfortable-looking chairs and a chaise waited for a reader to sink into the ample cushions. Beyond, the river burbled and played. On fine days, double doors could be flung open to the small strip of garden that ran between the cottage and the river's edge.

Millie joined Fern; her eyes were misty with tears of joy, and a large and infectious smile dominated her features. "Isn't it marvellous? Do you think the owner will mind terribly that my story turned their home into the bookstore of my dreams?"

Only now did a smidge of worry enter her gaze.

Fern snorted. She was going to enjoy breaking this to George and watching the mental contortions her uncle would have to engage in to explain the miraculous transformation of the stone structure.

"The house belongs to George. It had a tenant up until last winter when they moved to a small farm. It's been empty for a few months, so don't fear that you have evicted someone from their home. I think George will absolutely *insist* that you take possession of it." Fern stretched out a hand and caressed the spine of a book.

"I am so happy I might just expire on the spot." Millie pulled a handkerchief free of her pocket and dabbed at her eyes.

"Don't go doing that. I rather like having a friend at long last," Fern murmured.

Millie squealed and flung her arms around Fern's neck and hugged her tight. "Thank you, thank you, *thank you*! You not only rescued me from Bertie and that horrid nurse, but because of you, I now have the most incredible place to call home. And a friend," she added shyly.

Squib wriggled free of the embrace and flew to a shelf. There, he stalked along the rows of books like a miniature general inspecting his troops.

They continued exploring the cottage, and Fern catalogued all the changes the Stormborne Serum had wrought overnight. George's old desk had enlarged. The once-clear top now held a writing set and a stack of papers, waiting for stories to be penned on its surface. A shiny metal lockbox on one corner would hold the coins when villagers purchased a book. A generous fireplace had two armchairs and a long sofa placed before it, making a welcoming space to curl up in the cooler weather.

The rear of the cottage was a sunny kitchen with a table that would double as a workspace and where meals would be taken. Beside the kitchen, they discovered a tiny washhouse with a tin bath hanging on the wall. Up a winding staircase were two bedrooms, one slightly larger than the other.

The cottage was modest, but Fern suspected it would suit the widow and her pixie companion. After a quick look at the bedrooms, Millie practically ran back down the stairs to the bookshop part of the cottage. Fern took the balustrade. It provided a short but fast ride to the bottom.

Millie prowled the shelves, pulling books at random to see what treasures the cottage held.

Fern blew out a sigh. She would need a shoehorn to get Millie out of the place. "We need to tell George and Ambrose what has happened. If you are moving in, you need to pack your clothing and buy supplies for your larder. You cannot live on the written word alone."

The other woman hesitated. "What if we walk out the door, turn around, and all this is gone? It might disappear like a puff of smoke." She caressed a leather cover as though it were a precious prize.

"The vine didn't disappear, now, did it? Nor has Squib. Magic and your story gave this place life. Unless I douse your new home with the potion Lord Drakeman concocted, I suspect it will always be like this." Fern gestured to the cosy bookstore, or library, or whatever Millie would make of it.

Squib hissed and flapped his wings at the mention of the alchemist. He dove for Millie and curled his tail protectively around her neck. All the while, he glared at Fern while emitting short, angry puffs of steam.

"Oh, I would never do that *again*, Squib. So stop giving me the evil eye." Fern bit the inside of her mouth to stop herself from laughing. The pixie dragon was fiercely protective of Millie and appeared to have no difficulty understanding what they said. That shouldn't have surprised her, given he was crafted from words and ink ran through his body as blood.

"Once we have you settled in here, you will have years to examine every book under this roof. Assuming you want to stay in Drake's Bend?" *Assuming you'd like to be my friend,* Fern wanted to add but held her silence.

"Years." Millie breathed out the word. "Yes. I like the idea of years here. Imagine the stories I could write in the conservatory, with Squib and the river for company." Putting the book down (with some reluctance), Millie took Fern's hand. "Let us return to Nemython House and pack my little trunk. You will visit me here, though, won't you? So I'll not be alone?" Worry tugged at her eyes, and a faint tremor entered her voice.

Fern gathered up the nerves bouncing around inside her and squished them into a ball. If she wanted a close friend, she had to learn how to open herself up and expose her vulnerabilities. The armour around Fern's heart cracked a teeny bit. Just enough to make a tiny space within for the other woman.

"I thought we might spend much time together and become good friends. Only if you want to, of course." Fern tried an offhand tone to hide the delicate hope pegged to those words. Her dream was like a sheet on the clothesline. A strong wind might tear it away and set it adrift.

Millie squealed, and she hugged Fern's arm. "Oh, yes! I don't feel like I have to pretend to be somebody else when I am around you. Which is probably an odd thing for a writer to say since I make so much up." The frown returned to Millie's face as she sorted through some complicated, philosophical problem in her head.

Relief flowed through Fern like a gentle tide. "I know what you mean. We don't have to hide who we truly are around each other. Nor do we have to pretend to be the perfect, gently bred noblewomen that society expects of us."

A shy smile returned to Millie's face. "That's how you know you have found a true friend, isn't it? They like you for who you are on the inside. Not what everyone sees on the outside."

Fern nodded and held her silence for once. Taking her friend by the hand, she guided Millie towards the door and back out into the sunshine. Villagers lingered to stare at the transformed cottage. Millie placed Squib on her shoulder, and she caressed the cottage's stonework as Fern closed the door. Then, arm in arm, they hurried back to Nemython House to tell the news.

"My story came to life!" Millie shouted as soon as they walked into the kitchen.

Neither Ambrose nor George were there.

"That sounds lovely, Mrs Carlisle," Mrs Bentley said without looking up from where she worked at the bench.

Continuing on through the house, Fern and Millie found the older couple in the parlour.

Ambrose closed his book, and George looked up from the desk, where he was doing the household accounts.

"What came to life?" the large man asked, having heard Millie's loud announcement.

"Not so much came to life as...remodelled," Fern said.

George arched one eyebrow and put his quill back in its holder.

Ambrose rose and stood behind George. "Don't keep us in suspense. What did you find, and has it eaten anyone we know?"

Squib glided to the desk and rubbed his back against George's knuckles as Millie shrugged out of her coat.

The older men stared at Fern, waiting for her to explain.

"The storm altered your cottage, George, into the bookstore from Millie's story. Complete with a rather charming conservatory that overlooks the river." Having given a succinct explanation, Fern dropped to the sofa.

"A bookstore? Oh, that is wonderful news." Ambrose placed his hands on Millie's upper arms and beamed at her.

The two of them started gushing over the finer details and what books Millie had discovered in the brief tour of the cottage. Meanwhile, George narrowed his gaze at Fern, and his chest heaved.

"Magic, George. Just admit it was magic and circumvent the entire argument," she said with a suppressed giggle.

"Magic." He drew the word out as though testing how it tasted over his tongue. "Or...a troop of travelling builders who sought shelter last night picked the cottage because it is empty and decided to do a spot of work while they waited out the storm as a thank-you for the protection it offered."

Ambrose slapped his partner on the arm. "Really, George? Can you not, just once, admit that magic still exists without these contorted explanations?"

"Third time." George cleared his throat. "You, Squib, the cottage. Three lots of magic will do me."

Ambrose opened his mouth to argue for a fuller admission when Fern leapt into the conversation. "The *how* of what happened doesn't matter when there is a far more important question. Will you allow Millie to move into the cottage and run the bookstore?"

"But it is marvellous to have a fellow scribe in residence here, at Nemython. Mrs Carlisle is welcome to stay for as long as she wants, surely?" Ambrose glanced at Fern since Nemython House became her property after her father's death.

Before she could answer, Millie took Ambrose's hand and held it to her heart. "You have all opened your home to me and offered me a haven. But this is my dream made real. I could, finally, have a place of my own. If you and Mr Hawkins will allow it."

George rubbed his chin. "The stone didn't rebuild itself for anybody else. It's your cottage now."

Millie squealed. For a woman who didn't like loud noises, she seemed to make rather a lot of them. Then she threw herself at George.

After a fierce bear hug, he held her at arm's length and gave her a stern look. "You're part of this family now, and we're here if you need anything. We also expect you for Sunday dinner without fail."

Amid much excitement, Millie rushed upstairs to pack her belongings. Fern wandered back to the kitchen in search of a calming cup of tea, where Mrs Bentley and Alice were making pies.

"What was that all about?" the older woman asked.

Fern explained how magic had transformed a cottage into a bookstore and that Millie would move in as the new tenant. A serious look settled on Alice's young face as she made a pot of tea. She cleared her throat while pouring a cup and passing it to Fern.

"I'm going with Mrs Carlisle," Alice announced.

"What?" Mrs Bentley turned to her oldest daughter.

"Mrs Carlisle is a noblewoman and cannot live on her own. She will need someone to cook and clean for her. This is my chance to step out on my own, Ma." Alice placed a hand on her mother's arm.

Mrs Bentley set down the rolling pin and wiped her hands on her apron. "But you're my oldest, and we've worked together ever since you were a wee nipper."

Alice's features softened. "And you have taught me well, Ma. But you have our Lucy. She's quick as a whip and eager to learn. She just needs a chance."

Fern thought Alice raised a good point. Millie was used to living with staff who saw to her every need. The noblewoman probably didn't even know how to boil water, let alone feed herself. If writers even thought of such mundane things. It would be convenient if the magical transformation of the cottage included endless cups of tea and scones that simply appeared at the author's elbow. But the spell didn't work that way.

With Alice running everything, Fern didn't have to worry about Millie starving.

CHAPTER 3

Fern wondered if the idea of gently teasing loose the apron strings had been on Alice's mind for some time, but the opportunity had not arisen to step out of her mother's shadow. Becoming a housekeeper for Millie gave the young woman a chance at independence without being too far away from her family.

"It's a brilliant idea, Mrs Bentley. Mrs Carlisle will need help, and Alice will still be close by," Fern said as the housekeeper's grip tightened on the rolling pin.

The older woman turned away and dropped the rolling pin to the bench with a clatter. Lifting a corner of her apron, she dabbed at her eyes. "Very well, then. It seems it is time for my little chick to leap from the nest, and at least you are not disappearing off to London, where I wouldn't see you for months and months. Since you are staying in Drake's Bend, I expect you home for dinner on your day off."

"George has already told Mrs Carlisle she is expected to join us regularly for Sunday dinner, since she is part of our family now. Alice can come with her." Fern would make sure Millie brought Squib too. They all enjoyed his antics among the condiment pots while they ate and chatted.

By the time Millie came down the stairs, she had her own household. Albeit of one. Not that the little cottage had room for more staff than that. Alice would have a bedroom all to herself rather than having to share with her younger sister.

William hooked up the cart for the short trip, and George carried down Millie's trunk. Alice had hurried home and packed. Probably before her mother changed her mind and decided to grab her favourite knife to stop her daughter from leaving. Soon, a battered and ancient trunk was loaded into the cart beside Millie's larger one. Ambrose climbed onto the cart's seat, and George helped Millie up beside him.

"Are we all ready?" Ambrose called in a singsong tone before telling the placid horse to walk on.

George, Fern, and Alice walked behind as they made their way to the new bookstore and a new chapter for both the writer and their community.

At the centre of the village, Ambrose guided the cob off the road onto the grass before the cottage. Dropping the reins, he stared at the altered façade and the bay window that glinted like cut crystal in the morning light.

"Scribbles." He read the sign dangling beside the door. "How utterly perfect."

Alice paused and glanced up at the thick glass windows, and her hands tightened on her bag. Fern suspected nerves had sprung up inside the maid. It was one thing to bravely announce you were leaving the nest but another entirely to realise how far away the ground was as you jumped. Not that either Millie or Alice would be on their own, as they weren't that far away.

"When can we come in?" someone called out.

Millie blanched and glanced at Ambrose. It seemed the writer who dreamed of a bookstore hadn't realised that would include customers.

"Give her a chance to settle in first," Ambrose replied as he helped Millie down. "I'm sure the bookstore will be open in a few days."

People grumbled, but it was good-natured. The villagers had survived without a bookstore for so long; it would be a novelty to select the story they wanted rather than relying on whatever a traveller brought with them.

George dispersed the remaining crowd by telling them to bugger off. Then he planted himself at the end of the short path, crossed his arms, and glared.

"It gives me shivers when he does his stern bear impersonation," Ambrose murmured as he carried Millie's carpet bag inside.

Fern swallowed a laugh. She loved her uncles and thought them a wonderful example of a long-lasting love affair. But sometimes, you could glimpse a little *too much* of the inner workings of a relationship.

George carried in the larger trunks and hauled them up the narrow stairs. Alice explored the kitchen and ran her hand along the brand-new, cast-iron range. Ambrose marvelled at the rows of books, his eyes wide as he spied old favourites on the shelves. Or he plucked an unknown title down to skim the pages to find a new delight.

Millie sat at the desk and caressed the dark-green leather

insert. Then she opened the drawers to discover what was within. She soon made a stack of fresh paper, waiting for her to begin a new story. Squib perched on a wall sconce and watched like a dragon on a mountaintop surveying his domain.

"Let's leave Alice and Millie alone to settle in," Fern said after more than an hour, and when it became obvious there was nothing more for them to do.

"That includes you." George took Ambrose by the hand and dragged him away from a pile of books.

"I'll be back tomorrow," Fern promised Millie and waved as she was the last of her family out the door.

Back at Nemython House, Fern fetched one of the large canvas-covered outdoor cushions and set it in a sunny spot by the fish pond. Then she went to the stables to find Eurydice awake and snuffling around in the hay.

"Would you like to join me outside for a little while?" Fern asked.

On unsteady feet, the dragon slowly walked out of the stables and across the yard. Fern worried she might fall, but the creature was too large and awkward for her to carry. Once the dragon was settled on a cushion in the sun, Fern spent a quiet two hours tidying up the garden after the storm.

It lightened Fern's heart to see the iridescent shimmer of health return to Eurydice's scales as she snoozed. The dragon wasn't deeply asleep, though. If Fern ventured too far away, the creature cracked one eye open and scanned the garden for her. As she worked with the dragon for company, Fern made a decision. She would head out to Wyndham Hall and thank Lord Drakeman for allowing her to read the old journals. The knowledge they contained about broth made from fish caught in the river of Drake's Bend had set the dragon on the road to recovery.

She settled her weight back on her heels and wiped her hands against her trousers. "I need to go out for an hour or so. Would you like to stay here, or I can move your cushion close to George?" Her uncle by bonds of love was working in his shed, cutting and sanding a new project. He kept the door open to allow the swirling sawdust to escape.

Eurydice chirped and rose to her feet. Fern took that to mean she preferred company to solitude. And who could blame her after a month trapped beneath the fountain, thinking it would be her tomb.

Fern picked up the cushion, and the dragonet followed her along the path to the shed that butted up against the thick stone wall not far from the greenhouse. Her steps were laboured. The dragon would need slow, steady exercise to build strength and muscle tone. Fern watched the awkward shuffle and didn't want to contemplate if the creature would ever be able to fly.

That was another reason for venturing out to Wyndham Hall. She would ask for more time with the journals. The drake men of old might have written about how to help young dragons learn to fly.

"I hope you are prepared for company," Fern called out at the open door of the workshop. She placed the cushion in a sunny spot where the dragon could peer into the dim interior but wouldn't get sawdust up her nostrils.

George emerged wearing a thick leather apron not unlike the one the alchemist wore for his experiments. In his hands, he held a dowel or finial for some piece of furniture. "She can help me sand."

By *help*, George meant supervise since a dragon couldn't actually sand a piece of wood. She could gnaw the end if she were teething, but that probably wasn't the finished look George was after.

"Riddy might need a hand back to the stables. It's not dignified, but a wheelbarrow does the job." Fern worried that the walk might have exhausted the creature and she wouldn't be able to make the short return distance.

"I'll carry her back." George reached down and patted the dragon's head.

"That will work too, but please...be careful." Fern chewed her bottom lip, worrying about the dragon's fragile wings. In her mind, she imagined the bone structure breaking as easily as fine porcelain.

George glared at her.

"Right. Of course you'll be careful. Sorry. I'll leave you two to get back to work. I'm off to Wyndham Hall." Fern waved goodbye and spun around before concern for Eurydice made her say anything else foolish.

In the stables, she tacked up her mare since William was busy with other chores. The handy tree stump by the side of the yard was the perfect mounting block as she swung her leg over the saddle. She could have hopped up from the ground, but George always growled that it was bad for a horse's back and made one stirrup leather longer than the other.

Horse and rider strolled at a leisurely pace through the village. People were out clearing storm damage from their gardens and sweeping it from the road. Near the bridge, Fern glanced at the transformed cottage but couldn't see any sign of Millie within. No doubt she was buried in a book.

Once they were clear of pedestrians, the horse trotted along, and they soon reached the outer edge of the village. To one side lay the cemetery, sheltered behind a dense cluster of birch, beech, and oak. Both her parents rested beyond the trees, and she was overdue a visit to them.

Across the road, the ornate gates of Wyndham Hall were shut. Not that it deterred Fern. Dismounting and telling the horse to stay, she leaned on the protesting metal and prised it open far enough to admit them both.

"It's almost like they don't want any visitors," Fern said as she climbed back onto the horse.

They cantered along the curve of the driveway. Before them, the estate sat like a sulky child with a permanent scowl. The horse slowed her pace and halted on the overgrown lawn. Fern slid to the ground and looped the reins around a tree. The mare dropped her head to nibble the lush grass.

As she crossed the gravel drive to the house, Fern steeled herself to tangle with the surly butler. Grabbing hold of the dragon tail dangling from the brass knocker, she rapped four times. After a pause to listen for any response, she decided to keep on banging. That would make her harder to ignore, and she imagined Quint twitching with every firm smack of the metal.

At length, the door flung open just as Fern was about to start another series of knocks.

"What?" the butler demanded.

Fern smiled sweetly. "Oh, how did you know it was me?"

Quint ground his teeth but remained silent.

"I need to see Lord Drakeman. Where is he hiding today?" She peered around him, but the vestibule behind was empty.

The butler narrowed his gaze. He seemed to be mentally weighing up the odds that she would simply climb in through a window and cause a ruckus as she searched the place. Then he let out a sigh and stepped to one side. "He's in the library. I suppose you'll be wanting tea."

Without waiting for an answer, he walked off, leaving Fern to close the heavy oak door behind her.

"Tea would be lovely," she called out to his retreating back. "And perhaps a scone? Do you do a spot of baking in your free time, or is there some poor indentured waif chained to an iron ring in the kitchen floor?"

He paused and glared over his shoulder. "This isn't a prison. We have a cook."

"I think my mistake is understandable, given that the exterior of Wyndham Hall has all the warmth and welcoming ambience of a workhouse." She wondered if the building was built of dark stone or if the demeanour of the occupants had somehow stained it. A row of cheerful geraniums in pots would go a long way to alleviating the bleak mood.

If the house had a staff, that raised more questions. A large estate was usually the main employer for a village, with young people going into service and working their way through the internal hierarchy. Yet Fern couldn't remember a single person seeking employment at Wyndham Hall. Even if his lordship hired elsewhere, why didn't they ever wander the streets of the village on errands or pop into the tavern for a quiet ale on their day off?

Realising she was being left behind, Fern brushed away her scattered thoughts and trotted to catch up. Quint stalked along the hall to the double doors of the library. He pushed them apart and then growled, "She's back."

Fern dodged around his bulk and crossed the lush carpets.

Lord Drakeman sat at the desk before the window, papers scattered before him. Today, he wore a cream shirt without a cravat, the soft linen pulled to one side, exposing a triangle of skin. Over the shirt, he wore an earthy-brown waistcoat that matched the jacket hanging over the back of his chair. He glanced up, one paper in his hand. The eerie silver eye seemed to pierce right through her, the sensation only abating when he blinked.

"Miss Oakby. I gather you were successful at Warrington Manor." His attention resided on the letter in his hand.

"Yes. The potion erased the ink from Squib and rendered him inanimate. That allowed us to destroy the vine. I am pleased, though, that Mrs Carlisle's friend was brought back to life by the storm last night." Fern dragged a chair over, since there were none near the desk, and placed it to one side, with her back to the sharp midday light.

"Tea, Quint. And I believe there was mention of scones?" She waved a hand at the butler.

"You're staying?" Lord Drakeman dropped the paper to the desk and stared at his butler.

"Can't get rid of her. She's like mould in the north wing," Quint muttered.

Fern smiled. The grumpy man obviously knew very little about women in general or stubborn women in particular. Now that she knew she was under his skin, it made it all the more pleasurable to keep needling him.

"I thought you might like to hear what happened with the vine after I applied the potion to Squib and how the plant was fixated on Lord Warrington. We determined that was why the gardener was killed. He wore an old overcoat belonging to his lordship, and I believe it was able to scent him in the wool. We nearly lost another man who wore a handed-down waistcoat." Fern leaned forwards and couldn't keep the excitement from her voice. What a marvellous discovery had been lost to science and botany—a plant that could hone in on the odour emitted by a person. She still awaited any response from George's Romanian-speaking colleague to learn of any similarities to the other long-ago specimen.

Lord Drakeman leaned back in his chair and tented his fingers. "That is intriguing. How is a plant able to employ odour?"

Fern dug her nails into her palms to contain her excitement that he wanted to hear more. She thought she might burst if she couldn't share her ideas! As he listened, Fern lost herself in her theories. She explained how she believed that while plants were unable to smell like people and animals did through nostrils, they had the ability to sense odours.

"You think it might utilise some sort of chemical reaction?" The alchemist became more animated as they discussed the possible scientific process.

They hardly noticed when Quint returned carrying a

tray. Next to the teapot was a plate of scones and two small bowls. One holding jam, another clotted cream.

"Jam first, then the cream," he growled at Fern. "We're not like those monsters who put cream on first."

Fern and Lord Drakeman drank the entire pot of tea as they bounced theories back and forth. Eventually, the alchemist rose to his feet. "It has been...fascinating to discuss this topic with you, but I have kept you for some time. I would seek your opinion about the conservatory before you go."

Fern hadn't even noticed the passage of time as she talked botany and science with the earl. George would be wondering what had detained her. She followed the broad shoulders of the noble, expecting to go back out to the hall. But he approached a set of doors tucked under the mezzanine floor.

When he pulled them apart, Fern gasped. The conservatory butted up against the library. "Of course," she murmured. Both were double-height. She stared at the ceiling. "So the mezzanine above..."

"Looks out over the conservatory," he finished for her. "It used to be utilised for hatchlings to learn to fly. They could glide down from a safe height."

A conservatory built for dragons. The idea filled her with wonder. She wanted to run ahead and explore, but as she took one step into the grand glass structure, sadness washed over her.

CHAPTER 4

Fern stepped into a cemetery of neglected flora. Palms struggled to survive in the corners and dead vines were draped over trees like cobwebs. Light failed to penetrate the filthy glass and cast everything in a murky light. Leaves littered the tiled paths, and delicate plants had expired long ago. Reverently, she touched a withered orchid, its stem bare of any flowers as it leaned over brown leaves.

"Nothing has been touched for twenty years. This was always my mother's domain." He leaned on the door frame with his arms crossed but never took a step forwards as though he didn't want to venture within.

Even without a Lady Drakeman to stroll the paths, there should still have been gardeners to undertake the essential work of keeping the lush growth looking its best. "What about your ground staff?"

He huffed. "Do you think I employ groundsmen?"

A rhetorical question given the state of the place. "You should. There are keen local lads who need employment."

"I prefer my privacy. I am...selective as to who is allowed here. When necessary, Quint hires staff in London." His voice followed her. He must have entered the neglected space since Fern had disappeared behind trailing vines.

She stared up at a mass of woody stems that resembled grasping hands. She backed away, just in case they snatched at her if the recent storm had given them a taste for gardeners.

"You would find no more loyal staff than those drawn from the village. Drake's Bend protects her own, you should know that. Whatever your rank, you are still one of us. It is those in London who use words to cut others down." A raised stone platform called to Fern. It appeared to be made of slate, the surface mottled greys and deep greens that called to mind water flowing over stones. Around the edges of the platform, a few humidity-loving plants struggled on. Lacy foliage pushed through dead growth as the cycle of life fought on.

"What purpose did this serve?" Fern pointed to the raised area and searched for Lord Drakeman among the curtain of dead vines.

"It's a sleeping platform for a dragon. We have a hot spring on the estate that was redirected centuries ago to heat this place for dragons. This was originally built for use during harsh winters, for youngsters, or those recuperating from illness and accident. There is also a pool through those doors, although it holds only warm sludge these days." He gestured to the opaque glass coated in years of dirt and grime.

Ideas burst in her mind. The place was designed for young or sick dragons. Like Eurydice. The little dragon could sleep on the heated platform, swim in a warmed pool and perhaps, one day, learn to glide from the balconies above.

"It is my intention to hire one person to restore this conservatory." Lord Drakeman's voice interrupted Fern's galloping thoughts.

While she held a lingering grudge against conservatories, perhaps it was time to let go of her ill-feeling. Conservatories were not to blame for one cad's actions, nor her response to him. Time had healed the wound created in such a place, surrounded by lush growth.

"One person will be better than none. There are plants here that can be saved." A tiny measure of gloom lifted from Fern's soul. One person was a start. They could pull out the dead growth and nurse the struggling palms and ferns. It would be no different from lavishing care on Eurydice to help the dragon back to full health. Which might be an easier road if she could bring the dragon to the estate's conservatory.

Lord Drakeman cleared his throat. "Since you agree to take on the position, I will make a sum available to you for replacement plants in addition to a wage for your time spent here."

Fern was busy scrubbing at the glass with her nail to try to see the pool outside, and it took a minute for his words to drip through her occupied mind. "Wait. You mean to hire... me?"

"You have the required expertise and are the logical choice. And I find your presence tolerable. As does Quint." He frowned as though not entirely sure of the reaction his butler might have to that news.

Tolerable? He knew just what to say to charm the ladies.

Fern imagined he had been a stunning success with such pretty language when he went to London. Before his accident.

She blew out a sigh. It was, in many ways, her dream job. The neglected conservatory waved to her like a drowning person who had spotted a rescuer on the shore. It was also close to home, and she could fill it with rare and exotic specimens that wouldn't fit in her modest greenhouse. She could grow bananas and passionfruit! And it would aid Eurydice's recovery.

"Very well. On two conditions. One, that you agree to an hourly fee." Trying to keep the glee from her face, she named an outrageous amount.

His eyebrows lifted a tiny fraction, then he nodded. "And the second condition?"

"When I am working here, I will have Riddy with me." Fern would consult George about the logistics of getting the flightless dragon youngster to Wyndham Hall.

The scaled eyebrow above Lord Drakeman's silver eye lifted. "I said I would allow one person to work here. You are not to have an assistant."

Fern thought the dragon took a more supervisory role than one of an active assistant. "Riddy is a sick, young dragon I found trapped at Warrington Manor..."

"You would bring a dragon here?" He stepped back as though the idea of a frail dragon scared him more than a spider dangling from a dead leaf.

"Is that not the purpose of Wyndham Hall? You said this place was built centuries ago for the young, sick, and injured.

She is making small improvements and now desires company. The warmth of this stone will be good for her while I work. It will take some time for her to grow and build the muscle she needs for her adult form." Fern followed when he retreated. Her curiosity roused as to why someone whose family name and title were earned through service to dragons had such a reaction to one.

He stopped by the open doors and placed one hand high on the frame. His head shook with tiny movements as he waged some internal debate.

"I'll not work here without her. I'm sure you can find another gardener who will be...tolerable." The money would be a boon for her family, but they would survive without it. Fern wouldn't bend on Eurydice's presence just to line her pockets. Some things were more important.

Lord Drakeman turned, his jaw clenched and his gaze guarded. "Very well. The dragon will be allowed in the conservatory, but she is not to wander the house or estate."

Fern hadn't thought about letting Eurydice chase her along the halls until he mentioned her not being allowed inside. But she would content herself with access to the conservatory. Fern held out her hand. "We are in agreement, then."

After a moment of hesitation, he took her hand. His warm fingers tingled along her palm, and they shook on the deal. Then the first hint of a smile lit his mismatched gaze and full lips. "Since you and Quint are getting on so well, would you like to tell him yourself?"

Oh...she would very much *love* to tell Quint that he'd be seeing a lot more of her.

FERN RETURNED to Nemython House with her thoughts running in multiple directions like a family of rabbits chased by an exuberant dog. She handed her mare over to William and checked on Eurydice, who was curled up asleep in her blanket. Apparently, a few hours out in the garden and soaking up the sunlight had worn her out.

"I have found somewhere to help you recover, little one." Fern stroked the sleeping dragon's head and silently promised that one day, she would take flight from the conservatory balcony.

Entering the house, her thoughts were still in a daze over the events of the day. Ambrose and George were relaxing in the parlour before dinner.

"I have a job." Fern dropped to the padded seat of her favourite sofa.

"Of course you do, dear. And you are a very good botanist, no matter what anyone in society says." Ambrose glanced up from his novel.

Fern paused to dissect that statement. What was society saying about her botanical knowledge? A slur on her gardening skills would cut deeper than any barb about her character. Deciding to put that topic aside for another conversation, she blinked and returned to the employment she had accepted. "I have been offered a job at Wyndham Hall. Lord Drakeman has engaged me to restore the conservatory. It is a project that will take me some months." Or even years if he expected her to clean all that glass.

Ambrose nearly dropped his book, and George snapped the newspaper shut.

Fern had decided that she could spare up to three days a week to labour in the conservatory, clearing dead growth, restoring ponds, adding compost to beds, and finally replanting. Over the coming weeks and months, how many times would she encounter the reclusive owner with his dragon eye? The idea of being watched by him rippled over her skin, and she rubbed the idea away. Most likely, he would hide in his laboratory. She should worry about Quint up on the library mezzanine floor with a crossbow aimed at her.

"Did you overcharge him?" George asked.

"Of course. He didn't even blink." Part of her would have happily offered to pay *him* for the opportunity that now lay before her if it helped Eurydice. "When I asked if he was sure he wanted to hire me, he said my presence was *tolerable*. Somehow, I managed not to swoon when he said it."

George huffed. "He's lucky to have you. That accident must have burned away his ability to give a compliment."

"Such a shame what happened to him. I recall him being a kind young chap whenever he snuck away to play with the local boys in the river." Ambrose rose and poured a cup of tea from the pot on the low table. Then he passed it to Fern.

She sipped the tea and tumbled back in time through her memories. As a child, she vaguely recalled the group of boys who swam in the river or threw sticks off the bridge and chased them along the bank. If she remembered correctly, Lord Drakeman was just a few years older than her. But her mind failed to place him among the local lads. "I can't recall him as a boy. Although I spent most of my time with Mother and Father and thought boys weren't worth the bother."

George huffed in laughter. "*Some* boys grow up to be decent men."

Fern flashed him a smile. Admittedly, not all boys, or men, were a waste of time. The problem was picking the good ones. A handsome face could hide a beastly nature. Could the opposite be true, and a kind heart lurk behind a scarred face? Not that it made any difference to her; she merely considered it as an intellectual question. She relished the opportunity to restore the conservatory and would probably never see the owner.

Ambrose had a faraway expression as he stared out the window. Perhaps lost in his own memories of the cruelty of people. He spoke to whatever he saw in the shadows of the trees outside. "After the accident...well, as we all know, people can be savage. The previous Lord Drakeman insisted his son go to London to find a bride. A hunt that did not go well, despite him possessing both a title and a fortune."

Fern nearly choked on her tea. With a title and a fortune, anxious mammas would have thrown their daughters at him regardless of his odd scar. Young ladies would have stuck to him like he was covered in tar. How on earth did he avoid being engaged to at least one of them?

"After that season, he returned to Drake's Bend and shut himself away." Ambrose continued his story. "Since his father died a few years ago, it seems we never see anyone from Wyndham Hall in the village. Even what few staff he has, keep to themselves."

"This job will be a steady income for the rest of the year.

Perhaps while I am scratching in the dirt, I can dig up why the staff don't leave the estate." If Fern found out they were ordered not to pass beyond the gates, she would simply have to rescue them all as she did Millie.

The timing niggled at her. Why had Lord Drakeman decided to do something about the sad and neglected space now when it had languished for so many years? "Perhaps the passage of the years has eased his old wounds, and restoring the conservatory will be the start of his returning to society?" she mused out loud.

Somehow, she doubted they would see Lord Drakeman and Quint downing a pint at the Drake's Rest tavern. But stranger things had happened. Then she remembered the other marvellous thing about the job. "I am going to take Riddy with me. Did you know the conservatory was built centuries ago for dragons? It has a heated sleeping platform, a warm pool fed by the hot spring, and balconies for young ones to learn to fly."

"It will be the same hot spring that heats our bathhouse," Ambrose said. The village had a small stone bathhouse not far from Wyndham Hall. Ladies and gents used the pool on alternate days, but on Sundays, it was a day for youngsters to play.

George set down his book. "The conservatory was all stone originally, built five hundred years ago by skilled stonemasons. Then solid walls were replaced with glass."

"How marvellous that there will be a dragon back at the Hall. I read in a periodical that some estates still have their wyvernries. You must hunt out if one remains at Wyndham Hall and tell me all about it," Ambrose said.

"You'll need to take the cart when you go. It's too far for Eurydice to walk," George pointed out, ever practical.

"I shall worry about transport when I start there. Speaking of Riddy, I shall take her dinner before we have ours." Fern finished her tea and put the cup back on the tray.

In the kitchen, she collected the bowl left to one side by Mrs Bentley. With Alice now gone to live with Millie, the youngest Bentley, Lucy, assisted her mother.

Out in the stables, Eurydice had woken, and the dragonet wandered around the stall, poking her nose under the straw and exploring. She looked up and trilled on hearing Fern approach.

Unlatching the door, Fern sat on the straw. The prepared meal was less soup-like now, and the chunks of fish and vegetables sat in a small amount of broth. "You are looking much better. Would you like to accompany me to Wyndham Hall when I go there to work? The conservatory would be more fun to explore, and it will be warm."

She chatted to the young dragon as Eurydice enthusiastically ate her dinner. Fern marvelled at the change in the creature that had occurred in just a few days since they had added the nourishing local fish to her diet. Or was it the kelmsgale seeds?

Fern couldn't shake the feeling that the seeds had played an, albeit small, part in her recovery. But how? They were as solid as metal. Were they required in the digestive process? She had a vague memory of reading that some birds swallowed stones to help grind food in their gizzards. Dragons flew and were a type of bird. Perhaps their stomachs did something similar. Eurydice might have sucked the seeds from Fern's fingers because she instinctively knew her gut needed the hard kernels, and she had no access to pebbles.

"There is so much about you that is a mystery to me. I shall have to ask Lord Drakeman if I might read more of his ancestor's journals when I am at the Hall. They would know if you need stones in your stomach." Fern stroked Eurydice's side. The colour and warmth of her scales had greatly improved, and she was now almost entirely a uniform sea green with swirls of grey. All the youngster needed was to put a layer of fat over her ribs and build up the muscles in her body. "I hope you shall be able to fly when you are stronger."

As though understanding the words, Eurydice flapped her delicate wings, and straw stirred up around them.

Fern laughed and picked bits of the dried grass from her hair. "Perhaps we try that another day when we are outside?"

Or in a double-height conservatory. She imagined the little dragon peering over the side of the balcony before taking a leap of faith to glide to Fern below.

The next morning, Fern walked into the village to visit Millie and Alice and see how the two women were settling into their new home. She knocked on the door, but no one answered. Somewhat concerned that a carnivorous bookshelf might have swallowed the women overnight, she grabbed the handle and found it bolted. Not that a locked door ever deterred her.

Fern wandered around the side of the house, past the conservatory, and entered through the kitchen door. Which she found ajar.

"Good morning, Miss Oakby," Alice said. The maid wiped sweat from her brow using her upper arm as her hands were occupied holding a delicious-smelling loaf of bread fresh from the oven.

"Good morning, Alice. How was your first night away from home?" Fern scanned the bench. Alice had been busy baking as though she had a household of six to feed.

"A little quiet. Lucy makes these funny noises in her

sleep like a restless puppy, and I never realised how they helped me sleep. Mrs Carlisle says I can have this afternoon off to go visit them." She placed the bread on the bench and reached for the kettle. "I'll make tea. Mrs Carlisle is working on a new story."

Fern left the bright kitchen and entered the darker bookstore.

"Fern!" Millie called from the desk. She jumped to her feet so hurriedly she nearly spilt an ink pot by her hand. "I thought I heard a knock but was mid-sentence."

Squib squawked and launched himself from a shelf, and Fern held out her arm for him to land. The pixie dragon hopped up to her shoulder and puffed warm air in her face.

"The door was bolted, so I went around to the kitchen." Fern stroked Squib under his chin.

"People keep peering in the window and rattling the handle, and I have been ignoring them. I suppose I shall have to let them in, eventually." Millie heaved a sigh, and worry pulled at the corners of her eyes.

"How was your first night in your new home?" Fern glanced at the desk, covered in scattered papers. A few were scrunched up into balls and had been dropped to the floor.

"It is simply marvellous. My mind is crammed with so many story ideas I don't know which one to write first. I have to pinch myself to make sure this isn't a dream and that I am awake." Millie stretched out her arms and twirled around.

Then the frown puckered her pale forehead once more, and she glanced to the front window. "But I prefer quiet and solitude to write. Only now do I wonder if possessing a bookstore was such a good idea. Yesterday, there were ever so many people pressing their faces to the windows, and I could hear them chattering!"

"People are curious. It's not every day that a cottage they are long familiar with turns into something new and enticing. You will find that our little village is home to many devoted readers, and they simply long for new stories." Fern stared at the rows of books, finding it incredible how a magical storm and the power of words had brought them into existence.

"Let's go sit in the sun." Millie took Fern's hand and tugged her towards the conservatory. The fingertips of her other hand caressed the various spines on her way.

In the warmth and sunshine, Fern sat in one of the armchairs, and Millie joined her. Squib flew to a lush *Aspidistra elatior*, more commonly known as a cast-iron plant. The little dragon curled up underneath the dark-green leaves, which served as a shade tree for him.

Alice carried a tray out to them and placed it on the low table.

"I can already tell that Alice will be a blessing. Thank you so much for taking the leap to join me," Millie said as she set out the teacups.

Alice blushed and tucked the tray under her arm. "I'm glad of the opportunity, and I'm sure we shall rub along quite well. I suggested to Mrs Carlisle that I could make cakes and scones that customers could have out here while they read."

"A splendid idea, is it not? Although I don't want sticky fingers touching the books, so we will have to carefully consider what we serve. Or there will need to be a rule that customers can only eat after making a purchase." Millie leaned back in the chair and closed her eyes as she drank in the sunlight.

"It's hard to think that a fierce storm has brought such a change to all our lives. You have Squib and this place, and I have Riddy and a job at Wyndham Hall." Fern took her tea and cradled it in both hands.

Millie's eyes flung open. "Oh! You must tell me all about that. From the little I have gathered from your uncles, it sounds like a horrible, desolate, and gothic place with a dark and brooding lord who keeps a terrible secret hidden in the attic."

"Lord Drakeman does seem to favour a dark and brooding persona. I couldn't say if he keeps any secrets hidden in the attic, as he seems to prefer his laboratory. That's some distance from the house and across the meadow in case anything blows up." Pausing, Fern sipped the hot drink cautiously and considered the other elements in Millie's gothic outline. "While the Hall is rather desolate-looking from the outside, it is clean and tidy inside. I suspect it simply needs to have life breathed back into it. And some red geraniums. A splash of colour would make it far more welcoming." Sadly, nothing could be done to improve its butler, even if Fern made him an entire suit from the bright and cheerful flowers.

"A lack of ancient secrets hidden in the attic is a disappointment. Do you think he conducts wild and arcane experiments in his laboratory?" Millie's eyes sparkled as she spoke, and Fern could practically see her penning a new story in her mind.

"That I can confirm. Squib and I both witnessed him at

work." Fern shifted in her chair. For some reason, recalling the array of experiments laid out in the laboratory also brought to mind how he had wrapped his arms around her while she untangled her skirts.

"Oh, that reminds me! I have a story for Mr Reid. While I unpacked my trunk last night, I found one tucked in a pocket. Do you really think it might be good enough to be published?" The mischief vanished from her gaze to be replaced by a serious look. Worry practically oozed from her at the idea of handing over a story to be judged by an editor.

Fern reached out and touched Millie's arm. "I am certain that your stories are good enough to be published. Now, please reassure me that nothing in this cottage tried to eat you last night?"

Fern's belief in her new friend rippled over Millie. A quick smile flashed across the other woman's lips, and a little of the tension eased from her shoulders. She leaned back in her chair. "This storm had a different effect than the previous one, as I wrote quite a different story on Squib. It was one of hope and finding friends. The lonely heroine has been released from her prison, and so there was no need for her carnivorous guardian. Although, now I think about it, there was an odd growl coming from the cellar last night. But I'm sure it's nothing."

"What?" Fern set her teacup down with a clatter. Her mind leapt ahead to the sort of weapons and protection they would need before venturing down the steps to see what the magical ink and storm had brought to life. Only Millie's tinkling laughter made Fern narrow her gaze. "There's no monster in the cellar, is there?"

Millie sucked her lips together in an effort to hold in her mischief, and she shook her head. Unable to do it any longer, she expelled a long burst of laughter. "No. But you should have seen your face!"

The two women passed a pleasant hour together in the sun. Squib emerged from under the plant to find a more comfortable spot on a cushion. The pixie dragon flopped onto his back, exposing his parchment-coloured belly to the warmth.

"I wrote a letter to Bertie yesterday and told him that I won't be returning to Warrington Manor, as I have moved into a small cottage. I said I thought the peace and seclusion here would do much for my recovery." Millie chewed her bottom lip.

"Do you think he might try to drag you back?" Fern put her cup on the low table and leaned towards Millie. A bigger concern was that Lord Warrington might bundle his sister off to Bedlam—to hide his troublesome sibling away.

Millie sucked in her lip and wordlessly nodded.

Fern took her hand. "He will not succeed, should he ever try. You are one of us now, and no one will allow that to happen. If he turns up here, send Alice for help immediately."

With a shuddering breath, Millie uncurled herself, but she kept a tight grip on Fern's hand. "He's not really beastly, you know. We just never had much in common. Bertie was the heir and taught all those important things like mathematics, Latin, and politics. I was supposed to learn all the gentle arts, but Mother's nerves made her terribly ill, and she wasn't able to oversee my education. So Bertie is not to blame that I failed as a wife."

"You did not fail as a wife." Fern shook Millie's hand because it wasn't the done thing to grab a new friend by the shoulders and shake them vigorously enough to dislodge old ways of thinking. "Now, tell me all about the new story you will write."

It didn't take too much effort to unleash Millie's enthusiasm for her tale, and another pleasant hour passed by. As much as Fern wanted to stay all day, she had chores to do and letters to answer. Reluctantly, she rose to her feet.

"I had better get going..." She never finished her sentence as a shrill cry and a low roar came from outside.

With Millie on her heels, Fern rushed to the door of the bookstore. Out on the road, a fight had erupted. Two local men were exchanging blows while a woman screamed for them to stop. A crowd gathered, loosely encircling the combatants, but no one stepped between them.

"What do you think they are fighting about?" Millie asked as she peered over Fern's shoulder.

"I don't know, but let's find out before someone is hurt." Flinging the door open, Fern rushed along the short path to where people were gathered.

Fern recognised the fighters, two older men who should have been long past such youthful antics.

"Filthy, rotten swine!" Charlie Brayton struck out at his neighbour and life-long friend, John Linden. The smack echoed through the air.

It was a fair fight in that both men were of a similar age in their fifties and of a similar build. The lean muscularity of their youth had given way to the extra padding of middle age. Charlie's once-dark hair was now different shades of grey, whereas John's blond locks had lightened to a pale gold. Or what little hair John had left had lightened in colour, as most of it through the middle of his head had disappeared entirely.

"It's not what you think!" John yelled as he landed a punch on his friend's square jaw.

Sally Brayton tugged on her husband's sleeve. "Stop! You must stop!"

George strode across the bridge and pushed his way through the assembled locals to take hold of John. The blacksmith, Ben, followed behind. Fern's uncle must have been at the forge when they heard the commotion. The strong blacksmith wrapped his arms around the torso of Charlie. The fighting men were restrained, even though they continued to try to break free.

"What is going on here?" Fern stood between them, glancing from one to the other. She had known the men since she was small and had played with their children.

"He forced himself on Sally!" Rage fuelled Charlie as he struggled, and he nearly broke free of George's vice-like grip.

Gasps shot around the assembled villagers. The two couples had always been close friends, like George and Ambrose with Rowan and Delfie in their youth.

"She asked me to," came the quick retort.

That was followed by a low, *oohhh* noise like a ghost had joined in. Heads swivelled to stare at Sally. Whose face drained of colour, and one hand flew to her mouth.

"You should be hanged for abusing her! To think I once

thought you my friend," Charlie spat as he continued to struggle, but George held tight to his wrists.

"Please don't do this, Charlie. John and Megan are more than friends. They are like family," his wife pleaded with tears in her eyes.

"Family? He's a dirty criminal and needs to be held responsible for the horrible things he did to you." Some of the fight drained from Charlie as his wife laid a hand on his arm.

"It was a long time ago, Charlie. Let things in the past stay there," Sally said the words quietly.

Fern suspected there was a great deal more she wanted to say, but she refused to sate the curiosity of the audience.

"What is all this nonsense?" Megan Linden had been drawn from their cottage. She balanced one of her grandchildren on her hip. The Lindens had a large family. Their six children were all adults and had started families of their own.

"Did you know what he did to Sally?" Charlie cried out.

Megan appeared confused. The frown gathered up her forehead as though a sewer drew the folds together with thread. "What are you talking about? Are you both drunk again?"

"Why didn't you tell me?" Charlie's voice dropped, and he turned to his wife.

Sally's eyes were wet with tears. "This isn't the place. You were never meant to find out. How...?"

"Why don't we adjourn to the bookstore? It can be considered neutral territory, and Alice will make everyone a cup of tea." Fern linked arms with Mrs Brayton and steered her towards the cottage nestled by the bridge.

Mrs Linden's daughter hurried out to reclaim her granddaughter, and then she followed behind. George kept a hold of Charlie's collar and hauled him up a little taller to march him after the women. Ben kept a hand on John's arm and escorted him along the path.

The crowd muttered and lingered. Some were undoubtedly peeved that their entertainment had been ended, but the parties involved needed a private space to air whatever grievance had erupted between them.

When they reached the bookstore, Ben let go of John and then stood by the door to deter anyone else who thought they would slip in. Mrs Linden's daughter scowled, but her child began to cry, so she hurried back to their cottage.

Fern ushered the group inside to where the sofas and chairs were arrayed before the fireplace. That also put them out of sight of anyone looking in the window.

Alice's eyes widened at the sombre mood of the visitors.

"Tea, please, Alice. A good strong brew," Fern said.

George pushed Charlie down on an armchair opposite John. Then he stood by the fireplace and rested one hand on the mantel. He pointed a large finger at Charlie's head. "Start at the beginning."

Charlie swallowed and gave a sullen look. "John forced himself on Sally."

Megan gasped and stared from her husband to her best friend. "He would never!"

George held up his hand for silence. Then he pointed to Sally. "Did he?"

Sally twisted her hands in her lap. "No. I mean. Not like that. It's just...I wanted a child so much," she said in a small, faint voice. "When Megan announced she had conceived their fourth...I...it seemed so unfair." Tears rolled down her cheeks.

Megan dropped to the sofa beside her friend and took her hands. "You are like a sister to me. There were days I would have gladly given you two or three of the buggers. All I ever wanted was to see you happy, with a family of your own."

"Charlie and I fought about it that night, each of us blaming the other. He went out and got terribly drunk. John brought him home. Like the good friend he is." Sally smiled at the other man, who sat silently in a chair with his arms crossed. "I told John how I wished it were me carrying instead of you, Megan. He joked he would try if I wanted him to. Then at least we would know if it were me or Charlie who...couldn't." Sally's words trailed away, and she tugged a handkerchief from her bodice to wipe at her eyes.

"Oh, John. Tell me you didn't really make such a daft offer?" Megan turned to her husband and smacked him across the head.

CHAPTER 6

John swallowed, and his hands curled into fists on his thighs. "They're our friends. Family. Like you said. We would do anything for each other. I give you my word, Meg, I never did anything Sally didn't ask me to do."

"You let him?" Charlie gasped, emotions playing across his face. Rage vanished and was replaced by sadness and shock.

Cogs turned in Fern's mind as she tried to recall the ages of Megan's children and when she must have conceived number four. "How long ago did all this happen?"

"Twenty years," Sally said.

Now Fern remembered. Sally and Charlie only had one child, a daughter who was slightly younger than Megan and John's fourth child, a son. The pair would soon turn twenty, and they had grown up almost inseparable from one another. Everyone thought a romance might bloom between them, but it had been discouraged...

"Oh!" Fern slapped a hand over her mouth as she realised

why any romantic notions between the pair had been quashed.

"Were you willing, Sally?" George asked in a gruff tone.

"Yes," she rasped. She got up from her chair to kneel beside her husband, her hand curling in the fabric of his trousers. "I'm so sorry. John and Megan had so many bairns. I only wanted one. A son, or daughter, it didn't matter. A child we could both love and cherish."

Charlie shook his head and looked away from Sally as he emitted a low moan of pain. "Why didn't you tell me?"

Sally glanced over her shoulder at her neighbour. "John and I vowed to never speak of it. Remember how excited you were when I told you I was carrying a babe? The sense of pride when you first held her? You have always been our daughter's father. That has never changed. Would you take back the years of laughter and love she has brought into our lives?"

"Oh, I need to write this down. What a tale of maternal love and stretching the bonds of friendship," Millie whispered in Fern's ear.

While the story was overly dramatic, Fern hoped her friend would respect the privacy of those involved in any tale that incorporated the desperate act.

"Both of you should have told me and poor Charlie." Megan looked from her husband to her best friend. "I was so excited when you told me you were pregnant. It brought us closer when you had little Aggie not long after I had our Simon. I would never have denied you the joy of holding your child. Who would have thought that great lummox was the village stud?" A frown wrinkled Megan's forehead as she leaned towards her husband. "There aren't any more of your children running around, are there?"

John flushed bright red, and his eyes widened at the idea. "No! I promise you, Meg, there is only the one. And I swear I only had to touch Sally three times for us to get the job done."

"Yes, well, no need to brag, John." Ambrose halted that line of conversation before they all learned a little too much detail about the *village stud*.

Fern pieced the story together. "There is one thing I don't understand. This was twenty years ago, and you both vowed to never speak of it again. So who told Mr Brayton that Mr Linden had, supposedly, forced himself on Mrs Brayton?"

Charlie drew a shuddering breath. "No one told me. Not exactly. I was coming through the woods yesterday. I stopped to tell them how grateful I was for our daughter and that she had grown up to have her mother's smarts and beauty. The trees whispered back that she wasn't mine. That...that John had grabbed Sally in the dark and...did things to her against her will."

Those *trees* were the whisperwoods. The stand of magical trees a few miles southeast of Drake's Bend that had aroused Millie's curiosity. "But the whisperwoods hold secrets. They don't spread gossip. Where would they ever have got the idea from?" Fern couldn't make sense of it.

"Me." John blew out a sigh and scrubbed his hands over his face before taking his wife's hand. "I confessed to them a few years ago. I'm sorry, Sally. The secret ate at me over the years, and if I couldn't tell Meg, I had to tell something. So, one day I rode out to the trees and unburdened myself."

If you confessed your secrets and fears to the grove of old

trees, they normally whispered back reassuring wisdom. In all her years, Fern had never heard of the ancient stand repeating a secret. Let alone telling one person's darkest tale to another visitor. Or, in this case, adding a malicious twist to the truth.

"You daft buggers," Megan muttered. "I'm not happy about being left out of things, and we'll certainly be having words about this in private. But done is done. Aggie is your daughter, Charlie. John has never had any claim on her. And thank goodness our Simon has always considered her a sister, or we would have had a right mess on our hands."

Everyone drank their tea, which settled tempers and began the process of soothing old wounds. The two couples remembered all they had been through over the years and the tears and laughter their children had brought into their lives.

Millie sat at her desk, furiously scribbling notes.

Fern thought she would ride out to the whisperwoods and try to figure out why they were spreading nasty gossip. Perhaps one had boughs that had overreached.

With more to discuss without anyone else listening, the two couples left the bookstore for the privacy of the Brayton cottage.

"I hope they can work things out. Their motives were worthy, but perhaps all parties should have agreed to their plan beforehand," Fern said as she watched them cross the road and disappear under a rose-draped archway.

"I believe there is a saying about the path to Hell being paved with good intentions. Fortunately, both Sally and Megan have good heads on their shoulders. I am sure they will find their way to forgiveness once Aggie's origins are fully aired." Ambrose stood behind Fern and rested a hand on her shoulder.

"I'm going to ride out to the whisperwoods and have a word with them. They shouldn't be spreading gossip like old fishermen." Fern waved goodbye to Millie and left the bookstore.

The whisperwoods were only a short distance from the village, and curiosity itched at her. Neither her father nor any other botanist had yet ascertained how the whisperwoods spoke to people. Some said it was a form of delusion, and people heard what they wanted to hear. Her father hypothesised they used their leaves and catkins to vocalise. Other scientists thought the trees used psychic means to transmit words directly into a person's head.

With a course of action in mind, Fern set a brisk pace back to Nemython House. Once she had checked quickly on Eurydice and promised to take her to Wyndham Hall, she saddled up her horse.

The road south was quiet with no other travellers, and Fern let the mare canter along the worn path. Centuries of pilgrims to the mystical woods had left a mark that didn't need any signpost. At a certain point, the road dipped off to one side, where the trees leaned away from a narrow path leading through the ancient oak, birch, beech, and rowan.

The short dirt lane terminated at an old stone cottage. Its garden was long overgrown and its hearth cold. The elderly owner had died some years ago. George wrote letters trying to find the distant relative who had inherited the plot of land with both the cottage and the ancient grove of trees, but so far, his efforts were unsuccessful.

Before the cottage gate was a packed earth oval of just sufficient size to allow a carriage to turn around. Fern jumped to the ground and looped her horse's reins around the hitching post beside the gate to the cottage. Moss clung to the wood, but the rail was of sturdy construction, and even their most tempestuous winter had yet to rot away the timber. Although some horses did fine imitations of woodpeckers as they gnawed at the rail in boredom while they waited.

The next path was barely a person wide, as most people journeyed alone to the glade. Tree boughs mingled overhead, creating a dense canopy that filtered out the sunlight. The stand of magical trees huddled at the base of a hill. High above and barely visible through the dense leaves, an old abbey surveyed the land around it.

The whisperwoods formed a semicircle, drawing a person in towards the specimen with the widest trunk standing at the midpoint of the group. In appearance, they somewhat resembled a copper beech, with bark weathered to silver and knots and whorls resembling eyes. They were deciduous, and most of the year, they had a deep burgundy leaf that turned to glorious autumnal hues as the weather chilled.

Branches shook, and leaves brushed against one another to emit soft whispers. In winter, the whisperwoods hung with catkins that they rattled, and their whispers turned sibilant, like the hiss of a snake.

Walking among them was akin to passing through a crowded room. Around Fern was the low murmur of conversation, most of it indiscernible. Only the odd word or phrase made sense, but with no context, she didn't know what the trees talked about among themselves. They could have been discussing the weather, which seemed to preoccupy most old people she knew.

To make the trees speak required an exchange. First, those wishing to unburden themselves or seek advice had to tell a secret that resided deep in their heart. Then they waited for the sage wisdom of the ancient grove.

"I have heard that you have been spreading cruel gossip." Fern turned a slow circle, scanning each tree. They were all as different as people. Some tall, others short, wide and thin. The bark patterned in different ways. One seemed to have a wide-open eye that peered directly at you. Another had a half-lidded gaze. Only when their boughs intermingled did they become a uniform mass of rustling leaves.

Although none answered her accusation.

"It seems you will demand a secret from me." She approached the widest whisperwood. While not the tallest in the group, it had an ancient solidity, having stood in the same spot for hundreds of years.

What secret could she offer in exchange? Drawing a deep breath, Fern laid both hands on the smooth bark. "I didn't realise how lonely I was until I met Millie. Her friendship is filling the holes inside me, and it...worries me that she might decide she doesn't want to be my friend when she gets to know me better."

Fern glanced over her shoulders, embarrassed to make the admission and hoping no one overheard.

Leaves rustled.

"Beware. Mrs Carlisle...killed her husband," came the whispered reply from all around the glade.

"Well, that answers one question. You are not giving sage

advice but spreading horrid gossip," Fern muttered. In a louder tone, she addressed the trees. "You are wrong. I know that Mr Carlisle was killed in a duel, and his wife was not his combatant. She had no hand in his death."

After meeting Millie at Warrington Manor, Fern asked Ambrose what he knew of the widow. He recalled the tale of the duel over her honour and how her husband had failed to defend her name. She had retreated to the Warrington family estate and had not been seen in London since.

"The pen...is her sword." The words swirled around Fern. The mass of leaves spoke with one voice. "She used... her stories...to escape her husband."

Escape? That made Fern drop to the mossy grass. Crossing her legs, she mulled over the snippet of gossip that bore some similarity to what had happened only a few weeks before. Millie had written a story about escaping her brother, and her words brought a vine to life to save her. What if she had another sort of magical ink at her disposal and wrote a tale that urged a noble to call out her husband and end another oppressive reign?

"You are supposed to offer me wisdom. Not pass judgement on others." No matter how she tried, Fern couldn't erase the tinge of doubt from her words. If Millie had sought escape twice, both attempts had seen someone die. One—her husband, the other—a gardener the vine mistook for her brother.

"Would you be next...to fall victim...to her cunningly crafted plots?" What should have been gentle whispers had a harsher, sharp tone.

Fern closed her eyes and listened as the trees communed

among themselves. They all whispered at once. She caught snippets of secrets and confessions through the jumble of fractured sentences.

"...poisoned tea...unfaithful...stole from neighbour...smothered....lied..."

"Enough!" Fern stood and brushed the grass from her trousers. "For centuries, you have safeguarded the confidences entrusted to you. Why are you cruelly twisting those secrets? Have you grown bored that you now seek to drive people apart and cause harm?"

The trees didn't answer. They only rustled their leaves, and the murmured words became indistinct and unrecognisable.

Something had changed. But what?

Starting at one end of the semicircle and going tree by tree, Fern examined each with a critical eye.

Spring lengthened into summer. The trees were now in full leaf. Yet as she searched among the boughs and branches, she noticed that many of the purple leaves were marred at the edges. They curled with a brown, creeping death as though winter encroached on them. She searched for a pattern to the dying leaves. It seemed worse in the canopy of the oldest tree and spread outwards from there. Those at the outer edge of the semicircle, and farthest away from the old sentinel, were barely affected at all.

"What is happening to you?" Given the trees could talk, why didn't they just tell her what ailed them? They fell oddly silent when questioned about their health or anything affecting them.

Standing on tiptoe, Fern plucked a few leaves with the

odd decay pattern. Then she scrutinised the weathered bark, looking for any abnormalities. None had been slashed, so a direct wound didn't appear to be the problem. Before she left the secluded grove, she walked around behind them, scanning the undergrowth and clumps of grass for any indication of a wider issue.

Not far from the grove, the earth inclined to rise up and become a hill. Fern walked a little way up until the outline of the abbey emerged behind the canopy of foliage. Smoke puffed from two of the many chimney stacks.

"Huh. I thought you were abandoned." Apart from the slow curls of smoke that twisted up to the clouds, there was no other evidence of inhabitants. Not that much could be seen, given the towering walls and narrow windows that were more like arrow slits and built in a time before glass.

When she returned to the lane, a small carriage and a handsome, matched pair of chestnuts took up most of the space. The curtains were drawn in the carriage, and a driver slouched against the roof, catching a quick snooze while they waited for her to emerge.

The shiny black sides of the vehicle had a subtle crest in a deep navy. The light caught it on an angle as Fern walked past, revealing the silhouette of a lion battling what appeared to be a fish standing on its tail.

Privacy was valued by those who sought out the whisper-woods, and none ventured into the grove while another was there. Fern thought she had a duty to let the visitor know that the woods were twisting the words given to them in confidence. But she couldn't exactly yank the door open and tell the person waiting behind the closed curtains that they would hear salacious gossip.

While considering what to do, Fern collected her horse and climbed into the saddle. Only the clop of the mare's hooves awoke the driver of the carriage.

Fern paused as she drew level with him and spoke in a loud enough voice to ensure the passenger heard her. "There is a blight affecting the whisperwoods. Anyone who ventures into the grove should carefully judge the truth of anything they hear within."

The driver's eyebrows shot up, and he huffed. "Thank you for the advice, miss."

Fern nodded, then guided the mare along the narrow lane and back to the main road. On the ride home, she mulled over the spiteful gossip the grove had murmured. They alleged that Millie used her pen as a sword, cutting down those who stood between her and whatever freedom she sought.

Their friendship wasn't so firmly established that Fern was comfortable asking the other woman about the circumstances surrounding her husband's death. Nor did she see any need to cause Millie unnecessary distress by repeating old rumours. In fact, the more she thought about it, the more the tale sounded like what the newspapers might have reported at the time.

Once she returned to Nemython House and had tended to horse and dragon (who was awake and shuffling around her stall), Fern took the leaves plucked from the whisperwoods to her study. She laid them out on the desk. The foliage was larger than ordinary beech but small compared to the leaves of something like an oak. Each curled inwards from the tip, like a bent finger. Since the whisperwoods were deciduous, with the advent of the autumn chill, the leaves would have turned a vibrant orange before giving way to the death of winter. Only then did the leaves turn a muddy brown before falling to the ground.

There was something making the trees sick.

And turning them into bitter gossips.

CHAPTER 7

Fern twirled a dying leaf between her thumb and forefinger. "What is causing the change in you? Perhaps it is centuries of holding thousands of secrets. You might be like a well that has been filled, and now they spill back out."

Putting the leaf down, she turned her attention to the bookshelves. As Fern reached for a book, she paused and stared at her hand. Her fingertips were faintly smudged as though she had spilt a drop of ink on them.

"Now that is odd." She turned her attention back to the leaves. There didn't appear to be any residue on them, but the marks on her fingers had come from somewhere. Curious, she fetched a clean sheet of paper. Then she dragged a leaf over the surface, pressing down as she went. When she lifted the leaf away, the ghost of a trail of dark blue was brushed across the page.

"Huh. Leaves don't normally do that." In recent times, she had seen an animated cutting of a monstrous vine bash its leaf against a glass jar and smear its purple-black inky sap up the sides. But that sort of thing didn't happen regularly. Thankfully.

Searching in a drawer for her magnifying glass, Fern examined the leaf in more detail. Possibly it was cut and seeping minuscule amounts of sap. But she didn't find any visible cuts or breaks. Nor, from memory, did the whisperwoods have blue sap.

Dusk dimmed the light outside her window by the time Fern finished examining the leaves and had thumbed through a book about the history of the whisperwoods. After washing up for dinner and scrubbing the odd stains from her skin, she joined her uncles in the dining room.

"Something is affecting the whisperwoods. They have begun to spread gossip." Fern pulled apart a piece of bread as she pondered what to do about the cruel words whispered to her. Did the stand of ancient trees make up stories like a novelist, or did they distort secrets given to them in confidence?

John Linden's secret had been twisted and spread to Charlie Brayton when they both went to the trees about the same person—Agatha. Fathered by one man and raised by the other. Fern had confessed the depth of her loneliness until she met Millie. The trees had warned her about getting too close to the other woman lest she was placed in danger.

Fern followed that line of thought. The trees distorted what they were told. Which implied that either Millie or someone who knew her well had confessed to the grove.

"Did the trees tell you anything juicy?" Ambrose waggled his eyebrows.

Fern stilled as the secret whispered through her mind.

She had considered asking Ambrose about the duel over Millie's honour, but at the same time, it struck her as wrong to gossip about a friend behind her back. If she had questions, no matter how uncomfortable they made her feel, she should ask them directly of Millie. "They said something horrid about someone I know, and I don't feel comfortable repeating it. Even to you, sorry, Uncle Ambrose."

His handsome face fell in disappointment, but he reached out and patted her hand. "I understand. You are a good person that you won't repeat it, even to us." Curiosity simmered in his hazel eyes. Fern could imagine him mentally reviewing a list of everyone they knew, trying to figure it out.

"Good. There are enough gossips in this world." George handed her a bowl of vegetables. Apparently, he didn't think she had enough on her plate.

Recalling her afternoon visit made more questions burst into her mind. "Do you know if Sibylcrest Abbey has been sold or tenanted?"

"Not that I have heard. Why?" Ambrose tore a fluffy bread roll in two before taking a pat of butter to drop in the middle.

"I walked a little way up the hill today, and there was smoke coming from the chimneys." It wasn't that unusual to have fires lit late in spring. Sibylcrest was a cold and draughty old building. Any occupant would need a fire going year-round to ward off the centuries-old chill that inhabited its stone. Or it could have been a kitchen fire she saw, since they needed constant fuel to cook meals and bake bread.

"Perhaps it was a traveller breaking their journey to London?" Ambrose suggested.

"It was sold last year. The new owner must be doing something with it." George held his cutlery, poised, as he considered where to start eating.

Ambrose rolled his eyes at his partner. "And why did you keep that snippet to yourself and not tell me?"

George stared in response since his mouth was now filled. Long seconds passed as he chewed, and only when he had swallowed did he reply. "Luxton bought it. Don't like him."

"Luxton Davies? From our university days?" Ambrose's eyebrows rose in a quizzical expression.

George nodded and continued eating his dinner.

"I seem to recall he bore an unfortunate resemblance to a sprouting potato with all that sparse growth up top." Ambrose reached up and patted his own remarkable hair.

"He went bald years ago. Looks like a boiled egg now." George sliced a potato in two and stared at one steaming half.

"Well, we'll not be paying any social calls on him, then. Not that I can imagine him moving in there himself. It would be too old and gloomy for his tastes. Especially when he has a smart house in Grosvenor Square and that fancy country estate in Essex." Ambrose turned his attention to his plate.

Fern had watched the conversation and picked up on the undercurrent. "I assume this Mr Davies is not a friend, then? Did he know my father?"

"*Sir* Luxton Davies. He inherited the title of baronet at a young age. Despite being on the lowest rung of the nobility, he acts as though he were a duke. And no, he is not a friend, even though we all knew him. He's one of those people who will smile at you while he swindles you of your last coin. He would joke and laugh, but it was all so...

hollow." Ambrose stabbed a slice of carrot and popped it into his mouth.

"He only values money and himself," George muttered darkly, his brows pulled together as he recalled their years spent at Oxford University.

"And God," Ambrose added. "I recollect that he didn't like *our sort* and once called us unnatural while waving a bible around. Oddly though, for someone who loudly proclaims himself to be a Christian, he indulges in all sorts of unchristian-like behaviour."

George finished chewing, swallowed, and took a sip of his wine. "He thought we were stupid and only noticed what he said, not what he did."

"It sounds unlikely that he is at the abbey then, and more likely there is a tenant." Fern hauled the conversation away from events of the distant past and pushed it towards the dim gossiping grotto that concerned her. "I'm going to go back and widen my search around the whisperwoods for what might be blighting the trees. I found an odd residue on the leaves I brought home with me. I want to see if it is on the others." Another thought dashed through her mind—they might have rubbed against something on the inside of her satchel. Like leftover inky sap from the death vine. She would empty the bag and wipe it out with a damp cloth, just in case.

"What about Drakeman?" There were days when George refused to call him Lord Drakeman.

"Yes, good point, George. I want him to have to start paying me, and I promised Riddy I would show her the dragon conservatory. Tomorrow I shall make a start at Wyndham Hall. The trees can wait a little longer." After all, how much trouble could the tattling trees cause? She had warned one visitor, and Ambrose had suggested a notice by the path would alert others to not believe everything they heard.

SINCE THE NEXT day was Fern's first day at Wyndham Hall, she ensured her trousers were clean (not that they would stay that way) and her tools were sharpened and oiled. While William harnessed the cob to the little cart, Fern placed an old blanket on the tray. Eurydice had shuffled out from the barn to watch and sat in a ray of morning sun. As her body returned to health, her scales shone with a metallic gleam in the light.

When they were ready, George lifted the young dragon into the cart. Then he laid a sturdy plank of wood in the back.

When Fern cast him a confused look, he said, "You can use it to make a ramp for her to get in and out."

"Brilliant idea. Thank you." Fern climbed onto the seat and took up the reins.

Eurydice was alert enough to sit up, and she sniffed the air as they walked along the road and through the village. Children ran out, and the cry of *dragon!* went up among them. She chirped and trilled in response to the greetings. Fern worried the recovering dragon would be overwhelmed, but to the credit of the children, none tried to touch her as she passed.

Curious people followed them until she left the main part of the village and continued along the road heading north. When they reached the estate driveway, she pulled the cob to a halt and hopped out of the cart. The wrought iron gates weren't open wide enough, and Fern had to lean her weight on the metal to encourage it to give way. All the time, she muttered about the blasted butler who had probably tried to close the gates on purpose to keep her out.

When the house loomed into view, she guided the quiet horse as close as possible to the front door. She made a wager with herself—Quint would leave her standing on the doorstep long enough that she would think he wasn't going to let her in at all. Not that she wanted in, but she thought it only polite to inform him that she was there, needed someone to take the horse, and would be working in the conservatory.

Her third rap on the dragon tail knocker elicited a response. The door swung open, and the butler scowled at her.

"I left a window open. Thought that would stop you bothering me." He gestured to a ground-floor window that was raised a mere inch.

"An unlocked window, for me...you shouldn't have." Fern placed one hand on her heart and batted her eyelashes.

Quint crossed his arms. Today he wore a grey waistcoat and no jacket. His sleeves were rolled up to his elbow, exposing forearms that were covered in intricate tattoos. "I was busy. What do you want?"

"Busy baking scones?" She had to ask. The last batch he provided was light and fluffy.

He moved to slam the door.

"Wait! I'm starting work in the conservatory today. Is

there someone who can take the horse? Please." She added the last when he looked on the brink of telling her to sod off.

"Go around the side. I'll find someone." He gestured in the direction of the conservatory, just in case she hadn't noticed the enormous double-height construction.

Returning to the horse (who was snuffling at the gravel on the driveway), Fern took hold of the reins by the bit and walked around the side of the building. All the while, she wondered if *finding someone* meant releasing them from a prison cell. She would continue to believe that Lord Drakeman kept his staff confined in a dungeon until she actually met and spoke to any of them.

As they rounded the corner and made their way through the long grass, the vague odour of rotten eggs tickled her nose.

"Yuck!"

She stopped where the ground fell away in a jagged line. The horse snatched at seed heads while Fern took a step closer to the smelly hole.

"Good grief. It's the pool." Grass grew right to the edge of the long-neglected, tiled pool, giving the appearance that the ground simply gave way.

The swimming hole ran the length of the conservatory and was nearly as wide. Two adult dragons could happily bathe in it at the same time, or a dozen hatchlings could play in there. If it were full of clean, heated water—instead of the noxious sludge that bubbled in the bottom.

"His lordship cannot pay me enough to make me clean that out." Fern backed away and returned to the cart.

Using the wooden board, she created a ramp for Eurydice and guided her down, keeping her hands on the dragon's side to ensure she didn't fall. The dragon sat in the grass and nibbled a stalk, her grey-green scales blending in with the meadow.

Fern turned her attention to the gloomy, moss-coated exterior of the conservatory. Its long-ago origins as an entirely stone structure were evident in the massive arches that formed ribs. The building resembled half a cathedral with its soaring ceiling and vaulted roof that joined the solid side of the house. A legion of artisans must have laboured to remove the stone to allow for the glass panels that let light in below. All to give dragons a place to spend winter or for the injured and sick to recuperate. The size and scale of the conservatory hinted at the great esteem previous monarchs had for the creatures.

And the monarch's regard for his drake men who tended the dragons.

"Let's see if the doors open," Fern said to Eurydice, who had now edged closer to the pool to peer at the sludge in the bottom.

In the middle of the wall, double doors on sliding tracks could be opened or closed. Fern glanced at the metal that showed spots of rust and disuse. The task would be harder than she thought. Every door and gate on the estate seemed reluctant to admit any outsider.

Leaning on the ornate handle, Fern pushed. Metal screamed, the glass vibrated, and it moved a mere inch.

"At least it's not locked. That's a nice change." She might have to admit that opening the doors was beyond her ability and seek Quint's help.

"Miss Oakby!" a male voice called out.

Turning, a man approached, dressed in rough woollen trousers and a plain linen shirt with the waistcoat hanging loose. Somewhere in his thirties, he slid his cap from his head as he approached her.

"Mr Quint sent me to take your horse, miss. I'll unharness him and leave him to graze in a yard." He spoke to Fern, but his gaze was fixed on Eurydice.

Fern blinked in surprise. The man didn't appear to have been beaten, starved, or deprived of sunlight from being chained in an oubliette. She might have to re-evaluate what went on inside Wyndham Hall. The man also seemed vaguely familiar. As though she might have played with him as a child, or perhaps his family lived in the village.

"Thank you. Are you a local?" she asked.

"Born and bred, miss. I'm Denis Fawcett, and my family lives here still." He managed to draw his attention away from the dragonet, who appeared unsteady on her feet.

She knew the name Fawcett. They were tenant farmers of Lord Drakeman, and she recalled they had a number of sons. Some ran their holdings, while one had obviously taken employment at the estate.

"Have you worked here long?" She wondered if Quint watched her conversation from somewhere inside. Should she whisper to Denis that he should blink twice if he needed help to escape?

"Ever since I was a stupid lad and got myself in a spot of bother. His lordship offered me a job and a chance to make amends." He crushed the cap between his hands and stared at the toes of his boots as though embarrassed by his past behaviour.

Fern poked at her memory but couldn't recollect what *spot of bother* he might have found himself in. She would ask the font of local knowledge (Ambrose) over dinner.

"Before you take the horse away, would you mind giving me a hand with this door, please? It's rather stuck in its tracks." She gestured to the imposing glass door. Since Denis Fawcett wasn't an emaciated prisoner and had the air of robust good health about him, his strength would be useful.

"Of course, miss. I can't remember ever seeing these doors open." He shoved his cap back on his head.

"Let's clear any overgrowth first." Fern walked along the length of the door and checked the top and bottom. With her trusty trowel, she cleared away weeds that had curled around the bottom track.

Then they positioned themselves by the door. Denis wedged his fingers in the gap and leaned backwards while Fern pushed all her weight against the handle. Inch by inch, and screeching in protest, the door gave way.

CHAPTER 8

Three more times, Fern and Denis threw their combined weight at the door like plough horses leaning into their harnesses. Sweat tricked down Fern's back as she stood back and considered the gap they had made. She wiped her forehead on the sleeve of her shirt. There was sufficient room now to admit Eurydice and a wheelbarrow. Once she found one.

"That will be enough. Thank you," she said to Denis. "If you see Quint, could you please ask him to leave a wheelbarrow by the door for the weeds?"

"I can find one for you, miss, once I've seen to your horse." Denis tugged a handkerchief from his pocket and wiped his face. Then he led the horse, still attached to the cart, to the stables.

Fern stood at the threshold as warm, earthy air escaped. Eurydice waddled forwards to peer inside and gave a questioning trill.

"This place was built for dragons. I will show you the

heated platform where you can soak up the warmth while I make a start on the clean-up." Fern stepped inside and lifted away a collapsed frond that sprawled over the mosaic path.

Eurydice shuffled behind her with slow steps. Fern paused often, not wanting to overexert the recovering youngster. The rest stops gave her a chance to determine where she would start. The logical place would be by the door, but she wanted to keep an eye on the dragon.

After a few minutes, they reached the platform. The dragon placed her front legs on it and waited. Taking the hint, Fern hoisted her rear end up. Eurydice puffed short snorts as she wandered around the edge like a dog with a scent.

"Can you smell them—all the dragons who came before you?" Fern asked, but the dragon was too busy to answer.

Positioned at the south end of the conservatory, the platform was heated from below, and the sun caressed it from above. Eurydice picked a spot and flopped over onto her back with a contented sigh.

The dragon's tail made lazy sweeps back and forth, and she spread her wings, exposing as much skin as possible to the warming sunlight that penetrated the grimy glass. With her companion practically asleep, Fern picked a spot to start.

She tugged on leather gloves and, with her trusty short-handled shears, began cutting off dead growth. Some of the plants had died entirely, and Fern tugged them free of the desiccated soil. When she had a large pile of debris on the path, she wandered out the open door and found a wheelbarrow waiting for her.

"Thank you," she called out to the stablehand who had

placed the barrow by the door. Although she had hoped that Quint might appear with a pot of tea and a plate of fluffy scones. But perhaps that was reserved for guests, not employees.

Using the wheelbarrow, Fern created a pile of detritus next to the pool and a safe distance from the building for when the dead growth was burned.

Amongst the withered corpses of ferns, orchids, and bromeliads, Fern found the occasional survivor. A furry green frond pushed through the earth, and she cleared the dry soil around it and fetched a scoop of water. Like Eurydice, those plants that clung to life in the conservatory were sickly and starved of what they needed to thrive. Time, attention, and a well-matured compost were needed to nurse them back to health.

As she worked, the hairs on Fern's nape prickled, and a cold finger seemed to run down her spine. Even Eurydice opened her eyes and lifted her head, staring at the balcony.

"Who watches us, girl?" Fern murmured to the dragon.

As she tossed a dead fuchsia into the wheelbarrow, Fern turned and glanced up. She only caught a shadow retreating back into the mezzanine on the library side. Was it Quint or Lord Drakeman?

"It's probably Quint checking that I am toiling away hard enough to earn my pay." Fern shoved the trowel into a solid patch of dirt and broke up a lump. Or was it Lord Drakeman, and Eurydice's attention had caught the eerie silver gaze so like hers?

At midday, Fern sat outside in the shade and ate her lunch. She hadn't realised how stuffy the conservatory was until she caught the light breeze rustling the foliage of the surrounding trees. She drained half her water flask, and sweat trickled between her shoulder blades.

It was men's day at the bathhouse, so she couldn't go there to clean off. Fortunately, the weather had warmed over the last few weeks. A swim in the river before she returned home would be refreshing and sluice off the sweat. After her lunch, Fern worked for two more hours until Eurydice became restless.

"Let's stop for today, girl." Fern pushed off the platform to stand and arched her back. Every muscle in her body ached as though she were thirty years old. Then she snorted. She would reach that age before the end of the year. Once, young Fern had thought thirty impossibly old. Now that it was only a few months away, she would have to re-evaluate her definition of old and infirm.

"A thirty-year-old ruined spinster—there is a tale to terrify young debutants," she said to the dragon as they slowly wandered out of the conservatory. Her life had taken a darker path ten years ago, but she had no regrets. "If I hadn't been disgraced, I would never have met you, Riddy." Fern reached down to scratch the dragon's head.

A series of events unravelled in her mind. If she had been offered marriage during the season, as was expected of a noblewoman, she would never have taken up work to earn a living. Lord Warrington would never have employed her to investigate dead plants, and she would never have found the dragonet trapped under a fountain.

Tears burned in her eyes at the thought of the dragon dying alone, in the dark, with no one to rescue her. All because Fern had managed to behave herself in London. Thinking about it, there was another moral to be taken from the tale of her downfall. Being true to yourself could result in unexpected gifts. Like discovering a dragon. Or a new friend hiding from a storm. Millie and Squib would likewise never have entered her life if Fern had done well in London and married.

"Sometimes, the Fates place us exactly where we are meant to be," she repeated the words Morda had said to her.

Fern stepped outside just as Denis walked across the field with the horse and cart. She waved. He had perfect timing. Almost as if someone watched her and let the groom know when she was packing up for the day.

Using the piece of wood George had placed in the cart, Fern made a ramp. It took more effort to get Eurydice up the plank than it did to come down. Twice, she nearly wobbled off the side, and Fern had to steady her. But they got there. Once she was settled in the cart, Fern climbed onto the seat and guided the cob to the driveway.

"I know the perfect spot for a swim." Once through the wrought iron gates (which Fern refused to shut—let Quint do it), she urged the cob into a trot back towards the village.

They halted outside Scribbles, the bookstore. Fern jumped down and patted the horse.

"I'll not be too long," she told both horse and dragon. Children on the bridge ran down towards them.

Fern raised a finger at them. "You lot can keep an eye on both of them for me. But don't overwhelm Riddy, or she will burn your fingers and eat them like sausages."

The horrified looks on their faces told her the warning would be heeded.

As she walked up the path, a new sign hung in the window beside the door.

OPEN 1–4

Millie had decided to instigate limited opening hours to allow herself quiet writing time. Or more likely to protect herself from the chatter of customers all day long. Through the thick glass, a few people browsed the shelves.

Fern pushed inside to find Millie and Squib at the desk. The pixie dragon sat on the writer's shoulder like some sort of parrot editor as he peered at her writing and seemed to make comments about the work.

"Fern! I am simply run off my feet. I did not realise the village contained so many readers." Millie rose from her chair and nearly dislodged Squib, who squawked and fluttered to a bookcase. With arms outstretched for a hug, Millie halted before touching Fern, and her nose wrinkled. "You smell like a compost heap."

"I've been working at Wyndham Hall all day. I need a quick swim and was going to ask if I can leave my clothes in the kitchen and jump in from here." The cottage stood close to the river's edge, and as a child, George had taught her to swim there. When she had gained confidence in the water, her uncles used to sit on the grass and watch to ensure she didn't get into any trouble in the slow-moving river.

"Of course." Millie peered around Fern. "Did you bring company?"

"I took Riddy with me today. She's outside in the cart, and the children are supposed to watch her." Fern would have a very quick swim to scrub away the sweat. She had been jesting when she said the dragon would eat their fingers, but she wasn't entirely sure, and it had been a long time since her breakfast.

The pixie dragon hopped up and down on the shelf and trilled. Millie held out her hand to him, and he glided to her arm. "You go for your swim. I'll take Squib out to see Riddy."

"Thank you!" As she walked through the bookstore, Fern peeled off her jacket and undid her waistcoat buttons with one hand. She dropped the items over the back of a chair in the kitchen.

Alice was busy preparing dinner and turned with a curious look on her face and a knife in her hand. She froze as Fern tugged off her boots and then her shirt.

"I'm going for a quick swim," Fern said from under the linen as she somehow got stuck for a moment.

"I'll fetch a towel," came the reply.

Wearing only her shift (Fern wasn't stripping naked in the middle of the village), she ran out the kitchen door, across the soft grass, and leapt. Bringing up her knees, she hit the water with a splash and dropped under the surface.

Cold squeezed her body. Bursting back up, Fern let loose a string of oaths. The weather might be warming but no one had told the river yet. The water had the chill of distant snow still clinging to it. At least she would be clean and didn't have to either bother Mrs Bentley to heat water, or wait until tomorrow for ladies' day at the bathhouse. Not wanting to spend any longer being wet than necessary, she scrubbed her fingernails through her hair and rinsed off again.

Fern climbed out and walked, dripping wet, back to the cottage. Alice stood at the back door with a stern look on her face that was an exact replica of the one her mother used.

"You don't step inside until you're dry. I'm not having puddles on my clean floor." She held out the towel.

"I wouldn't dream of it." Fern rubbed her hair briskly, then her limbs. Last, she wrung as much water as possible from her saturated shift.

Once the maid deemed her acceptable, Fern was allowed back inside to pull on her clothes. Her trousers and shirt stuck to the wet shift, but she didn't have far to get home, and at least now the sweat was gone from her scalp and shoulder blades.

Passing through the bookstore, out on the front lawn, children sat on the grass around the cart. Squib and Eurydice appeared to be having a conversation, the two dragons trilling and clicking at each other, accompanied by flapping wings from Squib. The children were pretending to do voices and adding their own dialogue to the scene.

"They have simply marvellous imaginations. Although I don't think Squib is really telling Riddy to bite Joseph Parish on the bottom," Millie said.

"He might if he ever meets him. I believe he is the sort of boy who likes to throw spitballs made from wadded-up paper." Fern scanned the children and found Joseph scowling from the back. He also appeared to be chewing, so he probably had one of the infamous sticky blobs in progress.

"Ew." Millie screwed up her face. "I shall keep Squib away from him. Nor will he be allowed near *my* books."

"I'll be back to see you tomorrow for a longer visit." Fern promised her friend as she walked over to the horse and cart, shooing the children away as she went.

Squib flew over the tops of heads as he returned to Millie, and everyone waved as Fern turned the horse for home. As they walked up the drive, George came out to meet her. Eurydice lay slumped in the back of the cart. The excitement of the children and Squib had worn off, leaving her exhausted.

William took the reins as Fern climbed down.

"Riddy has had a big day. First, exploring the conservatory a little and sleeping on the heated platform. Then she visited with Squib and the local children while I took a quick swim." Fern explained her damp appearance and the tired dragon. She leaned into the cart and gently stroked Eurydice's head while calling her name. The dragon lifted her nose and blinked several times.

"We are home, little one. Would you like some dinner?" Fern asked.

The idea of food roused her further, and she managed to stand, although her legs wobbled.

"I wouldn't risk the ramp. She'll fall off," George said when Fern pulled the plank of wood out to ease the dragon's exit.

The barrel-chested man scooped the dragon up with his arms under her belly. He grunted as he set her down on the ground. Once the dragon was settled in her stall and had dinner in her belly, Fern tucked the blanket in around her curled-up form and left William to keep watch.

Fern's clothes were covered in soil, and her appearance would make Mrs Bentley wave a knife at her head. To avoid that, she stripped off her dirty and wet clothes on the doorstep and carried them straight through to the laundry. Wearing only the wet shift, she hurried to her room to dry off and put on a clean gown.

Over dinner, Fern told Ambrose and George about her day. "The conservatory is enormous. It will take me weeks to just clear out the dead growth. Then what survives will need careful nurturing. The soil is starved, and it will need loads of loamy compost to bring it back to life."

"And what of his lordship? Did the earl make an appearance at all?" Ambrose asked.

Fern recalled the moment the hairs on her nape prickled, and a shiver ran down her spine. Who had watched her from the shadows? "No. But I did meet Denis Fawcett, who took the horse and unharnessed him, bringing him back when I finished for the day."

Recalling the stablehand, who was a few years older than her, made a question for her uncle come to mind. "He said that Lord Drakeman took him in after he got into trouble as a lad. Do you remember what it was?"

"Denis Fawcett." Ambrose repeated the name as an aide de memoire. He leaned back in his chair and stared at the ceiling in silence.

Fern continued eating while they waited for her uncle to dredge up whatever he found about the man in the dim corners of his memory.

"Theft." Ambrose leaned forwards with a gleam in his eye. "I seem to recall that Denis stole a rather fancy horse from the stable at Drake's Rest. He didn't get far before it bucked him off. His bad luck continued, as the stead belonged to a noble passing through our village and who insisted the lad be charged with horse theft. He couldn't have been more than twelve at the time and would have gone to jail for some years. Or been sent to Australia as a convict. Lord Drakeman settled the matter, noble to noble."

"Now he is in charge of the earl's horses. I suppose that put his interest to use." Fern wondered what had motivated the old earl to save the lad. Did his son share the same sense of community and looking after the villagers?

"Probably taught him to ride a buck too," George said, to a snort of laughter from Ambrose.

CHAPTER 9

The next day, Fern rose early and answered her correspondence. Then she readied a box of rare plants purchased by the gardener at a large estate in Kent. The delicate package would be passed from one coach driver to another until it reached its destination. The lord having paid for a seat next to the driver to ensure its safety.

"Another scandal has shocked London society," Ambrose said over breakfast, the newspaper spread before him.

"What has some poor sod done now? Breathe the wrong way?" George asked over the rim of his mug.

"A light-fingered young buck has been accused of stealing jewellery from the boudoirs of wealthy widows. He claims they were gifts, but one woman's son is determined to press charges to recover the valuable pieces." Ambrose sipped his tea and continued to read the article.

Fern leaned over to see the accompanying cartoon. A buxom older woman clutched bedsheets to her chest, while a half-naked young man clad only in a shirt, pulled jewellery from a drawer. There was something about the drawing that itched at her brain.

She tapped a finger on the shield above the woman's head. A lion reared up on its hind legs to battle a fish. "I've seen that emblem before."

George glanced at the newspaper. "It's the crest of the Fishburn family. Lord Fishburn is pressing the suit."

A memory flared inside Fern. "I saw that crest on a carriage waiting in the lane by the whisperwoods. I wonder if Lord Fishburn had been inside."

Ambrose stared at the corner of the room as he worked through something in his mind. "If the trees are distorting confessions, perhaps the lord went to seek advice about his mother or possibly missing jewellery and was told about the other young man's involvement."

"From what we have seen so far, there is a kernel of truth in what the trees say. But they turn the words into a weapon to stab at where the visitor is most vulnerable." Fern recalled what they had whispered about Millie. That a quill was her sword to strike down whoever stood between her and freedom. "So how do we determine if Lord Fishburn did indeed pick up this bit of gossip about his mother and a younger man from the trees?"

Ambrose's eyes twinkled. "Leave that to me. I shall write to a dear friend who hears *everything*. She will have all the details that were far too salacious for the newspaper to print."

After breakfast, Fern asked William to harness the reliable cob to the cart once more. This time she would journey alone to the south, with a step ladder riding in the back of the cart instead of the dragon. She had promised

Eurydice they would go to Wyndham Hall when she returned.

Fern intended to examine the whisperwoods more closely, and they didn't have any convenient, low-hanging branches for climbing. Which is why the ladder was needed. A short time later, she guided the horse down the narrow lane and towards the lifeless cottage. Today, there was a grey horse tied to the hitching rail. The equine startled as the cart rumbled towards it and pulled backwards.

Jumping down, knowing her horse wouldn't move, Fern approached the startled one and whispered quiet, soothing words to it.

"Hush now. No need to be frightened of us," she murmured.

The grey horse rolled its eyes and snorted as shivers wracked its body.

"I just want to give you a scratch. Would you like that?" Slowly, Fern extended an arm and stroked the horse's neck. "You're a highly strung thing. I bet you don't like being here all on your own."

She talked to the horse and scratched its wither. After a few minutes, it let out a deep sigh and dropped its head. Only then did she slowly lead her horse around so they pointed out how they came in. Given the nervous nature of the other equine, Fern decided not to unpack the cart until the owner returned. Waving a ladder around might be too much for the grey horse, and she didn't want it snapping a rein and galloping off.

With nothing much to do except wait, she leaned over the neck of the cob and combed his long mane with her fingers.

She could have weeded the long-neglected garden of the cottage, but she rather liked the wild growth that sprouted in all directions. Instead, she wondered what she would say to the whisperwoods.

Part of her still struggled to believe the trees spread twisted truths. Nor had she plucked up the courage to ask Millie about the circumstances surrounding her husband's death. But she must. One afternoon while they had tea in the conservatory seemed like the best time. Preferably after the front door was bolted so no customers interrupted them.

Fern's tentative theory suggested that the trees took what a person confessed and found another secret, somewhat related, to maliciously distort. If she wanted to test that theory, she needed to give them a secret that involved someone else she knew about. But who?

The logical thing to do would be to pull Millie deeper into her investigation. There had to be an awkward conversation with her anyway, and it would give Fern more whispers to either verify or disprove.

The cob's head jerked upwards as someone crashed through the trees. Whoever had spoken to the whisperwoods returned and in an agitated state. A well-dressed gentleman pushed a branch aside as he muttered curses and condemned someone under his breath.

His hands curled into fists as he approached his horse. The animal took a step backwards, and its eyes widened.

Poor thing. No wonder it's nervous if his rider is like that. Fern watched as the man roughly untied the reins, paying no notice to how his high emotions were being absorbed by his horse.

The animal pawed the ground as he placed the tip of his boot in the stirrup. He barely swung his weight up when the horse did a small buck, snorted, and danced on the spot.

"Stop it!" the rider yelled, yanking on the reins. Then he booted the horse, and it cantered off with a choppy sideways stride.

"Well, someone must have heard bad news." A shame she hadn't recognised him. Then she could have scanned the newspapers for any scandals that hinted at his involvement. She spared a thought for the poor horse and wished she had let the thing run away while she had the chance.

"Perhaps the horse will throw its rider and gallop to freedom." Fern slid the ladder from the cart and carried it along the narrow track to the glade. The rustle of leaves and indistinct murmurs surrounded her, along with the rich loamy aroma of soil.

"You are supposed to help people and ease their worries, not make them all angry," she admonished the trees as she approached the central whisperwood.

The murmurs increased, and the occasional word became more distinct.

"...not...heir...gambling...deserved..." Branches shook, and the words faded away again.

There was a worrying new development if the trees were referring to the departed noble without her offering up a secret of her own. Or was her mind playing tricks on her, plucking unrelated words and trying to fit them together to make a story about the angry man?

"You are telling stories, and they aren't as good as the tales written by Millicent Carlisle. I believe she will become a famous novelist one day, and society will clamour for her attention." Sadness tinged Fern's words as she realised a tiny part of her longed for society to turn its warmth back on her. If only for a moment. What would it be like to once more have calling cards and invitations piled up beside her breakfast plate?

Shaking the old feelings away, she rested the ladder against the trunk of the central whisperwood and climbed the rungs. When she reached the extended bough, she hauled herself up so she could sit on it. With the solid trunk at her back, she had a better view of the canopy of leaves. The odd decay pattern seemed to affect the outermost leaves, and those underneath and closer to the trunk showed no signs of die-off at all.

As she studied the foliage, the whispers became clearer again.

"Millicent steals her ideas from others. They are not her own. She wants people to believe she wrote them. Because she has no talent." The leaves above Fern shook.

She sucked in a breath. "That's a horrid thing to say! Actually, I'm not sure what is worse, that you accused her of killing her husband or that you claim she has no talent and plagiarises others."

One could almost wonder if the spirit of a literary critic haunted the woods. There would be a plot twist suitable for one of Millie's stories.

From the satchel at her side, Fern pulled a strip of clean cotton. Folding it into a wad, she wiped at a bunch of leaves with browning outer edges. When she finished, the cloth was stained with a faint blueish tinge.

"Something is definitely causing your leaves to die, and I think it is airborne." It had to be something settling from above. If the trees were being poisoned from the roots, the dead growth would start in the centre and spread outwards. This moved from the outer edges inwards.

Using her pocket knife, Fern sliced through a small hand-sized bract. The tree hissed, and the branches closer to her rose a few inches as though they recoiled in pain.

"Given your size, this is comparable to trimming a finger-nail," she told the tree, which had overreacted like Squib. Perhaps all magical creatures were prone to dramatic outbursts? "I need a sample to figure out what is wrong with you before you sicken any further."

Treating the twig with care, Fern wrapped it in a clean cotton cloth and placed it back in her satchel. Then she lowered herself to the top step of the ladder. Once back on the grass, she pointed a finger at the trees. "You are supposed to be sage and wise. Not cruel. You would be far better to remain silent than to speak while you are sick."

She doubted the trees would heed her advice, but she had to try. Picking up the ladder, she walked back to the horse and cart. There was one more thing she wanted to investigate before returning to Drake's Bend.

Sibylcrest Abbey.

On her last visit, she noticed the pale smoke coming from the chimneys. That made her think of how upset Mrs Bentley got if she burned garden rubbish on laundry day. Sometimes the wind blew the ash over the clean washing and left a dark, sooty mark. A downdraft might have spread coal smoke over the surrounding forest and the towering whisperwoods.

At the top of the little lane, she turned the horse to the east and the worn path that wound its way up the hill to the abbey. The rambling buildings had started life as a Norman fort, and local tales said it had been occupied long before then. The Moray sisters spun fairytales of the Fae who once lived on the top of the hill. Their magic had flowed down and wrapped around the seedling beeches growing at the base.

Those saplings absorbed the Fae magic, and as they grew, they began to whisper and mutter. Travellers heard the strange voices. Others, when unburdening their darkest secrets to the grove, were gifted words of wisdom to ease their hearts. That was how the legend of the whisperwoods grew.

Even in Medieval times, the building perched on the mount had been known as Sibylcrest. Sibyl for the oracle from ancient times, which hinted at the nature of the whisperwood trees. The crest part of the name was obvious—the fort-turned-abbey sat on the pinnacle of the hill.

As they neared the top, the winding road turned into a stone-lined structure with a waist-high side that led to an imposing wall. Fern stared at the broody building.

"I never thought to find a gloomier place than Wyndham Hall." She jumped from the seat and told the cob to stay and not wander off.

England was littered with old castles and forts as though a giant had scattered them like seeds. Many fell into disrepair, either abandoned or the owners drowned in the cold ocean of debt required for their upkeep. From what she remembered of her local history, the abbey had passed to private hands—once it had passed through those of King Henry VIII.

Standing on the causeway, she stared at the chimney stacks. They occupied opposite ends of a steeply pitched section of the roof. They puffed pale smoke, and when she shielded her eyes from the sun, she thought she detected a faint blue tinge. It was doubtful the new tenant would stop lighting fires or switch from coal to wood to (somewhat ironically) save trees. But you didn't know until you asked.

Fern approached the portcullis, once intended to keep invaders at bay. Somewhere hidden in the wall would be the mechanism used to raise and lower the gate. Two strong men would be needed to turn the wheel and wind in the heavy chain. Grabbing hold of the cool metal, Fern shook it. Even after many centuries, the gate still did its job and didn't even wiggle.

While the portcullis had a conveniently sized square pattern that would make climbing easy, it descended from the stonework, and there was no gap at the top. The walls were over twenty feet high, and there were few finger holds among the carefully placed slabs. What windows it had were small arrow slits for shooting out, and even an inquisitive squirrel would struggle to climb in.

With no obvious way to gain entrance, she might actually be defeated by a door for once. If Quint ever heard it, he would install such a feature at Wyndham Hall to keep her out.

Fern pressed her face to the bars and scanned the courtyard beyond. Crates and barrels were stacked in a corner, but with no markers, their contents were unknown. There was no sign of life. Not a single dog slept in the sun, nor a cat looking down from a parapet. Not even a chicken scratching for insects between the ancient cobbles.

As she contemplated what to do next, a man trotted down a set of stairs that curved around an internal wall.

"Hello!" she shouted at him.

When he didn't turn, she cast around on the ground and found a rock. Sticking her arm through the gate, Fern threw it. She didn't hit him, but it did clatter to the ground by his feet, making him look up.

He startled, then cautiously approached. "Who are you?"

"I'm Fern Oakby. Is Sir Luxton Davies in? I'm assuming he is by the look of all the lovely fires going to warm him." She had decided to start at the top of who might be in charge at Sibylcrest and work her way down from there.

The man scoffed and rubbed his hands together as though they were chilled. "This place is so draughty; we'd need twice as many fires lit before we got warm. Not that he'd care; we're only allowed to light the ones in the main hall." Then he narrowed his gaze at her. "Why do you want to know if he's here? What business do you have with him? The stock isn't ready to ship out yet."

Well, that was an interesting titbit she would mull over later. They were making something and running some sort of business. "Oh, I'm with the welcoming committee from Drake's Bend. We realised we had been terribly remiss and hadn't welcomed Sir Luxton to the area when he purchased the abbey." Fern batted her eyelashes and tried to look like someone who belonged on a welcoming committee. It might have helped if she was wearing a dress and didn't look like she had just been climbing trees. Too late, she patted a hand through her hair, wondering how many leaves and twigs might be caught in its short length. Thankfully, she only found one bit of twig.

The man shook his head. "I already told you, he's not here."

What was it about male employees being overly protective of their employer's whereabouts? "Do you know if he will be at Sibylcrest this week? I was told to find out so we can deliver a gift basket." That sounded like the sort of thing you would do to welcome a new neighbour.

A gleam entered the man's eyes. "What sort of gift basket?"

"Um." Her mind raced. What sounded *welcoming?* "Scones, naturally. Locally made jam, a bottle of blackberry spirits." Ambrose and George had a bottle, and the fruity flavour delivered a powerful kick.

"He might be here next week. If that gift basket has cake in it, I will personally make sure he gets it." He grinned and revealed a couple of missing teeth. Probably because he liked cake.

"Oh. That would be ever so kind of you. What is your name, sir?"

"I'm Mr Sainsbury. I'm the steward here."

"Well, Mr Sainsbury, is there any cake in particular that, um, Sir Luxton might prefer?" Fern gushed.

"Ginger loaf. That's my...I mean, his favourite," the man replied.

"I will ensure it contains a substantial ginger loaf." She kept a pleasant smile on her face, but it was hard work when multiple questions were scratching at her brain, demanding to be let loose.

The employee raised his hand to rub his nose, and she noticed an odd mark.

"Did you spill some ink?" she asked.

"What?" He turned his hand over to stare at his fingers, which had a faint blue stain on them. "Yeah. I must have done."

The man didn't look the sort to labour over a column of numbers or write a novel.

"You might want to give that a good scrub. Ink does stain terribly." Not that she thought the stain was ink. The stain had appeared too regular on each fingertip as though he had dipped them in something. If it were the same as when she had touched the whisperwood leaves, it had taken a bit of effort to remove from her skin.

CHAPTER 10

"I shall be back next week with the gift basket and a special ginger loaf." Fern waved and returned to the horse. "Curiouser and curiouser," she said to the cob as she climbed into the cart and picked up the reins.

A conviction unfurled through her that the odd blue stain was being spread by smoke from the abbey's chimneys and that it had something to do with the twisted murmurings of the whisperwoods.

There was one person who would know for sure if the grime on the leaves was from the smoke—Lord Drakeman.

Before she consulted the alchemist, Fern wanted to see if the three witches knew why the whisperwoods were causing misery after centuries of offering quiet wisdom. Another thought popped into her mind. What if the grove had simply got sick of everybody's problems? She didn't know how they did it decade after decade without uttering a sharp word or telling a supplicant to sort their own problems.

After returning the cob, cart, and ladder, Fern slung the

battered satchel over her arm and headed out for the cottages shared by the magic casters. Today, they were outside. Nona and Decima worked in the garden, weeding and tending to the variety of plants they grew. Morda sat nearby in the sun, a contented chicken asleep on her lap. The blind seer stroked the chicken as she crooned to it.

"Hello, Fern!" Nona called out as she walked up the path.

Decima waved, a bright purple carrot dangling in her hand. While orange carrots spread in popularity, the witches grew old varieties that were purple or yellow.

Morda patted the grass beside her in invitation, and Fern dropped to the ground. Stretching her legs out, she leaned back and let the sun caress her face. Turning to the side, she cracked one eye open to find the chicken had done the same and regarded her with a half-lidded stare.

"Why do you appear to be hypnotising a chicken, Morda?" she asked.

"This lady is one of our best layers, but she's stopped for some reason. I am waiting for her to show me what has upset her." The youngest Moray sister continued to pet the chicken.

"George said a fox was sneaking around Nemython the other night. Until it came face-to-face with Riddy. Then it ran off. It might have passed through here." A dragon, even a small young one, was a brilliant guard for sleeping fowls.

"We will make sure they are in their coop at night until it has gone. Although it might have kept running until the next county after confronting a dragon," Decima said.

"How is Eurydice?" Nona asked.

"Improving every day. And growing." Fern loved having the young dragon for company, but how long would it be before she was recovered enough that she wanted to test out her wings and seek out others of her kind? "But I came to ask you about something else that is sick. The whisperwoods."

The chicken squawked and skipped its way to a shady globe artichoke as Morda's body jolted. The old woman turned her milky gaze to Fern as she spoke in a voice that seemed to echo from far away. "The trees cry out for help, yet spew malice with every word."

Fern let out a sigh. Of course the three witches would know that the trees spread horrid gossip that threatened to tear apart old friendships in the village. "That's why I'm here. The outer leaves of the whisperwoods are dying, and I think that is making the trees into cruel gossips. When I touched the leaves, it left a blue residue on my fingers, but I don't know what it is."

Nona stopped working and leaned on the hoe. "If it is a physical problem, you know who would be better to consult."

Fern plucked a piece of grass and tore it into pieces. "Drakeman," she muttered.

She was supposed to call him Lord Drakeman, but sometimes her mind had trouble with the noble title because he simply didn't seem very...*lord-y*. She had no difficulty whatsoever imagining him in some squalid East End tavern, managing a network of criminal activity and deciding who to rob or murder each night. That led her to wonder if that was where he dredged up Quint.

The more she thought about it, the more she doubted Quint was even his real name. The word referred to when a card player held five cards, all from the same suit and running in sequence. That thought tumbled her further into a dark hole. Her imagination placed Lord Drakeman in a dimly lit pub. The butler lost a card game to the earl, causing him to enter service until he had repaid the debt.

The three women cackled and pulled Fern's mind from a shadowy tale suited to grace the shelves of Millie's bookstore. The noise demonstrated why many thought of them as Macbeth's three witches as opposed to the Triple Goddess of maiden, mother, and crone. They were most definitely three crones. All they needed was a boiling cauldron in their front yard and a stack of frog's legs to toss in. And possibly some pointy hats to wear.

"You three had better not be interfering in my life." Previously, they had some sort of bet about whether she would gain entrance to the alchemist's laboratory. Morda won. You would think her older sisters would have learned to never bet against a seer.

Morda reached out and took her hand, gently squeezing her fingers. "The Fates can only show you a path. It always remains your choice if you walk it or not."

Fern huffed. She wasn't entirely sure the Fates gave her much choice at all. There were times that it felt as though they prodded her in the back with a knife to ensure she walked in a certain direction. "I intend to discuss the issue with his lordship when I am at Wyndham Hall later today. But I wanted your advice about the change in the trees."

She removed the bundle with the bract of leaves from her satchel and placed it in Morda's hand. The blind woman rubbed the surface of a leaf between her fingers, then sniffed and licked at the blueish residue. Once she had finished, Nona took the twig with its smattering of foliage to study, before passing it to Decima.

After they had all examined the small serrated leaves with brown, curling edges, they came to sit beside Fern. They conferred with one another in low, murmured tones.

Then Morda spoke in her usual cryptic fashion. "The nemeton bleeds, and the whisperwoods weep poison."

"The nemeton is sick?" Fern was familiar with the term. It meant an ancient grove sacred to the Celtic druids. Her family home bore a reference to such places—Nemython House being a corruption of the word. Her father thought it meant the old stand of kelmsgales that had once encircled the village green. But the whisperwoods were another and had long been a place where druids had performed their arcane rites.

Nona nodded, her fingers still weaving spells in the air. "Everything is connected. The sacred grove is the heart of the forest surrounding Drake's Bend. When it ails, all suffer. While this has a physical origin, I sense that it is no natural ailment."

"Someone has tainted the nemeton, and corrupted its magic for their own ends," Decima added.

Fern doubted she had to look far to figure out who. The residue had to be coming from the eerie pale smoke emitting from Sibylcrest's chimneys.

"To cure the whisperwoods, we must cleanse the nemeton. We will see what we can conjure to restore their balance. Young Benjamin has offered to take us out to the grove later today." Nona handed the bract of leaves back to Fern.

Decima cackled to herself. No doubt imagining how the strong blacksmith would have to lift each woman into his cart.

Fern wrapped the twig in the cloth again and placed it back in her satchel. She knew a little about nemetons, as the idea of ancient groves intertwined with magic had always fascinated her.

"Thank you all. I shall see what our local alchemist can tell me about this residue and if it is indeed connected to whatever they burn at the abbey." Her brain couldn't imagine what they tossed on their fires to leave such an inky residue. Unless it was books. In which case, they were monsters who had to be stopped.

Her task was twofold. If the smoke did indeed pollute the trees, she first had to put out the fires. Only then could they heal the nemeton. Fern silently hoped the witches would discover a simple solution, like adding fertiliser to the soil or waiting for a good rain to wash the leaves clean. She would have thought two thunderous and magical storms would have scrubbed away the smoky residue, or had it activated something instead?

"I'll call in again tomorrow, and you can share what you learned from the trees." Fern buckled up the satchel.

As she stood, Morda caught her hand. "Words have power."

There was a lesson she knew only too well. Words had caused her downfall in London, and they were wielded like weapons by the upper echelon of society.

Fern squeezed Morda's hand. "Yes, and I shall have a few

choice ones to give to Sir Luxton if his fires are damaging our forest."

She returned to her home and reclaimed the horse and cart. While George and William fussed with settling Eurydice in the back, Fern made a quick dash to the walled garden. There was another visit she needed to make, to people who were never far from her mind.

With her garden scissors in one hand, Fern made a bouquet of roses, sprays of lily of the valley, and forget-me-nots. Their stems were tied with string, and she placed them on the seat next to her when she climbed into the cart.

"We'll be home for dinner!" she called out to George and urged the horse forwards.

They trotted along the side of the river and through the village. Excited children ran behind, waving to Eurydice, who trilled in reply.

Despite the laughter of the youngsters, a tension built in the village. Two women argued and pulled each other's hair until an elderly woman rapped on one's arm with her cane. Men glared at one another as though suspecting the other would steal the money in their pockets.

The whisperwoods were well-known in Drake's Bend and only a short distance away. How many locals had gone for a walk or ride to see what gossip they could learn about their neighbours? Morda was right; words had power, and ones cruelly cast could tear holes in their little community.

"Will you come back, Miss Oakby?" one of the boys shouted.

Fern's thoughts returned to more immediate things. Like

curious children. "We'll be back later this afternoon, and you can sit with her then!" she called.

She had decided it was time to have a quiet, and no doubt horribly awkward, chat with Millie. Asking about her husband's death would either confirm her theory about the whisperwoods, or send her off in a new direction. The children could watch over the dragon while they talked in private inside the bookstore.

They lost their tail when they reached the northern tip of the village. A little further along the road, instead of turning right through the gates of Wyndham Hall, Fern urged the horse to the left. The road dipped between the closely grown trees, but once through the green fence, they emerged into sunlight.

Before them lay a meadow, surrounded by forest. The wildflowers were dotted with gravestones. Some with mossy, rounded tops. Others were more like obelisks, where entire families were interred over the years and names added by the local stonemason. At the farthest point from the road and with its back to the forest sat a modest church made from local stone. Drake's Bend was a secular community, the residents having no patience for either moralising or intolerance, but the old church was still used to celebrate and mourn.

Fern left the horse to snatch mouthfuls of grass while she hopped down. Eurydice seemed content to sun herself in the cart. Taking the bouquet of flowers, Fern walked towards the forest and a tall gravestone set not far from the base of a towering oak. A tree emerged from the granite, its roots running down the side of the stone while its bough stood above.

Two names were engraved on the stone. Kneeling, Fern placed the flowers at the foot of the tree, in a glass jar buried in the soil with the hole exposed. With one hand on the cool stone, she spoke to those interred beneath her.

"The whisperwoods are causing trouble, Father. How I wish you were here to help me. They have started gossiping like mean society ladies, and their cruel words are hurting people." She sat back on her knees. "Mother, how I want to talk to you about Lord Drakeman. I cannot take the measure of him. He is rude, abrupt, and shut away from all society. And yet..."

Here she paused, unable to find the words to describe what pushed her onwards. Certainly, her curiosity demanded she roam the halls of Wyndham and discover what mysteries and secrets it hid. But part of her also wanted to learn the secrets of the owner, not just the building. What experiment had caused scars that resembled scales, and how did the silver eye affect his vision? Did he withdraw from the world because of his appearance, or for some other reason?

She also wanted to know where he had unearthed Quint. It definitely hadn't been as a butler in another grand home. Fern suspected they had encountered one another in a dark alley.

Another part of her remembered the way he had held her when she became tangled climbing through his laboratory window. Her skin had warmed under her clothing, and her heart beat a little faster at the contact.

She snorted. Silly body, acting like a plant too long without rain. What she needed was a brief summer romance to burn away the memory of Lord Drakeman's touch.

"The kelmsgale festival is only a few weeks away now, and we will see many travelling merchants and entertainers in the village for a few days. There is bound to be a specimen among them who will divert my thoughts." Then she gasped. She really needed to learn to keep some thoughts inside her head. Her parents might be dead, but they probably didn't want to hear about her amorous activities!

Fern pulled a few weeds from around the headstone as she chatted with her parents, telling them of how their garden grew and the transformation of George's cottage into a bookstore. Then she placed a kiss on the granite before she left to check on another resident.

In the middle of the cemetery stood an odd little greenhouse. Barely reaching her waist, it was just two square feet in size. The thick glass was held in place with an ironwork skeleton. Gaps in the top allowed a small amount of rain in and for the air to circulate around the occupant. A door in the front opened, and Fern unlatched it and tugged it free.

Inside was an orchid. But no ordinary one. This was a spectral orchid. It had three thick, glossy leaves, each longer than Fern's hand. They tapered to a narrow point and hung over the exposed roots. Like gnarled finger bones, the silver roots jutted out of the soil and hung over the edge of the pot.

Fern checked to see if the orchid had any sign of a bloom. Spectral orchids only flowered in the presence of a spirit. One would have thought it would flower constantly in the middle of the village cemetery, and yet most of the departed villagers died content and without any need to linger.

Larger cemeteries had two or three of the caged orchids placed around their grounds. The bereaved found comfort in the ghostly white blooms, telling themselves it meant their loved one lingered. Often with a final message that needed to be delivered.

Her father had acquired a specimen after his wife had died. Both he and Fern had watched the orchid, sure that it would flower and show that Delfie returned to watch over them. But their plant never formed a bud. Fern wiped its rubbery leaves on a regular basis and consoled herself that her parents were together wherever they were. Even if it wasn't at Nemython House or the graveyard.

Today, the orchid had a barely visible bump on one side of its arching (and flowerless) stem. "I wonder if you are a flower or simply a bumpy bit of growth." Only time would tell if the distinctive bud would form and indicate a soul wandered the meadow.

Returning to the cart, and finding Eurydice snoring quietly in the back, Fern clucked her tongue to the cob, and they walked silently through the graves and back through the dense guard of trees.

CHAPTER 11

At Wyndham Hall, Fern jumped down from the cart to bang on the door and rouse Quint.

"Why are you bothering me? Do I look like a bloody stablehand? You'll find Fawcett at the stables," he grumbled before slamming the door.

She stared at the solid piece of timber for a long minute. It wasn't just the stablehand she needed to find, but his lordship as well. But that could wait until Eurydice was sunning herself on the heated sleeping platform.

Since she was directed to find the stables on her own, Fern took that as permission to explore the grounds. It wasn't her fault if she headed off in the wrong direction as she wandered through the overgrown gardens and neglected buildings, looking for the right place.

As it transpired, the stables were surprisingly easy to find. The rear of the estate opened up to a cobbled and packed-earth yard encircled by stone stables with a carriage house to one side. The other side of the courtyard was sheltered by what appeared to be double-height stables. Giant-sized doors ran on tracks along one side, rather like the entrance to the conservatory.

Fern halted, her attention fixed on the imposing building that was a ghostly effigy left from previous centuries.

"The wyvernry," she whispered to both herself and Eurydice.

"That's right, miss. Dragons used to live there many years ago," a cheerful voice said from beside her.

The unexpected sound broke the spell the wyvernry had cast over her. Fern spun around, grabbing the edge of the cart to keep her balance.

"Good morning, Mr Fawcett." Her gaze darted sideways as she tried to imagine what the ancient stone construction would look like on the inside.

"Just Denis, miss. Mr Fawcett is my father, and we don't stand on ceremony around here." He reached out and patted the cob's neck.

She had noticed the lack of ceremony at Wyndham Hall. Along with manners and any form of common decency.

"I'll only be here for a few hours, Denis. I'll come and find you when I'm done." That would give her a chance to explore the wyvernry.

Using the plank of wood, she helped Eurydice down from the cart. The dragon sat on the cobbles and stared at the building where her kind used to sleep.

"One day, Riddy, if you keep growing, you will be large enough to need such a doorway." Fern rested one hand on the dragon's head.

"It would be a marvellous thing to see a dragon in there

again. But she would be rather lonely." Denis led the cob and cart away to remove the harness.

"Yes. She would be all alone." For the first time, Fern considered Eurydice's future.

What would happen once she was big and strong enough to fly and hunt for herself? Would she take to the skies and never return to Nemython House? It was selfish to think the dragon would stay with her, like Squib with Millie, when there were no others of her species in the area anymore.

Could Squib's companionship be sufficient for a fully grown dragon? They would be a mismatched pair in years to come if Eurydice grew as large as the dragon Fern spotted flying over the garden some weeks ago. That was a question she couldn't answer. Nor was it her place to decide for the dragon who was her ideal companion.

Eurydice trilled and licked Fern's hand as though reminding her that she wasn't alone. They had each other, even if they were different species. That would have to be enough. For now.

Today, the walk to the conservatory was a little easier for the young dragon. As though she had recovered some strength from sleeping where generations of other dragons had once slumbered the day before.

The sliding door had been closed, and when Fern grabbed the handle and shoved her weight against it, it gave way so easily that she nearly toppled over and ended up on the ground. Only the fact that she was hanging onto the handle tightly left her dangling above the dirt.

"It appears someone has oiled the track." She swore she could hear Quint laughing from somewhere inside.

Regaining her balance, and plotting how to repay the butler for his kindness, Fern dropped her tools into the wheelbarrow and entered the conservatory. Eurydice followed behind, snuffling at brittle twigs and piles of dirt. The dragon had more energy today and explored under a group of drooping palms before wandering to the raised platform. She still couldn't hop up on her own, and Fern lifted the creature's rear end.

With Eurydice happily rolling on the platform and scratching her hide, Fern set off to find Lord Drakeman. "I'll not be too long," she called out.

The most obvious place to start was the library, just the other side of the wall shared with the dragon conservatory. Grabbing her satchel with its sample of leaves and odd, blue-stained fabric, she approached the panelled doors.

Sliding them apart, she walked across the library's rugs on the balls of her feet. She didn't want to drop dirt on the floor, plus it felt a bit clandestine to sneak in. The room was enveloped in silence. Not even the rustle of a paper or squeak of a scampering mouse broke the eerie stillness.

Having made it across the room without leaving a trail of muddy bootprints, Fern considered the next door. Since the earl wasn't in the library, he was either somewhere else in the house or in his laboratory. She knew how to find the squat building tucked into the hill, but she didn't want to waste all day wandering through the rambling Hall.

What she needed was her favourite butler with his cryptic clues.

Yanking the door open, she startled Quint, who walked along the corridor. His body jerked to a stop. He held a tray with a fat wooden box of polished wood with a fancy brass clasp. It was the sort of velvet-lined container used to store the best silverware. Beside it were a few separate silver condiment containers, a cloth, and a smaller container that most likely held whiting, a cleaning agent.

"Polishing the silverware or stealing it?" Fern asked as she leaned against the door frame.

Quint scowled. "Cleaning it. I wouldn't steal from the earl."

Interesting. He didn't say he wouldn't steal, just not from his current employer.

"Speaking of his lordship, where is he? I need to show him something." Fern hoped the butler was in a more co-operative mood today, and wouldn't send her off to become trapped in the attic. Or the dungeon. It was much harder to escape out the window of a dungeon since they usually didn't have any.

His gaze narrowed even further until his eyes were almost closed. Then he huffed. "In his lab." Then Quint carried on down the hallway.

Fern watched his receding back for a moment. That comment had been positively helpful when she had expected some sort of cryptic *not-in-but-not-out* statement.

"It must be fumes from the silver polish." That would be the only thing to explain the butler almost acting like one.

Not wanting to leave Eurydice alone for too long, Fern curled one hand in the strap of her satchel and marched towards the front door. She picked up her pace once outside and skipped across the meadow. At one point, she paused and glanced back at the house, not quite sure what she expected to see. Quint laughing from an upper window? Or perhaps Eurydice, tripping on the gravel and crying out as she tried to follow.

That thought spurred Fern onwards to the former storehouse nestled under its blanket of soil. With barely a glance at the partially open window, she rapped loudly on the thick oak door.

"What?" came the call from inside.

"It's Miss Oakby. I need a moment of your time, please, Lord Drakeman." When she heard no reply, Fern's gaze drifted sideways to the window. Should she...?

Before she could contemplate climbing through, the door was yanked open. "I have a few moments to spare while I wait for the Spiritus Aetherea to coalesce."

As she stepped inside, Fern wondered which of the many bubbling and smoking experiments was the Spiritus Aetherea. But if her time was limited, she couldn't indulge her curiosity. Walking to the square table under the skylight, she tugged the satchel strap over her head and opened the flap. From within, she removed the cloth-wrapped bract of leaves.

"The whisperwoods are spreading harmful rumours about people. I believe the root cause is something affecting their leaves, which are dying from the outer edges." She laid out the cloth and peeled back a side to reveal the twig hanging onto a small cluster of foliage.

Lord Drakeman heaved a sigh and placed both hands on the tabletop. He wore a stained leather apron over his linen shirt. The sleeves were rolled to his elbows, and she tried not to stare at his well-formed and muscular forearms or the odd scar that sliced down one. "Since we have had this sort of discussion before, I will assume there is more to this botanical problem."

"Yes. When I touched the leaves, I noticed an odd, blue stain on my fingertips. Yet, there is nothing visible to the naked eye. You can see it on the cloth." She pointed to the blue patches on the cotton. "There are inhabitants at Sibylcrest and pale smoke puffing from the chimneys. The steward there had a similar stain on his fingertips. I wondered if they were burning something that has coated the leaves?"

He picked up a leaf by the stem and twirled it before his silver eye. A noncommittal noise came from his throat as he then studied the blue impressions on the cloth. "It will not take me long to ascertain what this is. I shall deduct the cost of my time from your wages."

Fern drew a breath to retort, then swallowed it. Instead, she sucked in her lips to stop herself from saying something decidedly rude. On the point of sulking, he glanced up, and she swore his brown eye twinkled.

"It was a jest, Miss Oakby. No need to explode in temper and ruin my experiments." He carried the cloth and a leaf to the table, holding his microscope.

"A jest? What is happening at Wyndham Hall? You are being amusing, and Quint is almost acting like a butler." She crossed her arms and wondered if both men had been sniffing fumes from one of the gassy vials.

"Perhaps this is what happens when someone brings a dragon onto the grounds." Lord Drakeman snipped a leaf free from the bract and squished it between two squares of glass.

If dragons made the men at Wyndham civilised, Fern

thought it was a decades-overdue development. Although it seemed the previous Lord Drakeman had been more community-minded since he had shown an interest in the fate of the villagers.

"Speaking of dragons, I will return to my work in the conservatory and Riddy while you study the leaves. And thank you for your time." It was better to leave the laboratory than to stay and watch. Her hands itched to poke at the samples in bottles. Or worse, her eye was drawn to the breadth of the earl's shoulders, remembering how he had plucked her from the windowsill.

He didn't bother to look up as she left, already engrossed in whatever he saw under the microscope.

Fern walked slower back to the house, her attention on the dark windows despite the sunlight trying to lighten the panes. She ignored the front door (suspecting Quint might have barred it behind her) and carried on to the conservatory and the wide-open doors.

To her relief, Eurydice was asleep and had not noticed her absence. Dropping her satchel by the platform, Fern picked up a trowel and continued working. She sang old songs, taught to her by her mother, to fill the silence. At times, she had the eerie sensation of being watched, but when she glanced up to the balcony, no one was there.

"Quint is probably doing it on purpose to make me jumpy." Just like he had the conservatory door oiled so an unsuspecting gardener would use too much weight to open it and fall over.

When the sun was high overhead, and Fern's muscles protested the hours spent on her knees, she decided it was time to quit for the day. She emptied the last wheelbarrow on the growing mound outside. Returning the barrow to its spot by the door, she tugged off her gloves and collected her tools.

"Do you think you can walk back to the stables?" Fern asked Eurydice when she found the dragon exploring under fallen fronds.

She wanted to have a private conversation with Millie, and Eurydice could visit with Squib while there. She had no full-sized dragon companions, but at least the two appeared to speak the same language, despite the disparity in size.

With Eurydice at her side, they left the conservatory. Fern closed the sliding door behind her, and they edged around the stagnant water in the pond. The lack of staff on such a large estate prickled her nerves. As though the place didn't really exist at all but was some ghostly apparition that she had wandered into. As they approached the cobbled yard, there was no sign of the lone stablehand. Fern detoured towards the wyvernry, Eurydice snuffling along behind her. The dragon's nose was stuck to the bricks, scenting her ancestors, who had once called the place home.

"I think we can spare ten minutes to look inside, don't you?" Fern suggested to her companion even as her feet took her in that direction.

Up close, the wyvernry didn't seem much smaller than the main house. The weathered stone was a testament to its centuries-old existence. Beside her, Eurydice fidgeted, her scaled tail swishing with anticipation. The dragon was alert and eager to see where her forebears once lived.

"Ready?" Fern asked and rested her hand on the dragon's head.

Eurydice chirped in response, her eyes fixed on the building.

They approached the massive wooden doors that soared twelve feet above their heads and twice as wide. Fern pushed, her shoulder straining against the unyielding wood. These doors had most definitely not been oiled in recent times. With a groan of protest, the door inched open, revealing a sliver of darkness within. Eurydice darted forwards and squeezed through the gap. Fern followed, wincing at the screech of rusted hinges.

As her eyes adjusted to the gloom, Fern gasped. The interior was cavernous, the ceiling lost in shadows high above. Shafts of faded daylight filtered through narrow windows, illuminating motes of dust that danced in the stale air. The smell hit her next. A musty mixture of old straw, stone, and something distinctly reptilian that lingered even after all the decades empty.

Eurydice's claws clicked on the worn flagstones. Fern followed more cautiously, wishing she had a light to penetrate the vastness of the space. If only she could fling open a few more doors to let the sun in. Along the walls, she could barely make out the enormous stalls, each easily large enough to house a full-grown dragon.

Thick iron rings, their purpose unfathomable, were set into the walls and floor at regular intervals. Scratches marred the stone floors and walls. Some shallow, others deep gouges that spoke of immense power and, perhaps, frustration.

In one corner, Fern discovered a heap of rotten leather and metal. It appeared to be the clothing worn by a dragon rider to protect from the wind and elements. Fern pocketed a small brass clasp to marvel over later in the sunlight.

Eurydice's excited trill echoed through the chamber, and Fern hurried to find where the little dragon snuffled around an empty stall. Feed troughs were carved from solid stone and could have held an entire cow. Pipes to fill water bowls were rusted shut. Overhead in the gloom dangled a complex system of pulleys and chains. Once, they must have been used to hoist bales of hay and baskets of meat to feed the voracious inhabitants.

In one corner, mounded with mouldering straw, Eurydice clawed and sniffed.

Kneeling beside her, Fern thought she had uncovered an upturned washing bowl. Helping the dragon, she brushed away dirt from the rounded shape. Underneath, it was pale like creamy porcelain. Then, with a start, she realised what it was—an egg. Long abandoned and never hatched. She rested a hand on the cool, petrified surface.

"A life never lived," she murmured. Had the egg been forgotten when the last dragon left Wyndham Hall? Or had a female buried it in the straw, thinking it might be safe while she was away, only to never return?

A deep melancholy flowed from the abandoned wyvernry and into Fern, filling her limbs. As though sensing the waves of sadness, Eurydice let out a mournful chirp that echoed through the empty space.

Fern curled one arm around the little dragon and hugged her warmth. "It's sad to see it like this. Perhaps, one day, you will have many friends, and you will fill this place with the sound of wings and your chatter."

Eurydice butted her head against Fern and then licked her face. Which tickled.

"Enough sadness. Let's go fetch our horse and cart, and we shall pay a visit to Millie and Squib." Although, given Fern wished to discuss Millie's dead husband, the afternoon might hold more sadness.

CHAPTER 12

Fern found Denis at the stables, grooming a dark bay horse with a coat that gleamed like a silky hot chocolate.

"Done for the day, miss?" the stablehand said with a cheerful tone.

"Yes, if you could fetch the horse and cart, please." She walked closer to the horse, who snorted and pawed the ground.

Denis uttered soothing words, but the horse continued to grow upset.

Fern paused, wondering what bothered the creature, when she remembered Eurydice tucked behind her. "I don't think he likes dragons. I shall take Riddy and wait outside."

"He's a bit fiery, this one. Doesn't fuss when a big dragon flies overhead but gets upset by a small one nearby." Denis stepped out of the way as the horse lashed out with a front foot.

"I feel like that about spiders. I don't care how big they are, so long as they are far away from me." Fern ushered

Eurydice back out into the sun, and the horse settled in his stall.

Woman and dragon sat in companionable silence, each lost in their thoughts until the rumble of wheels over cobbles brought Fern out of her internal wanderings. Denis helped the dragon up into the cart, and they set off for the village.

At the bookstore, Fern halted the horse on the grass. By the time she set up the plank of wood and steadied Eurydice to the ground, a few children had appeared.

Today, a group of four girls promised to sit with Eurydice and keep her company while Fern was inside. When she glanced back from the front door of Scribbles, the girls were making a daisy chain crown for the young dragon.

The bell above the door tinkled as Fern entered. Millie sat behind the tall desk, dealing with her last customer of the day. The bookshop was bathed in the warm glow of late-afternoon sunlight that angled through the conservatory to one side.

"Fern! Lovely to see you. I'll be with you shortly," Millie said.

Squib, dozing atop a stack of books nearby, stirred and chirped a greeting.

Fern waited until the patron had paid their coin and left with a book clutched in their hands. Then she turned the sign on the door to CLOSED and slid the bolt across so they wouldn't be interrupted.

"Alice! Fern is here. Could we have tea in the conservatory, please?" Millie called out as she closed the ledger. Squib flew from his spot on the books to Fern's outstretched arm.

"Hello, Squib. Riddy is outside, if you would like to bask

in the last of the sunshine with her." Fern stroked the pixie dragon's papery hide.

He trilled and hopped up her arm to rub his little face against hers before glancing at Millie.

"I shall leave a window open for you. That way, you can get back in, but not any customers." Millie flicked the latch and tugged the window sash up enough to let Squib wriggle under.

Fern bit her tongue. If a reader was determined enough, the window would be easy to prise open and climb through.

Millie looped arms with her, and they headed for the sunlit conservatory. "Limiting the open hours has been brilliant. Although customers do chatter, and I swear their voices echo around here long after they have gone."

Fern dropped into an armchair. "Many will be browsing the shelves out of curiosity. The cottage did magically transform during a storm, and it will take a few weeks before everyone finds something else to talk about." Or, more likely, another argument would erupt because of the tattling whisperwoods, and people would be too busy fighting among themselves.

"You see, that is the problem. The people coming in actually want to talk about *books* with me! They are asking for recommendations, expecting me to find rollicking tales for them, or simply to rant about some poorly written tome they chose." Millie leaned back in her armchair and pinched the bridge of her nose.

Fern swallowed a laugh. It seemed Millie's dream of being surrounded by books was turning into a waking nightmare. "We all like to talk about books we love or hate. You might have to start a club. Perhaps once a month, there could be a get-together where everyone can talk about a particular book."

Millie blew out a sigh. "I like the idea, and I'm definitely keen to encourage their interest in stories. I just don't want them all here being noisy. Can't they do it somewhere else? And without me?"

A solution sprang to Fern's mind. "I will talk to Ambrose. He would love to host a literary gathering, and the Drake's Rest has a private room that would suit."

"Oh, that would be a perfect solution. I could supply the group with the books they read at a discount. Judging from the requests I have had over the last few days, most people seem to either want books about war or pirates." Millie cheered up once she realised she wouldn't have to host a noisy gathering.

"I'll not hear anything bad about pirate stories. I might have to join this book club if that is what they will be reading." Fern loved a thrilling adventure story. Especially if there were women swashbucklers capturing ships, evading the navy, and making their fortunes.

They chatted while Alice laid out a tea tray with gorgeous-looking scones to rival what Quint produced at Wyndham Hall. Fern held her cup in two hands, staring at the tiny wisps of steam as she pondered how to broach the topic she really wanted to discuss with Millie.

Her deceased husband.

And how he got that way.

"You keep chewing on the rim of your cup. What is

preying on your mind this afternoon?" Millie asked as she spread jam over her scone.

"The whisperwoods and their gossip," Fern said, considering her next words with care.

"Is it true, then? They really twist people's secrets?" Millie's eyes widened in curiosity and wonder. "I had to ask two people to leave today. They started to argue over a chicken of all things."

Fern put her teacup back on the table, so she didn't spill it as she squirmed with what she needed to say. "Yes, the trees are tattling. I went out there the other day to see what they might say. Since they require an exchange, I told them something about me. In return, they told me something about...you."

"Me?" Millie's hand paused halfway to her mouth with the scone. "Why would they say anything about me?"

Just like the whisperwoods, if she wanted Millie's secret, Fern would have to offer up her own. To make herself comfortable, Fern tucked one booted foot up under her. "Because I told them I never realised how lonely I was...until I met you. Your friendship has filled a hole inside me."

Millie reached out and squeezed her arm. "Oh. That is lovely, and I am grateful that events brought us together." The scone continued its journey, and she took a large bite.

Fern waited until she had chewed and swallowed before continuing. She didn't want to risk her new friend choking. "The trees told me something cruel about you. They said that you had caused your husband's death."

Millie coughed, a bit of scone getting stuck after all. Fern jumped to her feet and patted the other woman on her back.

"I thought you had swallowed. Sorry." Fern sat back down when Millie waved her away to take a slurp of tea. "I scolded them for such a hideous lie. Obviously. All of society knows your husband was killed in a duel with another noble. But they whispered that you penned the story that made them act that way." That was the bit that bothered Fern. Was Millie some sort of mastermind who could craft such compelling narratives that she could influence someone else's behaviour?

An awkward silence settled heavily over them. Fern squirmed in her armchair. She would rather climb into a moody alchemist's laboratory or face his possibly criminal butler than poke at her new friend's painful past.

"You said there is a grain of truth in what the whisperwoods say, and you are right. I did kill Peter with my quill." Millie placed her cup back on the table and turned sideways in her armchair so she faced Fern. Bending her knees under her gown, she wrapped her arms around them.

A scrabbling came from the partially open window as Squib climbed back in. Drawn by Millie's distress, he flew to her, landing on her shoulder. The pixie dragon glared at Fern and hissed.

"I'm sorry. I had to know if the trees are indeed spreading secrets confessed to them. Even if it is a distorted and malicious version." She placated the fierce pixie dragon guarding Millie. "You don't have to tell me, Millie. Not everything has to be shared." Some secrets were better left buried. Fern usually didn't stop and think long enough to kick hers into a hole and cover them over.

Squib huffed at Fern, then turned to rub his face against Millie and offer soothing coos.

Millie stroked the tiny dragon and closed her eyes. "No, I don't mind telling you. It seems fair. I was there, you know. That night. When you said those things."

Fern didn't have to ask to know what night Millie meant.

"My secret is no secret at all. I shouted across a crowded ballroom that I had given myself to Lord Talbot. How I had pressed my naked flesh to his, believing us two wedded souls. There is nothing the whisperwoods could say about me that hasn't already been said." The trees would have to try hard to find a deep, dark secret about Fern when she had a habit of shouting them out loud for all to hear. Possibly, she didn't quite grasp the concept of a secret.

"The ball was so crowded that night. All those people talking and laughing. I had desperately wanted to leave, but Father was squirrelled away with a group of his associates, and I couldn't go without his permission. Nor could I interrupt. Instead, I stood in a corner with my eyes shut, wishing that everyone would stop talking for just a moment. And then...they did." Millie glanced at Fern, and an embarrassed look passed over her delicately drawn features. "As though a giant hand had unclenched from around my heart, I could breathe again. Then I realised one person was talking, and everyone had fallen silent to listen."

"No one wanted to miss a word of my downfall." Fern made a joke of the events that had torn her heart in two. The man she thought she had loved and would marry...had betrayed her.

"You were so alone. It pained me that not a single one of

your friends stood beside you." Millie reached out and took Fern's hand.

"I can't blame them for staying quiet. If any of them had stepped forwards, they would have been cast into ruin with me." Odd how it still hurt even after ten years, even though she understood their silence. Some friendships were like autumn leaves. They withered and blew away with the first chill gust.

"Well, next time you decide to scandalise society, I shall be right beside you." The glint of mischief returned to Millie's eyes.

"I am sure we can concoct something between the two of us, should we ever visit London." The idea warmed Fern. What fun they could have, thumbing their nose at all the stuffy matrons and their silly rules. "But enough of my tale of woe. How did you meet your husband?"

Millie heaved a sigh and leaned back in her chair. Her eyes unfocused as she replayed old memories in her mind. "I debuted in London, as is expected of noble young women. But I hated every moment of it. The noise and press of people shredded my nerves. Father let me retreat to Warrington Manor and the company of books. I was content for a few years, left to my own devices. Then, after Father died, Bertie inherited and I became a problem that needed to be solved."

Fern filled their tea cups as Millie paused in her tale to sip the brew before it cooled too much.

"One day, Bertie informed me that he had arranged my marriage to Peter Carlisle. His family lived not far from ours, and we were acquainted. He was a good man. Kind in his way, but...I was not a good wife and ill-suited to marriage."

Millie lowered her feet back to the floor and cradled her cup in both hands.

"I think you are too hard on yourself," Fern said. The other woman constantly pointed out her perceived faults, which were no faults at all in Fern's eyes.

"We moved to London to do all the things one does in the season as a married couple. Meaning we went our separate ways. Peter did things with his friends, I was supposed to find my own. It was like being lost in a forest. Surrounded by tall, implacable giants who hemmed me in no matter which way I turned. Alone, I had no guiding light." Millie plucked at the hem of her skirt.

Fern understood how that felt. Other women had turned their backs on her until a handsome noble had asked her to dance. Then suddenly, others noticed her as though that first interaction had tugged aside a veil to reveal her underneath.

"I was invited to places, and I tried. I really did try for Peter. But I find it hard to talk to others. The ideas in my brain all seem to jam together, and then I blurt out something silly. Although not with you. Isn't that odd?" Her brows pulled together as she tried to fathom why she could talk to Fern but not other noblewomen.

"Because we were meant to be friends. Neither of us has to pretend around the other. We set our masks aside and can simply be who we are." Perhaps that was the advantage of finding another broken soul. They each understood what the other had been through.

"Yes. I think you are right. None of them dare show their true face in case London does not approve of it." Millie sipped her tea, and Fern broke off a corner of scone to nibble. "Over time, I realised how much they all liked to gossip. If one of them had a letter on them, it was always snatched and read aloud. That gave me an idea. I invented a character whose husband made her live on a remote estate. Bored, and left to her own devices, she led the most scandalous life and wrote to me about her exploits."

Fern could see the sense in that. For someone uncomfortable in a new place with people who appeared unfriendly. It would be like an actor pretending to be a character in a play and reading from a script. "So you penned a letter from this fictitious person?"

Millie nodded, and her eyes shone. "Yes. Detailing how her groom touched her leg when he helped her onto her horse and it made butterflies flutter in her stomach. I *accidentally* had it on me during one luncheon and had it peeking out of my pocket. When it fell out, it was leapt upon and read aloud. The other ladies were all horrified, of course, at the idea of a noblewoman conducting an affair with a stablehand. But at the same time, they couldn't get enough. My, how they all shrieked as they read it."

Fern could imagine the ladies would have seized on the salacious details. The easiest way to survive life in London was to ensure that someone else's life was being torn apart.

"After that, I was folded into their group and felt accepted for the first time. I went home and wrote another letter. And so my story took on a life of its own. The mysterious Lady X had a short affair with the stablehand and then a passionate relationship with her housekeeper. She also stole jewellery for the thrill of it when she was invited to dinner with other families." Millie's gaze darted around the conservatory as she detailed the adventures of Lady X.

"Did the fiction become real, like the vine and Squib?" Fern tried to figure out how the letters ended up in Millie's husband calling out another noble.

"No. Nothing like that. In hindsight, I rather think my idea worked too well. The ladies became ravenous for the next letter. Some demanded one a day! I mean, honestly, they had no appreciation for how a writer labours over their stories. It took me the good part of a week to craft each instalment for them and ensure it ended on a note of suspense."

"You should write a serial like that for the *Midnight Chronicle*. It would do wonders for their sales. All of society would clamour to buy the latest copy to read what happens next." That reminded Fern to prod Ambrose if there had been any response from his editor about Millie's story.

"That was when it turned. They became obsessed with figuring out the true identity of Lady X. Some suggested it was Lady Warrington since she and Bertie spent much time at the manor. You can imagine how that enraged him. He demanded that I reveal the mystery woman's identity. When I refused to tell anyone, it was put about that it had to be me. My denials were taken as proof. How ludicrous is that?" She threw up her hands and dropped back in her chair.

From what Fern had seen of Millie's strict older brother, she could well imagine his reaction to such a scandal touching his household. It would have been similar to that of Fern's uncle, the earl. Who had hastily cut her off, like a swift amputation, to save his family from rot.

CHAPTER 13

Millie closed her eyes and finished her story. "One night, the men were talking about it at one of those clubs they so enjoy. Peter's friend, a Mr Rourke, warned him to get me under control, as all of London knew of my affairs with the staff. Peter believed in my innocence and called out his friend for repeating the rumours. He said God would prove the allegations false and that his victory would show my innocence. Apparently, God wasn't listening."

Fern thought it foolish of Millie's husband to put his faith in God when he should have been practising with a pistol. People seemed to expect a deity to do all sorts of ordinary things they were perfectly capable of doing themselves.

Millie took another sip of tea and placed the cup back on the tray. "While I might not have killed him directly, I crafted his demise."

Fern knew what had happened next. Peter Carlisle was shot dead, and society took that as proof that Millie was an adulteress. "The whisperwoods took your secret and twisted it to give you evil intent."

Millie shook her head. "But they can't have. I have never been to the whisperwoods. So the grove cannot have heard the tale from me."

Curiouser and curiouser. If the one person who carried the most guilt about the death of Peter Carlisle hadn't told the whisperwoods, then who did? Fern considered how else the ancient trees might have learned about Millie's letters and the death of her husband. "Do you think it might have been your brother? He travels up and down to London, and the grove wouldn't be too much of a detour from his usual path."

A weak smile tugged on Millie's lips. "Bertie doesn't do secret confessions, especially if I am the cause of his headaches. He much prefers to shout at me in his study."

Fern had seen Lord Warrington berating his sister. His behaviour had compelled her to help the other woman escape and establish a new life in Drake's Bend. "I wonder who, then. Mr Rourke, who fired the fatal shot, might have unburdened himself afterwards."

"Yes. I suppose. Or any of the ladies who read my letters. One might have discovered a conscience and felt some pang at their involvement in spreading the gossip." Millie picked up her teacup and nursed it in her cupped hands without drinking. She glanced at Fern. "We are a pair, aren't we? Both of us broken."

Fern was rather tired of being told she was broken or flawed for simply...living. "No, we're not."

Millie tilted her head. "What are we then?"

"We're human. Beautifully flawed people, just like

everyone else. No one is perfect, unless they are made of marble. All of us make mistakes, take wrong turns, and have errors in judgement. But just like tribes that sacrifice a virgin to a volcano to appease old gods, society threw us upon the flames of their opinion. By casting us out for our mistakes, they all heave a sigh of relief that they have escaped notice for another season," Fern said.

Squib let out a trumpet of agreement. Then he stretched out his hind leg to show a tiny imperfection in his hide, where a purple-edged scale was a different size from the others.

"You are perfect in my eyes, darling," Millie cooed as she scratched under his chin. Then she met Fern's gaze. "What can be done about the whisperwoods? If they continue, who knows what secrets they will corrupt? So many people will be hurt, ostracised, or families torn apart, all based on twisted rumours."

"I need to determine the cause of the blight affecting them and put a stop to it. The three witches will find a way to restore the balance and their ability to hold their silence." Fern had hoped Lord Drakeman would have a solution by the time she left Wyndham Hall. Odd that for something he deemed a simple procedure, he had not gleaned an answer in a few hours. She imagined one of his experiments bubbling over and demanding his attention.

Millie worried at her bottom lip. "They hold centuries of secrets. Imagine if they spill them all forth. Part of me wants to sit in the grove with a stack of paper and my pencil to record what they say. But then it feels like such a betrayal of those who entered the sacred grove to unburden themselves."

"For now, the trees still require an exchange. For every

whisper you hear, you must give them something of yourself." Silently, Fern was grateful, and she was convinced the snatches she heard were not about the man who stood on the grass before her.

She didn't want to imagine what would happen if curious gossips had only to sit beneath the trees to hear all the secrets the whisperwoods held. The forest would become more crowded than Almack's at the start of the season. Although the Drake's Rest tavern would do a fine trade with all those travellers needing somewhere to stay and wait their turn.

"A Faustian agreement, is it not? But many will leap at such an arrangement for the advantage they think it might bring them." Millie's gaze had a faraway look as she contemplated the deal Faust had made with the devil.

The atmosphere in the conservatory had become heavy as they bared their souls to each other, shared their histories, and considered the fates of so many held in the rustling leaves of the old trees. There were two blights that Fern needed to heal. The physical one affecting the trees, and the unseen one that would reach for those further afield, as malicious gossip harmed lives.

Words have power, she reminded herself of Morda's words. And was there a better combatant to fight them than a writer who could parry with a raven's quill?

"As lovely as it always is to sit here with you, I need to search my books for anything about the whisperwoods." Fern stood and hugged her friend. Squib puffed warm air over her cheek, which was his way of greeting or farewelling someone.

"I have an idea for a new story. It will be about how a simple lie can distort and ruin lives." Millie followed Fern along the stacks. "I think it shall have a moral about not indulging in harmful gossip about people. Do you think the readers of the *Midnight Chronicle* would like such a tale?"

"I think they would. Especially if, at its core, it is about being true to yourself and not wearing a mask to suit society." Fern unlatched the door.

"Oh, yes! Excellent point." Millie's eyes flashed with inspiration, and she waved one hand as she hurried to her desk to find a clean sheet of paper.

Outside, Fern found the gaggle of girls surrounding a sleeping dragon. They appeared to be a guard circle to keep the boys away.

One leapt to her feet as Fern approached. "She fell asleep, Miss Oakby, and we did like you asked and made sure no one woke her up."

Fern ruffled the girl's dark hair. "Thank you. Do you think you could all help get her back in the cart?"

The dragon roused on hearing Fern's voice and opened sleepy eyes. While tired, she did as asked and slowly padded up the plank. The girls stood on either side and guided Eurydice when she wobbled.

"Thank you!" Fern called out as she clucked her tongue, and the patient horse turned his nose for home.

Once Eurydice was settled in her stall, and snoring softly from the mound of straw and blankets, Fern spent a quiet evening in her study. There were very few books about the whisperwoods. Every decade or so, a botanist would spend months or years trying to unravel the secret of how they formed words. And fail. The grove would be left in peace for several years until the next hopeful scientist came along.

Each was convinced that they would be the one to find the secret.

Fern's father had tried, even though his main interest was the kelmsgale. Rowan Oakby made occasional forays to the grove to study the trees. After some years, he had turned to Fern, shrugged, and said, "It's magic." She did wonder if he ever shared that opinion with George. Declaring that the whisperwoods were a secret of nature never meant to be revealed left her father free to concentrate on botanical mysteries he could understand.

Her studies found many causes of leaf curl and dieback in trees, but none linked to a mysterious blue residue. Fern made a list of causes anyway to work through a process of elimination. The invisible coating might not be responsible, and its presence merely coincidental.

That night, as she prepared for bed, Fern pondered Lord Drakeman's words when she asked for his help. He had commented that his attempt at a jest was what happened when a dragon returned to Wyndham Hall. An odd thought drifted through her mind as she pulled the blankets over her shoulders. What if his cold and distant demeanour was because he needed a dragon nearby? What if the king's drake men were linked to dragons in unseen ways? One might need the other to become fully what they were meant to be.

What a curious idea...

THE NEXT MORNING, Fern chewed her toast and sought the answers to a multitude of problems in her cup of coffee.

Ambrose chortled over the newspaper. "This will be known as the season of scandals. It seems every day brings a new revelation. This snippet hints at a rather tantalising morsel." He cleared his throat before reading aloud. "Rumours dart across London like sparrows. There are many things an Englishman forgives of his superiors. He may be a liar, a gambler, an adulterer, or a thief, but there is one line that cannot be crossed. This author waits to see if a particular sparrow-bearing Tea comes home to roost for a peer."

Fern frowned over the wording. "A sparrow with tea?"

"It's spelt with a capital T." Ambrose explained the wordplay.

"Treason," George muttered when Fern still couldn't unravel the hinted-at piece of gossip.

She let out a whistle. "The whisperwoods are speaking of treason?"

"Every parlour will be buzzing like a shaken beehive trying to figure out who and what they have done." Ambrose put the paper down to sip his tea.

"Do you think it will be something to do with Napoleon?" It had only been a few years since the emperor had been defeated and imprisoned on St Helena.

Ambrose hummed in thought for a moment. "Possibly. Our relationship with France is still rather chilly. Or it could be an older secret, perhaps about the loss of America? That does still sting for King George."

"Gossip is all well and good until it's about the wrong person. If a peer truly has a treasonous secret, they will raze the trees to the ground to ensure their silence." George sipped his coffee and returned to his periodical.

"But they can't! They belong to...somebody." The trees stood on land belonging to whoever now owned the cottage. For centuries, the owners had always let anyone who needed the solace or wisdom of the trees have free access to them. Perhaps the new owner would build a fence around them and charge an entry fee now they were so popular.

Fern's thoughts sprouted in different directions as she worried about the old stand of trees. There had to be some way to stop the slow death creeping over them and restore them to health. That would put an end to their tattling so people could unburden themselves with confidence again. But how to do that before someone took an axe to them?

"We still haven't found old Mrs Rawdon's great-grandson." Ambrose looked up from the newspaper.

"The village will continue to look after both the cottage and the grove until we do." George put his coffee down to shovel an entire egg into his mouth.

"We need to organise people to protect the trees so no one sneaks in at night and saws them down. Or sets fire to them, which will put many at risk if the entire forest burns." This was a rare occasion where Fern needed to enlist the support of the Botanical Society. They would be as aghast as her at the thought of losing the rare stand of trees. She rather fancied the idea of stuffy old men forming a protective guard armed with books, quills, and wads of paper to throw.

"I'll talk to some lads. We'll set up a watch," George said. "One person can raise the alert quickly. Especially if the witches can supply a magical light to release."

Fern smiled her thanks. George would swing into action and have the locals keeping an eye on the grove. As she mentally prepared a suitably polite letter to the Botanical Society in her head, William Bentley appeared in the kitchen doorway.

He waved a folded piece of paper in her direction. "Message for you, Miss Oakby. Came from the Hall."

He handed the missive across the table and then glanced at his mother before retreating back out the door—retracing his footsteps exactly so as not to leave more dirty marks on her clean floor.

Fern flipped the folded sheet over and stared at the seal—a dragon with its wings and claws extended. *What have I done now? I might have been fired,* she wondered as she picked up a knife and broke the seal.

To the contrary, far from being told to stay away from Wyndham Hall, it was a summons. "His lordship needs to see me and requests my presence this morning."

Ambrose's eyebrows shot upwards, and then he waggled them.

"Don't go getting ideas. He will want to discuss either the conservatory restoration or the leaves I left with him yesterday." Fern tapped the note against the tabletop as she organised her day. "I have a letter to write first to alert the Botanical Society to recent events. I can post it in the village on my way through. I'm sure his lordship can wait an hour or so."

The general store that sat in the middle of the main street also collected and delivered their mail. Fern would take the road through the western side of the river and then cross over by Scribbles to reach Wyndham Hall.

It took a little longer than she anticipated to write her

letter. Her first attempt showed her contempt for the society a little too clearly. Even the near-sighted fool who read the thing would have spotted her barbs. Not having Millie's way with words, four sheets of paper were discarded before Fern had a brief, and to the point, letter about the whisperwoods.

Satisfied, she addressed it to the chair of the society and used her father's seal—his namesake rowan standing on a small hill. Tucking the letter into her satchel, she hurried out to the stables to request the horse and cart from William.

Eurydice greeted her in the aisle. The dragon had her nose to the cobbles as she snuffled along behind a beetle. Since Fern had read the advice about fish from the local river, the dragon had improved every day.

Or was it the kelmsgale seeds she ate?

That idea wouldn't go away, despite Fern's efforts to dislodge it. The only way to disprove the niggling doubt was to find another deathly sick dragon and feed it the seeds that were as solid as metal. Or find any mention of them in the old journals kept at Wyndham Hall.

"I reckon she's putting on weight now, Miss Oakby. Her ribs don't show as bad," William commented as he lifted Eurydice into the back of the cart.

"I think you are right, William. She has been hungry for more solid food, and that must be helping." Mixed emotions swirled inside Fern. Relief that Eurydice improved daily and would soar one day, mingled with a profound sadness that she would lose the creature's companionship. Thinking of company reminded her of someone she'd not seen recently. "What has Daniel been up to? I've not seen him the last day or so, and he normally spends a bit of time with Riddy."

"He's off-colour, miss. Ma thinks it's a spring cold and has him tucked up in bed drinking chicken soup." A tinge of worry lurked in William's eyes for his younger sibling.

"Tell him I hope he feels better soon. Riddy will be missing him," Fern said as she climbed into the cart.

Eurydice trilled as though agreeing with her. The dragon leaned her head over the seat of the cart and nudged against Fern.

"I'm sure he'll be running around and getting in my way before the end of tomorrow." William waved as he turned back to his chores.

Fern picked up the reins, and the cob headed out of the stables and along the drive.

They turned in a different direction today and took the western side of the river. The main street was busy with people running their chores and conducting business. The homes here were more regular in appearance, with wide bay windows on the street level and living upstairs and at the rear. Hanging baskets contained geraniums in bright reds and pinks. Frothy alyssum spilt over the edges and reached for half barrels with potted roses and lavenders.

Shop windows displayed a variety of wares, and as she returned to the cart after handing over her letter, Fern's eyes were drawn to a gown with sparkly green beads and embroidery that advertised the modiste. The locals didn't have any need for evening gowns, but the seamstress lived in the hope that she would sell one. Trousers might be practical for her working day, but Fern still appreciated a beautiful dress and how it made her feel.

"Summer festival is not far away," she reminded herself.

At the rate she was overcharging Lord Drakeman, she could afford to buy the fancy gown to wear to the outdoor dance. That would certainly help her find an eager gentleman to scratch the itch that seemed to be growing under her skin.

CHAPTER 14

When Fern arrived at Wyndham Hall, she handed the horse and cart over to Denis and then settled Eurydice in the conservatory. That left her pondering one question in her search for Lord Drakeman. Should she enter the library via the conservatory or walk around and use the front door?

As she stood by the wooden doors with their ornate carving of dragons, her dilemma was answered when Quint shoved one side open.

"He's waiting for you, you know," he grumbled, then he stood aside to allow Fern to enter.

She paused for a moment and stomped her boots to dislodge any dirt. There was no need to deepen the butler's foul mood by treading mud into the rugs. As she walked further into the room, it became apparent that wherever Lord Drakeman waited for her, it wasn't in the library.

Turning, she arched an eyebrow at Quint. "Where? Or is this a game of hide-and-seek?"

She had been quite good at that as a child due to her

ability to scamper up things. As she got older, young people preferred sardines. In that game, if you found the person hiding, you squished yourself in with them and waited to be discovered. All sorts of things could happen in the dark and close quarters, depending on who you found and how long you waited.

"Study," Quint said as he strode across the room and out the other side.

Fern yanked her mind out of a dark cupboard of heated memories and ran to catch up. The butler turned right, went along the hall a short distance, and then rapped on another door.

"Enter," came the alchemist's voice from within.

Quint pushed the door open and swept a bow to Fern.

The study was a smaller, and far messier, version of the library. One wall was lined with books. Opposite that was a cosy fireplace with a marble mantel and two worn and comfortable armchairs before it. A large desk sat at the end of the room, positioned in front of the window.

Lord Drakeman stood at the bookcase, flicking through the pages of an open book that rested atop a pile of volumes. He appeared to be trying to find something. He glanced at Fern and slammed the book shut.

"I need a sample of whatever they are burning at Sibyl-crest. I recognise one ingredient, but not the other. Although I am sure it is something organic." His attention scanned the books, and he selected another from a shelf at the upper range of his reach.

Gathering samples was beyond her agreed brief to restore the garden next door. But then she wanted to cure the whisperwoods, so if it helped, she would try. "That will be difficult, milord."

"Can't you get in?" Quint asked from the doorway.

"They have a portcullis." Fern resisted the urge to sulk as her mind conjured the ancient steel contraption that had barred her way into Sibylcrest.

"Windows?" Humour flared in Lord Drakeman's brown eye as he mentioned how she gained egress to his laboratory.

Fern huffed. "Mere arrow slits."

"What about just climbing the wall, then?" That idea came from Quint, who now lounged against the door jamb.

"Well-constructed stone with tight seams, twenty feet high with hardly any hand holds." The blasted place defeated her.

Quint barked in laughter. "I like the sound of this abbey. Think you could get the owner to swap with us? That'd keep her out."

A soft chuckle came from by the bookshelf, but Lord Drakeman's expression had returned to its previous serious one when she turned around. One long finger scanned an index as his attention returned to the book in his hands. "Then you must get them to raise the portcullis for you. I need the samples as soon as possible."

"I spoke to a man there and mentioned I would go back with a welcome basket. He seemed quite keen to know if it would include ginger loaf. Perhaps Quint could provide some baked goods I could use to bribe my way in?" Fern smiled at the butler. No matter how hard he denied it, she would continue to imagine him in the kitchen wearing an apron with an edging of lace, baking scones.

"Quint, ask Nancy to make up a basket." Lord Drakeman waved a hand in the direction of his butler.

"Who is Nancy? Does she work in the kitchen?" Fern asked her question of the alchemist, then turned to the butler when it became obvious no answer was forthcoming.

"He. Mr Nancy is the cook. I told you it wasn't me." Pushing off the door jamb, Quint disappeared into the hall.

A question stuck in Fern's mind, and she asked it now that she was alone with Lord Drakeman. "You said you identified one component. What was it?"

His body stilled, only his head tilted to stare at her with his silver eye. "Dragon's blood."

The air left Fern with a whoosh. "Dragon's blood? Are you sure?"

It didn't seem possible. Her mind struggled to imagine what they were burning in the old abbey that contained blood from dragons. Had some long-ago occupant stuffed and mounted a dragon in the great hall, and the new resident chopped it up for firewood?

A dark eyebrow arched, and the silver eye narrowed. "I have some familiarity with the blood of a dragon."

The word *how* flew to her lips, but at the last second, Fern was able to slam her mouth shut and stop herself from saying it aloud. Not that she had to say it. The question must have been written all over her face like the looping words on Squib's hide.

"There are many old samples here from various species," Lord Drakeman said in an off-hand manner as his gaze dropped to thumb through the pages of the book.

That answer prompted more questions. Fern's mind

imagined what relics were stashed around the Hall, taken from the dragons who once lived in the wyvernry and swam in the heated pool.

Now that she could gain access to the house through the adjoining conservatory, she might need to do a little wandering to discover what lay hidden in dusty corners. However, if she struck off to explore, no work would get done, and little Eurydice would be alone out there.

"While I wait for Quint to bake some scones and a ginger loaf, I shall continue my current job in the conservatory." Since Lord Drakeman didn't reply or look up, Fern assumed she was dismissed. She wandered back through the quiet house, taking her time and staring at the old portraits.

In the entranceway hung a life-sized painting of a man dressed with a Tudor ruff around his neck. A dragon sat behind him, its scales an inky blue like an evening sky. The man rested one hand on the creature's bent leg.

"You must have been the last drake man," Fern murmured as she peered at the date on the brass plate. 1598. Five years later, Queen Elizabeth died, and the distraught royal dragons set fire to their wyvernry near the Tower of London. King James refused to keep the beasts when he came to the throne, and the royal drake man was no longer required.

Dragons still resided at Wyndham Hall for some decades afterwards. The king could issue a decree, but he couldn't stop the majestic creatures from wintering in the warm conservatory, swimming in the thermal waters, or sunning themselves in the middle of Drake's Bend. Since the mid-

1700s, their numbers had dwindled, and the wyvernry fell into disuse.

Fern worked for two more hours in the conservatory before Quint found her. He carried a basket covered with a cloth that wafted delicious aromas.

She closed her eyes and inhaled. "You have outdone yourself. That smells incredible and is sure to gain me access to Sibylcrest."

"That's the ginger loaf you can smell, but you're not to eat any of it. And I already told you Nancy does the cooking, not me." The scowl on his face deepened as he thrust the basket at her.

Taking it, Fern lifted one corner of the towel to peek underneath. Fluffy golden scones were nestled beside the divine-smelling ginger loaf. "Why don't I get ginger loaf with my tea?"

"You didn't ask for it." He turned on his heel and walked away.

"I will be now!" Fern shouted to his retreating back.

Putting the basket out of reach of the sleepy dragon, whose nose was twitching, Fern trotted around to the stables and asked for the horse and cart. Then she quickly emptied the wheelbarrow and tidied up her tools.

At Nemython House, she left Eurydice in the care of George. While William hitched up the cob and cart, she hurried upstairs to her room to change into a dress. Fern even tied a bonnet under her chin. Experience had taught her that some men greatly underestimated the intelligence of women. Especially those wearing dresses and bonnets and who fluttered their eyelashes. She wanted to be able to use such tactics if necessary to gain access to the abbey.

Oddly, men were less susceptible to eyelash flutters when dressed in her work attire of trousers and a waistcoat. She had a theory that the trousers confused them—men could be such simple creatures who were easily befuddled.

Soon, she was on the road to the whisperwoods with the basket safe at her feet on the floor of the cart. She slowed the cob as they approached the narrow lane that led to the cottage and gossiping grove. Soft whinnies and nickers drifted on the light breeze. Not one but two carriages waited in the dappled shade.

Given how narrow the access was, Fern wondered how the drivers had managed to pass each other. One would have given their occupant a bumpy ride as they lurched off the road and over the rough clumping grass to avoid hitting the waiting vehicle. Continuing on her way to Sibylcrest, she passed a rider cantering towards the woods.

"No good will come of their curiosity," she said to the horse.

George was right. Soon, people would realise they could make specific confessions to elicit secrets about the person they mentioned. What if the rumour of treason truly did touch a high-ranking peer or even the royal family? The grove would be razed to the ground in a matter of days if it meant keeping the secrets of the upper echelon.

Fern drew a deep breath to stop herself from kicking the basket by her foot in frustration. She clucked at the horse and urged him into a trot as they approached the twisted road that curled its way to the top of the hill. Plumes of pale-blue smoke spiralled from the chimney stacks and drifted to the sky. Knowing those innocent-looking puffs might contain dragon's blood made a chill run down her spine.

A tiny part of her had hoped that today, the portcullis would be raised. It was not. Drawing the horse to a halt before the causeway, Fern turned the small cart so they were heading back down the hill. She looped the reins around the front of the cart and gathered up her skirts to hop down.

Sliding her arm through the handle of her basket, with her free hand Fern ensured her bonnet was still on her head and at the correct angle. Striding across the stone causeway, she approached the metal portcullis. Peering into the court-yard beyond, nothing appeared to have changed from her last visit. Nobody stirred, and there was no sign of habitation. Only sparrows dived to the cobbles in search of any insects to eat.

Where was a person to open a gate when you needed one?

"Hello?" she called out. Attracting the attention of anyone within was not unlike rousing Quint. Someone would be along if she made enough noise.

At that point, she realised a bell was hanging to one side high above her head. Staring up, the clapper was still inside, but someone had removed the rope needed to ring it and alert those within that someone stood at the gate.

"Probably a relative of Quint." Undeterred, Fern placed the basket on the ground.

Then she picked through the stones at the edge of the road to find a rounded one.

"I should have worn trousers," she muttered as she

wedged the stone into a pocket hidden in the seam of her skirt. Then she used a skirt hike to lift the fabric away from her boots.

With her hands free, Fern climbed the portcullis to reach the bell. Looping one arm through the metal to steady herself, she pulled the rock free and banged on the weathered brass.

Repeatedly.

She didn't have to do it too many times before a door opened at the bottom of the rambling building, and a man appeared in the doorway. He froze for a moment before hurrying across the courtyard.

Fern imagined she presented quite a sight, hanging from the portcullis with her skirt hitched up to her knees. She should probably explain her behaviour.

"Hello, Mr Sainsbury! I brought a basket of baking. Just like I said I would." Fern recognised the steward of the abbey from her previous attempt to get inside. With care, she climbed back down, undid the skirt lift, and shook out the fabric. Picking up the basket, she held it up to the gate as an offering. "There's a ginger loaf that is still warm. I am sure Sir Luxton will enjoy it with a cup of tea."

"He's not here. His visit's been put off." Mr Sainsbury slowed as he approached, his gaze on the basket with the cloth cover pulled just to one side to tease what lay beneath.

Fern frowned and peered at him from under lowered lashes, which was hard to do while also wearing a bonnet. "Oh, that is a shame. I hope you have a few friends inside who could help you eat this lot. That would save me from having to carry it back to Drake's Bend as it's ever so heavy."

He grinned and stood a little taller. Men were odd creatures; when they heard a woman say something was heavy, they puffed out their chests.

"I wouldn't want you tiring yourself out. Let me take that from you. We'd all much appreciate a bit of warm baking, miss." The steward walked to one side and reached up to take hold of something out of sight. When he returned, he held a long, black key in his hand. It fitted into a lock in the portcullis. With one hand, he swung a portion of the gate open to reveal a person-sized door. With his other hand, he reached for the basket.

Fern stepped towards the door and angled her body to tuck the basket close to her side. "Could you show me inside, please, Mr Sainsbury? I've never been in here before, and it would give me a tale to tell the other women when I get back."

"No one is allowed in. Sorry." He blocked the little doorway.

Bother. A little more eyelash fluttering might be required. "I don't take up much room, and I'd be as quiet as a mouse if you could show me the great hall, please. The other women in the village will be ever so jealous." Fern batted her eyes at him. In case he needed further persuasion, she lifted the cloth covering the basket to reveal the treats underneath, rather like a woman revealing her ankles beneath her skirt.

His gaze brightened. "That is a fine-looking ginger loaf. I can't see a quick look around doing any harm, but you'll have to stay close to me and not wander off."

"Oh, thank you," she said in a breathy tone. She could take to the stage with the performance she put on.

When Mr Sainsbury reached through the open door, Fern shoved the basket at him, which caused him to take a step backwards. That allowed her to slip through the narrow door before he changed his mind. Passing through the ancient portcullis was like tumbling back through the centuries. A solemn stillness clung to the stones that surrounded her. The cobblestones beneath her boots were worn into grooves from countless footsteps that told a silent tale of the abbey's long history.

Between the gate and the building stretched a patchwork of stone and stubborn weeds that pushed through the cracks. Moss clung to the lower portions of the walls, painting them in hues of vibrant green that seemed almost out of place in the otherwise austere setting. Sibylcrest Abbey loomed over Fern, its weathered façade a testament to Norman craftsmanship and the passage of time.

Her gaze traced the lines of Gothic arches and ornate buttresses that supported the structure. Gargoyles peered down from their lofty perches, their grotesque faces frozen in eternal vigilance. The abbey was a rambling affair, with wings and additions from various periods creating an architectural hodgepodge. A squat Norman tower hunkered in one corner while delicate Georgian glasswork adorned a more recent extension on the opposite side. Ivy climbed the walls in places, its tendrils seeking purchase in every nook and cranny.

"Come on. I'll let you look in the hall, then you'll have to leave," the steward said as he gestured across the courtyard.

"Oh, thank you. I really appreciate it. I'll be sure to tell the girls how gentlemanly you are," Fern gushed. She would have to find an excuse to slip away if the fires weren't burning in the hall.

CHAPTER 15

Fern's escort pulled on an iron latch embedded in a battered door, weathered to silver by centuries of wind and rain. She followed behind, her boots clicking against the worn flagstones as she followed Sir Luxton's steward through the labyrinthine corridors of Sibylcrest. The musty scent of age and neglect permeated the air, a stark contrast to the vibrant, earthy aromas she was accustomed to in her botanical pursuits.

Her attention darted from the uneven floor to the towering walls. Faded tapestries hung limply, their once-vibrant threads now dulled by time and dust. Portraits of stern-faced ancestors watched her passage with judgemental eyes.

They entered a square hall with a twisted staircase on one side and imposing double oak doors on the other. They had wound inwards to the great hall. Beyond the doors, she hoped, lay whatever produced the pale-blue smoke that coated the whisperwoods below.

The steward hauled one door open and stepped inside. Fern on his heels.

"Oh..." she breathed out.

Fern's feet halted as she took in the vast expanse of the hall. Its sheer size overwhelmed her. The vaulted ceiling soared high above. Intricate stone ribs arched gracefully to meet ornate bosses. Faded frescoes, barely visible in the dim light, hinted at long-forgotten stories painted across the ceiling's surface.

Massive stone pillars, their surfaces worn smooth by centuries of hands reaching out as they passed, rose from the flagstone floor to support the lofty roof. Around the top clustered gargoyles, their claws curled around the stone as they peered down. Along one wall was a row of tall and narrow windows that allowed thin shafts of light to pierce the gloom. The view looked back over the valley and took in Drake's Bend.

The opposite, windowless wall held a collection of wooden barrels stacked two high with unmarked sides. They reminded Fern of the kegs used to store spirits. Next to them was a neat woodpile, with chopped lengths piled up as high as a man could reach. The timber ready to supplement their coal usage.

Are they making alcohol? Fern wondered as she moved further into the imposing room.

A banqueting table that could have seated a hundred people occupied the middle of the room. More barrels were stacked on the tabletop at one end. The middle held a variety of funnels, ladles, and bowls. None of the equipment laid out appeared to be used for making brandy or other sorts of liquor.

A grand fireplace dominated each end of the hall, with granite surrounds some twelve feet wide and ten feet tall. Each was easily large enough to roast an entire ox. Two grown men could have comfortably stood inside the fireplace. And they did. Or slightly to one side since a fire burned in the grates. Both fireplaces had metal lug poles sunk into the stone that were sturdy enough to lift an ox or horse. A chain dangled from the curved hook and supported a pot large enough to stew an entire cattle beast. Coal embers heated the containers as the men stirred the contents with what looked like a boat oar.

But it was the steam that truly captured Fern's attention —a peculiar, pale-blue mist that rose in lazy tendrils before disappearing up the vast chimneys. Whatever they simmered in those pots contained a trace of dragon's blood. Were they making dragon stew?

"Goodness, you look like you are cooking dragon soup!" Fern joked, hoping the steward didn't confirm her worse fears.

He laughed. "You can't eat that stuff." Then he raised the basket to his companions at either end of the hall. "We have a visitor who has brought us scones and cake."

"Good. I'm famished," one man called back. He hauled the oar out of the pot and left it leaning against the mantel.

Mr Sainsbury set the basket down on a clear spot on the table. "Right, you've had your look. Time to show you out." He gestured for Fern to turn around.

Blast. She needed a sample of whatever was in the cauldrons. She walked a few more paces closer to the fireplace closest to the doors.

Her escort grabbed her arm. "You need to go, Miss Oakby, or I'll get in trouble if Sir Luxton hears."

"Oh, I would not want that to happen! I do apologise. I am simply fascinated by the size of these fireplaces." She feigned an interest in the carvings of the supporting pillars and hoped the innocent look on her face covered the frantic workings of her mind. "Are the kitchen fires of a similar size? They must have fed armies centuries ago when this was a fort."

Step by step, she edged closer to her goal. Movement caught Fern's eye. A smaller table to one side appeared to be a workbench similar to what George used in his little shed. A man selected a piece of firewood from the orderly pile and placed it into a vice. Then he picked up a plane and began shaving. Curled pieces of wood fell into a tin bath placed under the table.

Given the size of the hearths, which could have used stacked children as logs, there was no need to further reduce the size of the lumps of wood. Nor did any dragon stew require wood shavings.

Fern gestured to the man creating the pile of light-coloured shavings. "Whatever are you doing here? Why, my little brain simply can't make sense of it! If you would be so good as to explain it to me, I'll not tell a soul. It shall be our secret. In return, I can make a weekly delivery of baking if you like?" She rested one hand on his forearm and added an eyelash flutter for good measure.

Mr Sainsbury's face screwed up as he considered the offer.

"If you don't tell her, I will," came a muffled voice from one of the other men. He had dug into the basket, selected a scone, and was happily munching on it. "These are delicious. Just like my Ma used to make." He leaned over and took another scone for his free hand.

The steward let out a sigh. "We're making paper. It's some fancy stuff Sir Luxton intends to sell to his noble friends."

"Paper?" Sibylcrest used to be an abbey, and paper-making seemed apt given its former life. Monks would spend their days making paper, binding books, and illuminating manuscripts. It seemed fitting if a new papermaking business was established in its great hall. Fern didn't know much about how wood was turned into pages. Did it always involve gigantic cauldrons that could boil an entire cow? She pointed to one. "What part of the process is that?"

"The pulp has to be boiled down. Sir Luxton has a special method he doesn't want anyone else copying. His paper is extra fine, you see." A flicker of unease passed over Mr Sainsbury's face at giving away trade secrets.

Fern would consult Ambrose and George about both how paper was made, and if Sir Luxton had an expensive paper business. The wisps rising from the cauldrons were unlike anything that came from Mrs Bentley's cooking, due to the odd colour and being more substantial than normal steam. Then it occurred to her that given the size of the containers, could the inclusion of dragon blood have been accidental?

What if, decades ago, they had been used to render down a deceased creature?

"I wouldn't mind just a tiny peek at how it works. It sounds fascinating." Fern walked towards the fireplace.

Mr Sainsbury moved quickly to intercept her. "That's not possible, miss. We wouldn't want you getting splashed. There's a reason those two wear thick aprons." He gestured to his companions, who did indeed wear tough leather aprons.

Fern forced a smile. "Of course, I wouldn't dream of being a bother. Perhaps you could tell me more about the wood you're using?"

As if on cue, a gust of wind down the chimney sent a waft of steam in their direction. Fern inhaled deeply, trying to pick apart the bouquet of aromas. Beneath the acrid smoke tang, there lingered something that tugged at the edges of her memory.

"It's just ordinary wood. Nothing special. The lads cut it down from the forest around the abbey." Sainsbury reached out and took her upper arm, turning her around so she faced the door.

Fern wasn't so sure about that. She'd not seen any evidence of felled trees in the nearby forest. Although, thankfully, they hadn't taken their saws to the whisperwoods, which stood on a sliver of land owned by someone else and weren't part of Sibylcrest.

Lord Drakeman had tasked her with getting a sample of whatever was in those cauldrons, but how to obtain it? The steward watched her like a hawk and was herding her towards the door like an anxious sheepdog. Her chance was about to slip through her fingers. There must be something she could do.

As they walked back along the worn flagstones, Mr Sainsbury dropped his hand. Fern took the chance to stumble, deliberately losing her footing. She flung out her hands to balance herself on the long table. Letting one hand drop to the floor, her fingers closed around a wood peeling that had escaped the bath or been kicked along by the men's feet.

"Silly me. I must have caught my toe on a bit of flagstone." She tucked the scrap of wood into her pocket as she rose. "Goodbye! I'll bring more scones next week, and perhaps a pie," she called out to the men who returned to their positions at the fires.

"Let's make sure you don't fall over again," the steward said as he took her upper arm again and marched her back through the twisting corridors and across the cobbles. He only released her at the narrow door in the portcullis, giving her a little push to ensure she left the abbey.

The iron swung shut behind her with a clang, and the long key turned in the lock. Fern waved and then headed for the patient horse and cart. Checking over her shoulder to ensure Mr Sainsbury was no longer watching, she dug into her pocket and studied the flake of wood she had managed to snatch.

It had a soft, golden colour, like the first blush of a sunrise. It wasn't much—barely larger than a fingernail. Raising it to her nose, she inhaled the faint scent.

"I know you," she murmured. The memory of it scratched at her mind, trying to break free. She'd probably jolt wide away at three o'clock in the morning and suddenly remember.

Taking out her handkerchief, she laid the flake in the middle and wrapped it with care before returning it to her pocket. She hadn't managed to sneak a sample of what bubbled in the cauldrons, but this was a start.

Climbing into the cart and untying the reins, Fern cast one last look at Sibylcrest. The thick stone walls held tight to the secret of whatever bubbled in the great hall. Tendrils of eerie smoke curled from the chimneys and reached up to join hands with the clouds above.

Whatever the men brewed, if it sickened the whisperwoods, Fern was going to get to the bottom of it. Somehow.

When she returned to Nemython House, Fern found William in a sombre mood.

"Is everything all right?" she asked as he undid the harness from the horse.

"We're all worried about Dan," he said in a quiet voice.

"Is he no better?" Fern had expected the young lad to be back on his feet in a day or two. A chill and the sniffles shouldn't have been enough to keep him away from Eurydice.

William shook his head and patted the horse as he removed the bridle. "No. Ma summoned the doctor, and she thinks it might be pneumonia."

A chill of fear washed over Fern. Pneumonia plucked many lives far too soon. "Oh, no! I am going to visit the Moray sisters. I shall ask Nona for a brew while I am there."

Fern's cry of concern pulled Eurydice from her stall, and she padded along the aisle to butt against Fern's leg.

"That would be most appreciated, Miss Oakby. None of us like to see Dan sickly." William led the horse into an empty stall.

The dragon followed Fern out of the stables and refused to be left behind. She considered shutting the creature in the stall but thought that rather mean. The dragonet seemed much recovered now, even though she didn't show any inclination to fly.

"I think you can come with me, Riddy. But we shall walk slowly, and if it is too far, I will leave you with the sisters and run back for the cart," Fern told the dragon of her plans.

It was a slow walk as Eurydice veered off the road to snuffle at flowers or to follow a scent that caught her interest. When they turned up the path to the whitewashed cottages, the chickens squawked at Fern's companion.

The old women were out in the garden, and three heads turned in greeting.

"Oh, Morda, Fern has brought the other dragon to visit." Decima placed the hoe she had been using on the ground and took her blind sister's arm.

"Ladies, this is Eurydice, or Riddy for short. Riddy, these are the Moray sisters. They can mould magic, and they are very wise." Fern stopped by the spreading tree, and the dragon sat with a relieved sigh.

Nona and Decima helped Morda to kneel down, and the seer placed her hands on the dragon's face.

"You will restore the balance, my beauty," she crooned as

her fingertips brushed over the dragon's head and down her neck.

The dragon trilled and spread her wings, stirring up a light breeze. The three women cooed over Eurydice, admiring her form.

"While I am here, Daniel Bentley is sick. The doctor thinks it is pneumonia. Could you make a tonic for him, please, Nona?" Fern asked the oldest sister.

"Of course. I have some already made up with a healing charm to ease the lungs and reduce fever." Nona squeezed her arm. "These two can tell you what we discovered in the woods while I fetch it."

Fern helped Morda to the wooden bench under the tree. Decima sat next to her while Fern sat on the grass at their feet. Eurydice padded to a sunny spot and then flopped onto her belly with a contented groan.

"Did the whisperwoods tell you anything useful?" Fern asked.

Decima's attention was fixed on the dragon rolling on the grass. A curious chicken edged closer but ran out of bravery when Eurydice snorted, and the hen darted under the shelter of a rhubarb leaf. When Decima turned to face Fern, her gnarled fingers wove patterns in the air. "We have gazed into the heart of the sacred grove. What we saw troubles us deeply. The nemeton is indeed out of balance, but the cause is more complex than we first believed."

Morda, her blind eyes seeming to focus on the invisible, added, "The sickness of the grove is both old and new. A wound from the past, reopened by present greed."

That wasn't particularly helpful, but Fern bit her tongue.

The sickness was new and most likely triggered by whatever the smoke from the abbey's chimneys contained. But one thing did catch her interest. "An old wound? Like one being cut down or poisoned before?"

Decima took up the narrative when Morda fell silent. "No, child. There is a presence that slumbers deep under the grove. An ancient spirit is woven into the roots of the whisperwoods. It is the guardian of the confessions passed to it over the centuries, gathering the secrets that pass through leaf and limb to be buried in the ground. Whatever taints the trees has seeped into the roots of the nemeton. As the spirit is twisted, so are the words it was bound to protect."

That confirmed what the sisters had told Fern earlier. Only when she removed the blight could they settle the whisperwoods and restore their peaceful balance. She needed to find some way to either stop whatever was creating the smoke at Sibylcrest or cleanse the leaves.

"You must act." Morda caught Fern's hand and her attention. "For more than the whisperwoods suffer."

"There are other trees affected?" Anything else should be easier to deal with since the whisperwoods were the only ones spreading gossip. Unless the surrounding oak, beech, and elm decided to start talking.

Morda let go of Fern's hand to throw hers wide. "Everything in nature is connected."

Fern leaned back and mulled over their words. Everything was connected. The chickens scratched in the earth and pecked bugs from leaves. Or ate the silver beet, stripping it to the white stems. A willow fence protected those vegetables the chickens liked a little too much. In turn, they ate the eggs the chickens produced. There was a cycle to life. But Fern doubted Morda meant the chickens would suffer.

"Trees..." A realisation burst into Fern's mind, and she sat upright. "Trees bear fruit, and plants have crops. If they are also tainted somehow by the smoke, what might happen when we eat them?"

CHAPTER 16

Nona returned with a healing brew. "This should help the lad."

Fern reached for the dark-green bottle, her mind racing ahead. "Wait, you said you already had this made up."

Nona took a seat beside her sisters. "Yes, Daniel is the third to fall ill this week with the same cough and fever. Doctor Dodd asked us to brew more."

"Who are the others?" A horrible idea took root in Fern's mind and refused to be dislodged.

Nona named two boys, their names familiar to Fern.

"They're the same age as Daniel." They were probably friends. What if the three lads had all touched or eaten the same thing? They could have been climbing trees in the woods surrounding Sibylcrest and have the taint on their hands. Boys were notorious for sticking their fingers in their mouths without washing up first.

She had to talk to Daniel. "We must leave you, ladies.

Come along, Riddy." Fern tucked the bottle into her coat pocket and rested an encouraging hand on the dragon's head.

Riddy snorted as she rose to her feet and followed Fern back along the path to the road. It was hard to stop herself from running all the way home, but Eurydice would never have been able to keep up. Instead, they walked as briskly as possible.

The dragon's feet dragged by the time they walked into the stables. "Can you put her to bed, please?" Fern called out to William and then raced across to the Bentley family cottage.

She rapped on the blue-painted door, and it was opened by Lucy, the youngest at just ten years of age. She favoured her father in appearance, with dark-brown hair and light, almost amber eyes. Lucy also inherited her father's height and was already as tall as her mother.

"Hello, Miss Oakby. Does Ma need me in the kitchen?" Worry creased her young face.

"No," she reassured the youngster. "I need to see Daniel, if I may. I have some tonic for him." She patted the bottle tucked in her pocket.

"He's upstairs, miss. I'm sure he'd like a visitor." Lucy closed the door behind her and gestured to the narrow stairwell that ran up one side of the hall.

Fern took the stairs to the loft bedrooms. William and Daniel shared the one to the left that overlooked the stables. Lucy and Alice had the one on the right-hand side that peered over the front garden of Nemython House.

She paused in the doorway. Two single beds were pushed

against opposite walls. One had a shape under a blue-and-green patchwork quilt.

"Daniel?" Fern called his name gently, not wanting to disturb the lad if he slept but hoping to find him awake.

The shape under the blankets rolled over, and an arm pushed them away from his head. "Hello, miss," Daniel rasped. The lad tried to push himself up.

"Let me help." Fern tucked his pillow up and helped him lean back against it. Then she tugged up the quilt to keep his chest warm.

The boy coughed, and it seemed his lungs rattled against his ribs. His eyes were red, and his skin flushed.

Fern sat on the edge of the bed. "I have a tonic for you. Nona brewed it to ease your breathing."

On a shelf by his bed sat a glass of water and a spoon. Fern poured a little of the amber-coloured medicine, which reminded her of honey and summer flowers, onto the spoon. Daniel opened his mouth like a baby bird and swallowed the brew.

Replacing the cap on the bottle, she placed it on the shelf.

"I hear that Joseph and Edward are sick too. That seems an odd sort of pneumonia that you all caught it." There were many illnesses that spread through families or communities. But no one in any of the boys' families was sick, just the lads.

"We've been swimming in the river." Daniel paused to cough, but it didn't have the horrid hacking sound now he had taken a little syrup. "Must've caught a chill."

Fern had also been swimming in the river and hadn't come down with pneumonia.

"Or perhaps it was something else that the three of you did?" She tried to nudge him in the right direction.

The lad plucked at his blankets, and as he did so, Fern noted a faint blue tinge on the fingertips of his left hand. He remained silent and held tight to whatever secret the boys had shared.

Fern tried a different approach. "You're not in any trouble, Dan. Far from it. You see, the whisperwoods are sick, and I think it is coming from the smoke puffing from Sibylcrest. But the smoke might have settled over more than just the grove. There are lots of trees around that hill, and I'm worried that you boys might have climbed one and touched the leaves. That might be what is making you all sick."

He didn't answer. A shiver wracked his lean body, and he nestled a little deeper under his blankets.

"The tainted smoke leaves a blue smudge. You can't see it when you look at a tree, but it appears on your skin after you have touched it." She picked up his left hand and splayed his fingers.

Daniel swallowed, the lump visibly moving down his throat. "I think it was the apples, miss. We didn't steal them. Honest. It's a wild one, not from someone's garden."

"I believe you. There are many fruit trees scattered around, seeded by birds or discarded fruit." Her stomach rolled with dread. "But I need you to think hard for me, Daniel. Can you remember if you noticed the blue smudges of your skin when you climbed the tree or after you plucked the apples?" There was still a chance it was only foliage affected.

His young face screwed up in concentration. "Only Joe

climbed the tree. Eddie and me caught the apples he tossed down."

Bother. But at least she now knew it wasn't pneumonia. Instead, they had eaten poisoned apples. Fern drew a long breath through her nose and exhaled as she planned what to do next in her head. There had to be a way to cure the boys and the whisperwoods. Which meant she had to go and see Lord Drakeman and tell him she failed to gather the sample he required. She had put it off long enough.

In her mind, she could hear Quint snorting, and he had probably already written away to acquire a portcullis to install at the end of the estate's driveway.

Fern patted Daniel's arm. "I am going to find out what was on the apples that has made you, Joseph, and Edward sick. Then the Moray sisters can make another tonic to cure you all."

Leaving the cottage, Fern found William in the stables and reassured him that she would discover a cure for what ailed his younger sibling and his friends. When she peered into the end stall, Eurydice was tucked under her blanket, fast asleep and snoring.

"That walk must have worn her out," Fern murmured.

Each day, the dragon grew stronger and could walk farther. How long before she marched down the drive and never returned? Or would she ever leave when she couldn't fly? The dragon had not shown any sign of wanting to test her wings.

Fern walked her mare to the mounting block and then rode towards Wyndham Hall. Trotting through the village, they had to quickly jump to one side as a carriage rumbled through. The driver cracked the reins and refused to give way or be mindful of the villagers.

"Another gossip-seeker. Everyone will want to know which peer was plotting treason." Patting the startled mare, they carried on their way.

At the Hall, Fern left her horse with the stablehand—now she knew the estate had one. Not bothering with the main entrance, she walked through the conservatory, stomping any dirt from her boots as she went. Then she cracked the library door open and peered inside hoping to find Lord Drakeman at his desk.

Empty. Bother.

Closing the door, Fern strode back through the long-neglected greenroom and headed for the laboratory. She could have roamed the house in search of either Quint or his lordship, but instinct told her if he wasn't in the library, he was most likely huddled over his alchemic equipment.

"Quint should hang up a chalkboard by the front door and write where Lord Drakeman is so I can find him," Fern muttered as she walked through the flowering meadow. The cornflowers were beautiful with their vibrant blue blooms, and she plucked one on her way past, tucking it behind her ear.

When she stood before the squat stone building, Fern rapped firmly on the silvered door and called out, "It's Miss Oakby with news from Sibylcrest."

Within a few seconds, the bolts were drawn back on the door, and it was flung open.

"You have the sample I need?" Today, the heavy leather apron was absent. Nor did Lord Drakeman have the helmet and goggles balanced on his head. He seemed dressed to spend time in the library, not sniffing fumes, and almost appeared civilised—even with the unnerving mercury eye and scales.

"Yes, and no. I have a sample, just not the one you wanted." Fern pushed past him before he had a chance to slam the door on her.

She moved directly to the square table positioned under the skylight and tugged open her satchel. She carefully pulled free the handkerchief that held the tiny wooden flake.

"Mr Sainsbury, that's Sir Luxton's steward at Sibylcrest, was swayed by the basket of baking and Quint's ginger loaf in particular." Until she saw Mr Nancy, the Hall's cook, Fern would continue to believe that Quint spent time in the kitchen happily baking while he hummed tunes. After all, nobody could be that dour and grumpy all the time. He had to have a hobby that lightened his heart.

"I wheedled my way into the grand hall. From the outside, I thought that the most likely place with the fireplaces in use, producing the oddly tinged smoke." The abbey had so many chimneys, most of them cold and unused. In hindsight, she wondered why they didn't use the kitchens. Or perhaps those fires weren't large enough for the giant-sized cauldrons.

Lord Drakeman grunted and pulled the handkerchief to his side of the table, but he remained silent. Apparently, he was disappointed in Fern's sleuthing ability.

She carried on so that he would understand the relevance of the scrap of wood. "The grand hall has two fireplaces, one at either end. Both were large enough to roast an entire cow.

Each had a cauldron sitting above coal embers. The steam drifting off them is producing blue smoke. To one side were stacks of wood. A man was using a plane to turn them into flakes that were then thrown into the cauldrons. When I asked what they were making, Mr Sainsbury said it was paper."

"Paper?" At last, he looked up, and his brow furrowed.

"It is a possibility, is it not? Papermaking does involve wood pulp, which was something traditionally done at monasteries." Although it didn't usually poison the surrounding forest and apple trees, causing grief and sickness for all those it touched.

"Papermaking doesn't usually involve dragon blood." That silver eye bore through her.

"I hoped it might be accidental. The cauldrons appeared very old. Is it possible that they might have been used long ago for some purpose related to dragons?" Fern struggled to imagine how blood might have seeped into the iron. She doubted the creatures did laundry. But an injured one might have required some sort of dressing. "Perhaps bandages that were blood-stained were then boiled to get them clean?"

Lord Drakeman rapped his blunt nails against the table-top. "Possible. But in such a situation, there would only be a small trace unless the cauldrons were coated with blood. I need a sample of the boiled pulp, which is what you were supposed to obtain."

Fern relived the last few days in her mind, trying to pinpoint when she became some sort of maid he could send on errands. "They weren't exactly going to let me dip a container in. Nor did I have anything to hold the bubbling concoction." That was his fault. The alchemist should have given her one of his bottles. What was she supposed to do, swipe her hand into the hot mixture? "Mr Sainsbury said it was a secret recipe of Sir Luxton's that produced finer paper."

The tapping stopped. "I don't recall him having any interest in paper products. There isn't sufficient margin to satisfy his appetites."

"There is another complication. Three village lads have fallen ill. After speaking to Daniel Bentley, all three ate apples growing at the edge of the forest surrounding Sibylcrest. Whatever is in this smoke is making the villagers sick." Physically and mentally, as the twisted words of the whisperwoods sewed dissent and fuelled anger.

"Do you know what sort of tree this flake is from?" Lord Drakeman didn't seem to acknowledge that the sickness had spread to the boys. He turned to fetch a pair of tweezers to pick up the sliver and hold it close to his dragon eye.

There was another failure on her part—and they were certainly piling up today. What sort of botanist couldn't identify a bit of wood?

"I think it is a hardwood. It has a dense, close grain. There is a faint scent that is achingly familiar. Combined with the rich golden colour of the cut edges..." At long last, memory supplied the answer, and Fern nearly fell over the table as she gripped the edge with both hands. "No."

The alchemist shot out a hand across the table to steady her but stopped before he touched her skin. Instead, his curled fingers grazed the air by her side. "You don't know?"

"I mean, yes, I know. But I cannot believe it could be so. I think it's kelmsgale." How did they have a stack of wood from the rare and magic-imbued tree? George would know for certain, with his woodworker's ability to identify a tree from grain, hue, and aroma.

"Kelmsgale is unique. It will not take me long to ascertain if this is from one." He placed the curl on a piece of glass and flattened it with another. Then he disappeared into the dim rear of the laboratory where the shelves held samples and books. When he reappeared, he carried an open book and another slide.

Fern paced while he worked. Unable to stand still as her mind spun.

"Rowan leaves and dragon's breath, are the key to life and death," she whispered the old rhyme, the words echoing through her bones.

In her mind, she saw the drawing in the front of her father's journal—the dragon curled up asleep at the base of a tree. *What have we stumbled into, Father?*

As she waited for Lord Drakeman to compare the shaving to his book, she tried to make sense of the two ingredients. The whole thing could still be accidental. Blood from centuries ago could have seeped into the iron and then leeched back out during the cooking process. The men who cut down the tree probably didn't even know what species it was and merely hacked down something convenient. Apart from the one in Drake's Bend, there weren't any kelmsgales in the area, except...

Her brain sparked into life again. Except for the felled giant at the midway point between the village and Warrington Manor. The one that her father had left off his map for some reason. What if that tree was the origin of the wood shavings?

And the dragon's blood. She recalled what she had discovered in the long grass at the base of the tree. A horrible scene played out in her head as Mr Sainsbury and his men cut down the kelmsgale and then slayed the dragon for its blood.

Her skin itched to do something to put the pieces together. She was close to understanding something, and a certainty in her core whispered that when she did, it would unlock the secrets surrounding her father's research and death. But she needed to be certain first. Were the ingredients of the wood pulp by accident or design?

Her main concern was the health of Daniel and his friends. Would the blue tinge poison the lads, or was it something temporary that would pass through their young bodies? The Moray sisters said the whisperwoods could be healed, and she hoped the same was true for the lads.

Please let this all be a mere coincidence. She made an entreaty to the Fates.

Mutterings came from the microscope, and after several too-long minutes, Lord Drakeman straightened, and his eerie silver gaze settled on her. "It's kelmsgale, and yet not."

"It is, and it isn't?" How could a tree not be a tree? Her father might have known the answer to that riddle.

CHAPTER 17

Lord Drakeman gestured to the open book with its detailed drawings of wood samples taken from the magical tree. "It is predominantly kelmsgale rowan, but there are slight variants in the structure of the wood fibres. So it is not exactly a kelmsgale."

"Oh." Fern let out a long sigh as the tree's omission from the map made sense. Her father only included known kelmsgales. "It didn't *look* like a kelmsgale. Perhaps the leaf was different."

Lord Drakeman frowned. "How can you tell that from a shaving?"

Excitement bubbled under her skin at having solved one mystery that had plagued her. "Between here and Warrington Manor, I found a tree stump. Beside it was a kelmsgale seed pod. I thought the tree had to be a kelmsgale. Except it's not on my father's map that marks the location of every specimen in England. He even painted them silver when they died or were cut down—like the four in the village green. This particular tree wasn't on his map, and I couldn't determine why. Most likely, it was because the outward appearance wasn't the same."

"That would seem a logical explanation." He slammed the book shut.

"There was also a dragon skeleton," her voice faded to a whisper as she recalled the sad bundle of bones.

"What?" The alchemist froze, his body tense as his gaze drilled through her.

"Beside the stump. I found a skeleton. It was covered in long grass, and I didn't notice it at first. From the size, I would say it was only a hatchling. Like Riddy." She tried not to think about how Eurydice was almost entombed under a fountain.

Silence dropped as heavy as the air before a summer thunderstorm. Lightning seemed to flash in Lord Drakeman's silver eye, and he certainly wore what Ambrose would call a *thunderous look.*

"Take me there." He spun on his heel and grabbed a coat from a hook, shoving his arms into the sleeves as he roamed his laboratory.

"I can't do it now. I have to find the apples that most likely poisoned Daniel and his friends." Nothing would restore the dragonet or tree, but she could determine what made the boys sick and help them before they became worse.

"No. Show me this creature first. After that, I will find an antidote for whatever has made the boys ill." He flung open a cupboard and retrieved a battered leather bag much larger than Fern's old satchel.

There was no harm in having a cure from an alchemist and a witch. One or the other would have to work.

He shoved items into the bag. "Tell Fawcett to saddle my horse."

Fern didn't move.

"Fawcett. He's my groom." A drawer slammed as he closed it after failing to find whatever he wanted.

"I am acquainted with Mr Fawcett. He cares for my horse while I am in the conservatory." The man who worked in the stables had a cheerful disposition at odds with the other residents of the Hall.

He pulled a roll of vials from a shelf and added it to the bag. "Then did you not hear me? Go tell him at once."

Oh, I heard you. While technically she was on the staff since she took payment for her work in the conservatory, she also had noble blood in her veins and didn't respond well to being ordered about.

The alchemist glanced up when she still hadn't moved.

Fern met his gaze and remained silent. Waiting.

Lord Drakeman ground his jaw. "Could you tell Fawcett to ready my horse...please."

She smiled. "Of course, Lord Drakeman. I shall meet you at the stables."

That wasn't so hard, now, was it? She thought.

The earl and his butler could both do with learning a few basic civilities. How fortunate for them that huffy, moody men didn't intimidate her. Another thought occurred to Fern. Perhaps she should bring Mrs Bentley and her rolling pin out one day. The stern housekeeper would have both men *minding their P's and Q's* in no time.

Outside, the weather was on the turn, and a chill wind chased her back across the meadow. Fern found Denis mucking out a stall in the quiet stables.

"His lordship needs you to saddle his horse, please," she said as she leaned on the cool wood. "We are riding out immediately. I'll tack up my mare."

She didn't want the stablehand having two equines to worry about, especially not when one had the capacity to turn into a snorting, impatient beast. And the other was a sensitive mare.

By the time Fern was mounted on her horse waiting in the yard (who had only the occasional foot stomp of impatience and eye roll at the stallion who was standing a little too close), the earl came barging from the house. He had found a dark grey greatcoat, and it swirled behind him like an ominous cloud. He grabbed the reins of his horse and put one foot into the stirrup, swinging his body up and over as the horse moved off.

"We're off, then," Fern muttered as he cantered away along the driveway.

Not that the mare needed to be told twice that they were leaving. The horse leapt into a rhythmic canter as soon as Fern thought of it. They easily caught the other horse and rider, who had to slow for the narrow gap in the ajar gates.

Once on the main road, Lord Drakeman urged his stallion onwards, and the eager horse flew over the ground. Fern's mare proved that smaller didn't mean slower. The equine was fleet, sure-footed, and just as keen to stretch her legs with a good run along the tree-lined road.

It was an eerie ride. Lord Drakeman didn't speak and set

a fast pace. Long stretches of canter were only occasionally broken by a bit of walk or trot to let the horses catch their breath. The stallion would roll his head to the side to make sure the mare was still close by. Even the weather joined the mood of the day; the sun hid behind dark clouds, and the threat of rain hung above them.

Fern thought she followed on the heels of Death, the way the alchemist leaned over the horse's mane, his coat billowing out behind him.

"I must tell Millie, she will love this for a story," she said to the mare as his lordship hadn't spoken a word since she made him say *please*.

Only two carriages rumbled past them. One with the curtains drawn tight, the other with a woman's face pressed to the glass. Both drivers veered off the road as the galloping riders approached. Or perhaps they thought the grim reaper bore down on them, and it was better to let him pass.

Fern wondered if the occupants headed for the whisper-woods to hear gossip about their peers, or to learn who among them had plotted treason. Every day saw more travellers passing through Drake's Bend on their way to the ancient grove. Some stopped to pass an hour or two in the tavern or to stroll alongside the river to stretch their legs.

The ride of an hour to the spot Fern remembered was cut considerably shorter by their urgent speed. She couldn't fathom the alchemist's hurry. The dragonet was long dead. Or did he have some horrid secret process that could resurrect it? Galvanism would most likely be involved.

She glanced up at the darkening sky. He probably

wanted to lay his hands on it before a lightning strike. The bag hanging at his side might contain metal rods to direct the electricity. Not that she saw him shove any in there.

"Here!" Fern called out as they approached the curve in the river that had been her halfway point marker as she journeyed back and forth to Warrington Manor.

They guided the horses off the road and jumped to the ground. The mare gave a warning squeal for the stallion to keep his distance when it appeared he might follow her to the river for a drink.

Keeping one eye on her horse, Fern gestured to the stump and the secret hidden beside it. Lord Drakeman walked his stallion to the other side of the felled tree before tying the horse to a low-hanging branch.

"Sorry girl, but I don't want you two becoming *better acquainted*," Fern murmured as she found a branch within reach of both water and grass to secure her horse.

Lord Drakeman unslung his bag and waited a short distance from the stump.

"It's on that side, closest to you." Fern pointed to the long grass between him and the tree. Edging around the remnant of the kelmsgale with care, she leaned down and tugged aside a clump. Pale bones were revealed beneath the bright, spring green.

"You're certain it's a dragon?" He stepped closer, tugged the fabric of his tight breeches up a fraction, and then knelt.

Delicately, as though she weeded around the finest crystal glasses, Fern eased strands of grass free from the soil. Piece by piece, more of the creature was exposed. The gentle arch of wing bones was clearly visible against its ribs. Even the tail had been curled around the dragonet, and the bone at the tip rested close to the skull. Fern imagined the dragon laying down its head and wrapping its tail around its body until the end covered its nose.

When they had uncovered all of the skeleton, the alchemist grunted and sat back on his booted heels. "Since you knew a dragon was here, why didn't you bury it?" He spoke without looking at her, his attention fixed on the sad pile of bones.

His question struck her as an accusation. Fern opened and closed her mouth as she struggled with a reply. If he were any sort of drake man, why didn't he know hatchlings were being trapped and dying?

"It seemed more disrespectful to expose the poor thing and move it to bury than it did to leave him or her undisturbed and hidden by the tree. Whatever happened, do they not deserve to be left to rest in peace?" As she watched his hands glide down the thin ribs, something else struck her. The skeleton appeared intact and undisturbed. Not even a hungry nocturnal creature had dragged any part of it away.

"I would guess it died a year ago. Do you think that is consistent with when the tree was cut down?" Only now did he look up and fix his all-seeing gaze on her.

She was no witch to peer into the veil of time. "I can only guess. The timber has weathered, but no rot has crept under the bark. A year is possible, but I cannot say with certainty if they were taken at the same time."

"If the wood was taken a year ago, why have signs of

poisoning in the whisperwoods only shown now?" He reached into his bag, pulled out the odd glasses that covered his human eye, and examined the bones.

Fern recalled the dinner-time conversation with George. "Sir Luxton Davies bought Sibylcrest last year. The residue from the smoke might have taken time to accumulate on the leaves before the trees showed any effect. Any winds would change the direction of smoke drift, and rain would wash it away. The Moray sisters say it spreads through leaf and limb to the roots, and that has twisted their words."

Before he could answer, hooves clopped along the road at a steady trot. An odd, short, rectangular, and enclosed cart driven by a dark-clad wraith halted by them. The conveyance reminded Fern of a hearse. One that would conceal the occupant rather than display the coffin like the glass-sided carriages used in larger towns and cities.

As the driver hopped down, she realised it was no wraith. Just Quint.

He grinned at Fern and tapped the solid wooden side of the cart. As though reading her thoughts about hearses, he said, "Just your size, I reckon."

"I much prefer to ride than recline. But thank you for the kind offer." She wondered why the butler or henchman, or whatever he was, had to join them. The trip was uncomfortable enough with her and Lord Drakeman. Millie would say the addition of Quint added dramatic tension.

"Today, Quint. Before it rains," Lord Drakeman said.

The butler opened the rear door and reached in, pulling out a folded length of canvas. Fern kept her vigil beside the skeleton as he walked towards her and opened the waxed fabric. Lord Drakeman removed his glasses, then took one side. They laid it out like a picnic blanket beside the dragonet.

Now she understood what they meant to do. The skeleton would be removed and transported back to Wyndham Hall. But to do what?

"What will you do with them?" Fern asked as the men guided the canvas under the bones.

"There is much of value to be learned from the skeleton." The alchemist slid bones onto the fabric with one hand when they hit a rough spot of ground, and couldn't ease the pile on any further.

Of value. How horrid. She thought he would take the poor thing away to bury in the dragon graveyard that hid among the trees on the estate. But no, the creature would be rendered down in his laboratory. He probably had potions that needed dragon dust or teeth.

"You criticise me for not burying the wee thing when you are going to use it for ingredients in your experiments." She glared at Quint and curled her fingernails into her palms before she said more.

Lord Drakeman stared at her, the slit of pupil in his silver eye narrowing further until the slice of black almost disappeared entirely. "You overreach, Miss Oakby. I do not have to explain my actions to you."

Fern brushed aside his comment as anger built inside her. Blast the man. Was he built of the same solid stone as his laboratory? "Do you feel nothing at all when dragons sicken and die? You treat this poor thing like it is just supplies on a larder shelf. Riddy would have met a horrible end if I had not found her, and yet, you show no interest in her recovery whatsoever." Although, to be fair, she couldn't blame the alchemist because Lord Warrington's hounds had chased the dragonet into a hole.

He stilled, and the oncoming storm seemed to pause around them. When he moved, he took one long stride towards her. His frame filled her vision as he closed the gap and stood so close that his angry exhales warmed her face like Squib puffing heated air. Staring down at her, he closed his normal eye and tilted his head. That silver gaze pierced straight through her.

Fern refused to be silenced or intimidated. She met his dragon stare and dared him to justify his hideous behaviour when the magical creatures had raised his family and given him so much.

"I am not scared of you," she hissed to fill the silence.

"No. You are not." At last, he blinked. As though satisfied with what he found in her soul. Slowly, his scaled lid lowered, and the slit pupil returned to its normal size. Without answering her accusation, he returned to the pile of bones laid out on the canvas.

"You should be scared," Quint muttered.

Oddly, it was him saying it that caused a chill to ripple down her spine. Yet she went nose to nose with the alchemist without any sense of fear.

Anger and righteous indignation can carry you through many a difficult situation, she thought.

The rain began to fall, and they moved quickly to cover up the skeleton. The two men carried it to the back of the cart. Quint slammed the doors and threw across a bolt. Then he hopped back onto the seat and pulled a hood over his face to protect his bald head from the rain.

"You have done your part of our deal, and I will do mine. Bring me a poisoned apple, and you shall have your cure for the boys." Lord Drakeman took a knife from his satchel and carved off a piece of bark and trunk from the remains of the kelmsgale, and then he stored them away. After he retrieved his horse, he leapt up into the saddle and cantered off down the road.

Fern's mare called after the departing stallion and pawed at the ground. Apparently, she had now decided she liked having the other horse for company.

"Give me a minute, girl." Fern mimicked the alchemist's actions. Taking out her pocket knife, she sliced a sample from the tree. Perhaps George could tell her how it differed from the kelmsgale that stood in the village. Her father had a sample of the wood from one of the trees that had sickened and been felled before it toppled on an unsuspecting villager.

She drew her hood up and kept her chin tucked in as she rode back to Drake's Bend. At times, she glimpsed Lord Drakeman in the distance up ahead of her. But he never slowed or glanced over his shoulder.

"Men." He did callous things and then got upset when she pointed out how cold his actions were. "You're being hysterical!" she shouted at the distant figure.

He didn't hear her, but it made her feel a little better to let the words out.

All the way home, her mind picked at what she had learned, trying to unravel what Sir Luxton was really doing at

Sibylcrest. It obviously wasn't artisan *paper*. Blood from a dragon and shavings from a kelmsgale were simmered together in a cauldron and poisoned the surrounding forest. How did one get blood from a dragon?

She knew what hunters did.

A carcass was hung to drain before skinning and dressing.

CHAPTER 18

Fern kept seeing the dragon curled up beside the tree as though it had huddled there in its final moments. Seeking comfort or solace from the ancient kelmsgale. With other game, a hunter would bury what little remained after they had taken everything that could be used.

In Fern's mind, anyone callous enough to stab a dragon for its blood wouldn't bother burying its body afterwards. Nor would they curl it up by the tree so that it appeared to slumber. How did she reconcile the two possible actions? Someone could have found the dragon afterwards and arranged its limbs. But why do that and not bury it so there was less chance of scavenging animals?

And why hadn't any stray dog or other predator dragged off a bone to gnaw on? What would stop a hungry critter from having a chew on the slain dragon? Even if the imagined executioner had taken away the meat, the bones remained. Although she didn't know if dragon bones contained much marrow.

Disease. Or magic. If someone hadn't reverently arranged the deceased creature, something else had ensured the dragonet lay undisturbed long enough for the grass to cover its remains and conceal it from view.

Oh! Could that be why Lord Drakeman had taken away the skeleton, to find any trace of sickness or magic? He could have said, though, instead of being all ruffled and offended like a broody chicken over her comments.

She put her thoughts aside as the rain intensified. The mare shook her head, dislodging water that trickled into her eyes.

"Let's get home, girl. I promise you'll have a good rub and a warm feed tonight."

Fern still needed to find the apple tree with its poisoned fruit. Lord Drakeman had promised to help in return for her showing him the dragon skeleton. That was a promise she would hold him to.

Thankfully, the rain had eased a little by the time they reached the village and home. Fern rode into the stables before dismounting. Both rider and mount were soaked. Eurydice waddled from her stall and arched her neck as she gave a questioning trill. The curious horse lowered her head and bumped noses with the dragon, unafraid to be near the other creature.

Mares are much more sensible. Fern unbuckled the girth. Then she amended her thoughts, given how Lord Drakeman had reacted to her questioning his lack of feelings for dragons. *Females, in general, are much more sensible.*

William's boots rang out on the cobbles as he entered the barn. Worry tightened his eyes. "I'll do that, Miss Oakby."

Fern pulled off the saddle and placed it over the half wall. "How is Dan? Has the tonic helped at all?"

His concern would be for his sibling since it wasn't the first time Fern had returned from a ride drenched through.

"A little better. The cough is not so bad, so that is good." He took hold of the reins and led the mare into her stall before unbuckling the bridle and slipping it off.

"I need to head back out soon, to find the apple tree Daniel told me about." She stomped her boots, shaking water free from her clothing.

"I'll give madam here a good dry but won't give her any feed. You could do with the same if you don't mind me saying so." William reached up for a towel hanging nearby and briskly dried the horse's damp coat.

Water trickled down the back of Fern's neck. "I'll give it an hour for the worst of the weather to pass over. But a little rain can't stop me when the lads are sick. The sooner I find an apple, the sooner the Moray sisters can brew a cure."

And Lord Drakeman, of course. She would hold out a poisoned apple to him. If he took a bite and the fruit sent him into a cursed slumber, who would rouse him with a kiss?

"Ugh!" Fern shook herself like a wet dog to dislodge water and certain thoughts.

Inside, she shed her wet coat and hung it to dry in the kitchen. Next, she tugged off her boots and, after a pointed look from Mrs Bentley, tucked them inside the little porch outside. The housekeeper tutted under her breath as Fern ran across the kitchen and up the stairs to her room.

Her flesh erupted in goosebumps as she pulled more damp layers off her body. After a quick dry with a towel, Fern dressed again. Her wet clothes were dropped into a basket that she carried back downstairs. Mrs Bentley released the rope holding up the drying rack that hung from the ceiling by the range, so that Fern could place the damp items on the wooden dowels. Then she raised the rack back up and tied off the rope, to allow her things to dry near the oven's warmth.

By the time Fern had finished, a steaming mug of sweet tea and an omelette waited for her on the table.

"Thank you, Mrs Bentley." Fern took her seat and wrapped her hands around the mug.

As she warmed up, Ambrose came into the kitchen, clutching some sheets of paper.

"Ah, there you are. I have news from London." He waved the papers covered in a curling script written in black ink. Ambrose sat across from Fern, plucked his reading glasses from atop his head, and placed them on his nose.

"More gossip?" she asked between mouthfuls of delicious and cheesy omelette with fresh tomato from their vegetable patch.

"Yes, the salacious kind. My chum has given me all the details that are far too sordid for the newspapers to print." He flicked the pages over to find a starting point.

"I didn't think newspapers recognised any boundaries of behaviour?" From what little she knew, some didn't even bother to verify if what they printed was even true or not. Some articles were less *news* and more works of fiction.

"It seems widows and orphans are still treated with some care." He waggled his eyebrows over the top of his glasses. Clearing his throat, he began. "We start with Lord Fishburn..."

Fern recalled the name. That was the lord whose family crest was the fish fighting a lion. Which, when she thought about it, should have been an easy match to win for a lion. "He was the lord waiting by the grove."

"That's him. It appears his elderly mother has a much younger lover, and she has been giving him exquisite pieces of jewellery for, shall we say, *services rendered*. Lord Fishburn is unhappy with the arrangement, since it is depleting his inheritance. He wants the man charged with theft and deception and restitution paid. The gossip is that Lady Fishburn is not the only wealthy widow to fall for the young man's *charms*." Ambrose paused to take a sip of tea.

Fern digested that news along with a mouthful of omelette. Lady Fishburn shouldn't be shamed for finding companionship with a younger man. However, if he had indeed coerced the expensive jewellery from her, then he deserved to be charged for his actions. But given what she knew of how the whisperwoods distorted the confessions entrusted to them, she suspected the truth was far less salacious and was simply a lonely woman looking to fill the void in her heart.

"What of the treasonous peer?" Fern moved on to the next rumour that interested her.

"Ah. That one. Speculation is rife across London. Some little lord is trying to gather support to have the woods silenced."

"No!" That made fear clench Fern's heart, and her hand tightened on her fork.

Ambrose turned the page over. "We have some time yet, I believe, to reverse what ails the whisperwoods. Lord Blair is being very vocal that an Englishman cannot go around destroying another Englishman's property just because it offends him. Then he gives the most excellent example of Lord Hyland's garden."

Fern nearly choked on her mouthful at the mention of that particular abomination. Lord Hyland had a townhouse with a patch of garden between it and the road. He crammed it with flowers of clashing colours in such bright hues (some of them painted to further exaggerate the look) that ladies angled their parasols as they passed so they didn't have to look at it. The chaotic display destroyed the harmony of the area, and his neighbours raised many a protest, trying to make him change it to green shrubbery and subtle flowers. The Botanical Society magazine usually had at least one article devoted to whatever mismatched horror he had planted that month.

"Lord Blair raises an excellent point. While George has yet to find Mrs Rawdon's great-grandson, he is still the owner of the land beneath the grove. An absent owner doesn't make it permissible to destroy the trees." The name Lord Blair rattled around in Fern's mind. She had once been acquainted with a Lady Blair. Was she a sister or daughter of the man who now defended the whisperwoods?

"I suspect the lordling's strings are pulled by another hand. If someone did, or was, plotting against England, they would hardly step into the full gaze of society to reveal themselves." Ambrose read the rest of the letter for snippets but didn't find anything relevant to their conversation.

"Let us hope common sense prevails. If people stopped feeding the woods their secrets, there wouldn't be all this gossip flying around the countryside." No good ever seemed to come from spreading malicious tales. Words thrown to entertain some wounded others.

"I shall have my friend keep their ears open." Ambrose poured himself more tea and wandered back to the parlour.

Once Fern had warmed up, she fetched an old waxed canvas cloak and ventured back out to the stables. Eurydice called from her stall, the dragon able to recognise Fern without seeing her by either the sound of her tread, voice, or scent.

"You will need to stay here, Riddy. It is too cold and damp to take you out." She opened the door to kneel in the hay, scratching the dragon's neck and finding an itchy spot that needed attention. "I promise I shall take you to visit Squib tomorrow. If it is a nice day, perhaps you might like to try a little paddle in the river?" There was a shallow spot where the dragon could play.

Eurydice butted at Fern's hand and made a rough, purring noise which she took as consent to that plan. Checking her friend had fresh water, she closed the stall door and walked to the mare.

When she grabbed the saddle and blanket, the mare danced sideways and snorted.

"I know girl. But once we find the apple tree and deliver them to the sisters and Lord Drakeman, you can have your dinner." The horse was fond of her feed and could usually be cajoled along with promises of warm barley in her bucket.

As she led the mare outside, the rain eased to a steady drizzle. Once in the saddle, Fern arranged the waterproof fabric so the drape of it covered the saddle, her legs, and the mare's flank.

"Last ride for today," she promised the horse as once more they set off along the packed dirt road.

Daniel had told her the apple tree was a wild seedling that grew between the edge of the forest and Putnam's field. That was where wheat grew, which supplied the mill on the river with the grain that produced their flour.

A rich, earthy scent surrounded Fern as the cool rain hit the sun-warmed soil. She didn't mind the spring rain because the smell always made her think of happy times with her family. Her mother used to grab her by the hand and urge her outside after a summer shower to inhale the aroma of warm, damp earth. Her father would tell her how the combination of water and heat from the sun created the magic needed for plants to break free of seeds. The memories triggered by the smell of wet ground made Fern smile.

At a crossroads before the lane that led to the old cottage and ancient grove, Fern guided the mare to the left. They headed northwest and rode the line between the dense forest that encircled the hill and the fields that stretched back to Drake's Bend.

Wheat and barley grew and ripened as spring edged into summer, and the meadows transformed into rippling golden carpets. Fern approached Putnam's field. The road formed one boundary to the meadow. Another butted up against the forest, and a small creek created the third side.

Leaving the mare to munch on the lush clover growing by the sheltering trees, Fern set off to walk the path worn between forest and field. She didn't have to go too far to find the likely poisoner. The apple tree had probably grown from a seed deposited by birds. On its limbs hung fruit that would have tempted anyone. The apples were the size of her hand and a deep, glossy red that made her lick her lips, wondering if the fruit was as sweet as the appearance promised.

"I imagine the evil queen offered something similar to Snow White." No wonder the boys hadn't been able to resist. Or perhaps the perfect outer form of the fruit and colour were a warning from nature that all was not as it seemed inside.

She climbed up the tree and balanced herself against the trunk as she plucked a perfect specimen and wrapped it in cloth. It had worried her that the rain would have washed away any residue from the smoke, but the faint blueish tinge stained her fingers when she turned her hand over.

With one apple secure in her satchel, Fern selected another and wrapped it in a separate cloth. Then it was nestled next to its companion.

"Done." She buckled up the straps and then dropped from the tree.

The mare gave a snort as they turned for Drake's Bend. At times, Fern had to steady the eager horse as the rain made the road slick, and she didn't want to risk a fall in their eagerness to return home. It wasn't too long before they trotted up the drive of Nemython House. Once the horse was in her stall, dry and tucking into a well-deserved feed, Fern cast a longing look at the warm lights coming from her home. She couldn't rest just yet. Tugging her hood up, she set off on foot to the three witches.

The rain had decided to linger, and she walked quickly to

the quaint cottages. The sooner she handed over the poisonous fruit, the sooner she could strip off her damp clothes and curl up by the fire, eating her dinner. Even the chickens had abandoned the garden today, but smoke curled from the chimneys. Fern knocked on the cottage door and didn't wait long before it was flung open by Nona.

"Come in, Fern, you must be drenched. Decima, a hot cup of soup for our damp friend," she called over her shoulder as she pulled Fern inside.

"Oh, no. I won't stay long, and I don't want to get your floors all wet." She stood at the very edge of the slate floor.

From under her cloak, Fern tugged free her satchel and reached inside for a cloth-wrapped apple. The cream cotton now showed slight blue patches. She paused before handing it over to the old woman. "This is what Daniel and the other boys ate. Please be careful. I don't want any of you to sicken as well."

Nona chuckled as she eased the bundle from Fern's hands and unwrapped the perfect red apple. "We are a hardy trio. It will take more than a sour apple to harm us. But we shall handle this beauty with care. Don't you worry about us."

"Lord Drakeman has also promised to distil a potion to counter the effect of the blue smoke. But I have more faith in you." Nor did she want to journey out to Wyndham Hall to discover what the alchemist was doing with the dragon skeleton. She would remind him of his promise to help the lads tomorrow.

Morda cackled from her spot by the fire. "It is not a matter of faith but of fate."

CHAPTER 19

Fern returned home, her thoughts as dark as the rain-filled clouds overhead. If anyone tried to meddle in her life and push her in a certain direction, she would push hard in the *opposite* direction.

"Take that, Fates," she muttered at the sky as she shook out the cloak and hung it up in the porch before slipping in through the kitchen door.

Over dinner with her uncles in their cosy dining room, they plotted what to do next.

"The sisters are going to use the apple to brew a cure for the boys," Fern said after swallowing her mouthful. "I'll take the other apple to Lord Drakeman tomorrow. But I think we need a village meeting first."

"Already organised." George used a carving knife to ease another slice of ham onto his plate. "People need to know what made the lads sick."

Ambrose dabbed at his lips with a linen napkin. "George has also organised a guard for the grove. The fellows are taking turns sitting in the Rawdon cottage and keeping watch."

That eased a little of Fern's anxiety. If anyone from London tried to silence the trees by hacking them down, a villager would raise the alarm.

"The witches made an alarm. If a man shoots an arrow in the sky, it will signal us in the village." Next, George selected more potatoes and beans to add to his second helping.

"How?" Fern wondered what the three old women had concocted.

"I believe there was some mention of peacocks." Ambrose winked and reached for the wine.

Fern worked at many grand gardens where peacocks roamed. The birds had a rather distinctive and shrill cry. She imagined one screaming across the village. "A peacock cry would work."

After a quiet evening, Fern was grateful to sink into her bed. But her dreams were restless ones and cast in shadows. Peers crept through the forest, plucking secrets written on leaves from the trees while she tried to chase them down and snatch them back. When she lunged to grab one, they disappeared in puffs of smoke, leaving behind a blue smear on her palms.

THE NEXT MORNING, they walked into town for the village meeting. Drake's Bend had no mayor, but George and Nona were considered the elders, and their voices were listened to. Not that either Fern or Ambrose would tell George people saw him as an elder. His hair might be turning silver, but he still retained most of it. The role had less to do with his physical age (as there were older men in the village) and more because his level-headed and reasoned opinions were respected.

People assembled on the village green, and there was a festive air to the meeting. Chairs were brought out for the older residents to sit on. Others laid out blankets and sat on the grass. Children ran around the trunk of the kelmsgale, singing and laughing.

Nona took up her position in front of the Drake's Rest, facing the river and the kelmsgale. A chair had been carried out from the tavern for her, with carved arms that resembled a throne for their wizened queen. George stood beside her, one hand resting on the wooden back. Fern stood on the other side. The old woman reached up and squeezed her hand, indicating she could begin.

"Thank you all for coming," Fern called out when she figured most of the village was gathered.

Millie sat at the edge of the grass closest to the bridge. Squib perched on her knees and puffed comforting breaths over her face as the volume of conversation rose. The writer had her arms wrapped around her legs and her body hunched over so that she resembled an armadillo turned in on itself.

As Fern began to speak, voices were hushed. People fell silent as they paid attention, and some of the tension eased from Millie's body.

"As you probably all know, the whisperwoods are sick. They are cruelly twisting the secrets and confessions that have been entrusted to them over the centuries." As she scanned the faces of those present, some averted their eyes. Curiosity nibbled at her as to what made them drop their gazes. Guilt that they had crept to the woods to hear the gossip, or had they played their part in spreading it?

An uncomfortable quiet fell over those assembled. Furtive glances were exchanged between some. At least a dozen people who Fern knew of had come to blows over the gossip spread by the trees. Old wounds were opened, and salt rubbed deep.

"There's some truth to it, though, isn't there?" Charlie Brayton yelled out. Learning the true parentage of his daughter was still a raw scar.

Rippled mutterings flowed over the green.

"If some of it is true, they might know who killed the princes in the tower," someone near the back called out.

Fern hadn't considered using the trees to solve old mysteries. "Possibly. But it would rely on someone involved long ago having stopped at the grove to unburden themselves. And you would need to share a secret that somehow connected you and the princes."

"I could be a descendant of Richard, you know. Some say he escaped and lived to a grand old age. My Ma says I have a noble chin." The man puffed out his chest and tilted his head.

"That's not a compliment, Percy!" someone else retorted to much laughter.

Fern held in a sigh. Her rally for help had quickly gone off the side of the road and into a ditch.

Nona thumped her staff to the ground, and while it made no sound, a *whump* vibrated across the soil. "The trees have guarded our secrets for over a thousand years. They need our help."

Fern flashed her a grateful smile. "People in London are travelling here to learn gossip that they are spreading through society. Scandals grow daily, and there are whispers of treason. Other voices are calling for the whisperwoods to be silenced forever."

As much as Fern wanted to see Daniel and his friends healthy and running with the other children, she also had a need to save the ancient trees coursing through her veins. How to explain to everyone that their world would be diminished without the whisperwoods?

"Some men have volunteered to watch the woods, but we could do with more eyes." George's voice carried across the green, even though he didn't seem to raise it.

Among those who raised their hands to say they would help, were others with a differing opinion.

"They're just trees, Fern. Trees get cut down all the time," Ralph, a man of her age, called out.

When they were children, she often got into fights with the fellow as they had differing views about the wonders of nature.

Tears burned in Fern's eyes, and she blinked them away. Why could they not see how important the grove was? "Yes, we cut some species down for firewood. And we ensure there are seedlings to keep providing firewood in the years to come." Everything they did had to be in balance with nature. "But would we cut down the kelmsgale?"

"No," several answered in unison.

"Or what about Mrs Emley's peach tree? When it had

blight, we healed it and didn't cut it down." Fern smiled at the old woman, whose peach pudding was legendary.

"What affects the whisperwoods will spread. The smoke from Sibylcrest is tainted. Already, we have sick lads who ate fruit touched by it," Nona spoke out.

Alarmed conversations spread as those assembled could see how the blight might affect them.

"The doctor thought our Daniel and his friends had pneumonia. Fern discovered it was the apples by the forest." Mrs Bentley stood as she spoke.

Fern took up where the housekeeper finished and hoped no one would overreact. "There is a chance the smoke might spread to our crops. Putnam's field borders the forest, and that's where the boys found the apple tree. If the smoke affects the wheat, then our bread might make us sick."

People jumped to their feet as everyone started talking at once. Some demanded they storm the abbey and douse their fires. Fern would have suggested that first if she knew a way in. Other people wanted to know if the water was safe or their potatoes. Those were questions Fern couldn't answer.

She had to raise her voice to be heard over the chatter as people surged forth to offer to help or bombard her with questions. "I hope Lord Drakeman might be able to tell us more. I will consult with him later today. Even once we stop whatever Sir Luxton is doing at Sibylcrest, we need to be aware that the effects could linger for some time."

George arched his bushy eyebrows. "If you wanted to prod them all into action, you should have started by telling them about the apples."

"I didn't want to panic people. But it seems we will have

more than enough help now." She stood on the tips of her toes to see over the heads.

Millie had jumped to her feet and rushed over the bridge back to the bookstore. Squib flew on ahead of the retreating woman. The sudden outbreak of noise must have been too much for her.

Fern would make sure her friend was all right before she headed to Wyndham Hall.

"There are things...there are..." Fern tried to be heard as everyone spoke at once.

"Quiet!" George roared.

The chaos dissolved in an instant. Everyone fell silent, and some people even sat back down.

"Thank you," Fern whispered. Addressing the villagers, she said, "There are things we can do to make sure no one else falls ill. Wash your fruit and vegetables. The residue from the smoke can't be seen, but it leaves a blue stain on your hands."

George and Nona organised people to help in two different ways. Some were rostered to be part of the watch over the whisperwoods. Others would wipe their fruit and produce to test for the blue stain. A third group formed, intent on riding to Sibylcrest and demand they immediately stop using the chimneys. Fern wished the group good luck with their endeavour. They agreed to stop at Nemython House on their way back to tell George if they were successful or not.

When the village meeting concluded, Fern walked over the bridge to Millie's cottage. She would share a cup of tea with the other woman before embarking on the rest of her day. Or perhaps she needed the friendly company to fortify her for the chilly atmosphere at Wyndham Hall. A gentle warmth wrapped itself around Fern's cold soul as she pushed into the serene bookstore as though the other woman's presence was a comfortable blanket. Or perhaps that was what a true friendship felt like?

"Tea, Alice!" Fern called as she stomped mud off her boots at the door. Then, somewhat belatedly, she added, "Please!"

Millie was bent over her desk, the raven feather quill scratching across the page. Fern walked towards her friend. "Are you all right? I saw you and Squib hurry back here, and I worried the meeting got too loud for you?"

"Oh, no. Well, a little. But I had the most brilliant idea for some dialogue for my villain and wanted to write it down before I forgot. I won't be too long." She smiled and waved Fern away.

Relieved that the woman hadn't been escaping the noisy villagers and not wanting to disturb the author while penning a monologue, Fern browsed the shelves. Every time she visited the bookstore, she found a new treasure. It seemed the magic that transformed the cottage also replaced some volumes. Or there might be a mundane explanation, like Millie purchasing books by mail and they arrived in crates. But Fern preferred to think it was a magical process.

As her fingertips grazed the leather-bound spines, the bell over the door gave a gentle tinkle. George had replaced it with a smaller and quieter one so as not to disturb Millie. Fern cast a sideways glance as a well-dressed woman in a long coat of deep maroon entered. Dark hair was tucked up under a bonnet with a ribbon that matched her coat. Fern's brain froze. There was something familiar about the profile with its aquiline nose.

A name that she first encountered long ago flared across her memory. More recently, it had been mentioned in Ambrose's letters from London. "Lady Blair?"

The woman turned, her sharp features cooly composed as her dark gaze settled on Fern. They stared at one another. An awkward silence enveloped them, so thick it seemed to press against Fern's skin. Once, she had thought the smartly clothed woman was her friend. Circumstances revealed it had only been a fleeting and shallow acquaintance.

"Miss Oakby, I need to speak to you." She stepped into the stacks.

"You need to speak to me? I cannot imagine what you have to say after ten years." Fern tapped her fingernails against a shelf. Words jumbled together in her mind, some of them rude, as she struggled with how to phrase what she desperately wanted to say.

"I watched that village meeting and recognised you. There is a matter that you can assist me with." Her gloved hand reached for a book and tugged it free from its companions. A glint sparkled in her eyes as she read the title.

Fern laughed a short, dry, and incredulous sound. "You cannot seriously be asking for my help?"

The other woman sighed and pushed the novel back into place. "And why not? Speak plainly, Miss Oakby. Both of us prefer openness."

"None of you ever said a single word in my defence or wrote to me afterwards." That was what had hurt her the most ten years ago. While she understood their silence in that crowded ballroom, not a single so-called friend had written to her. "Why should I do anything for you?"

The other woman huffed and waved a dismissive hand as though Fern's pain was nothing in the face of her needs. "And you never gave a single thought to the damage you inflicted on those of us left behind."

Damage to them? What was she talking about? "Lady Blair..."

The other woman cut her off. "Stop calling me that. I am Mrs Garrick."

The sound of that name was so surprising, it took some of the old heat from Fern's anger and diverted her tirade. Mr Garrick had been an older and unpleasant widower who had prowled the ballrooms during her disastrous season. He had tried to acquire Fern as his fourth wife. Or was it his fifth? "You married *him*?"

A coldness dropped over Mrs Garrick's face. "What else was I to do? After your performance, his offer was the only one I ever received. My father made it plain to me that I either accepted Mr Garrick, or I would be turned out into the street."

"I..." Fern's mouth opened and closed. Her brain tried to fathom what had happened to the women in her circle after she scandalised London, and her father rushed her back to the comfort of their home in the secluded countryside.

Alice appeared with a tea tray, but she seemed unsure what to do as she stared from Fern to the newcomer.

Millie placed her quill back in its holder and approached.

"Hello, I am Mrs Carlisle, the owner of Scribbles. Would you care to join us for a cup of tea?"

"Mrs Carlisle?" Mrs Garrick arched one dark brow. "So it is true what they say about birds of a feather flocking together."

"Mrs Carlisle has been a true friend to me and understands what it is like to have society cast you out." Fern crossed her arms over her chest and narrowed her gaze. If Mrs Garrick thought to say one word against Millie, then Fern would call her out, and society could add petticoat dueller to her list of crimes. That brought the warning from the whisperwoods to her mind. Millie wielded her pen as a sword, and people were killed.

"A cup of tea would be lovely. Thank you, Mrs Carlisle." Mrs Garrick smiled and swept past Fern to the sunny conservatory.

Millie raised her eyebrows, and delight sparkled in her eyes.

"I better not read any of this in the *Midnight Chronicle*," Fern muttered as she trailed behind.

CHAPTER 20

Alice deposited the teapot, cups, and a plate of sliced currant cake. "I'll fetch another setting, Mrs Carlisle," she said before hurrying away for an additional cup and saucer.

Mrs Garrick made herself comfortable on the chaise. Fern took her favourite armchair next to the one Millie liked. They all stared out the window at the river until Alice returned with the additional cup, set it down, and hurriedly retreated.

Once Millie poured tea into each cup and handed them around, Fern curled up in her chair with hers and waited. She was the one owed an explanation after all. With the village rallied to save the whisperwoods, stop Sir Luxton, and cure the boys, she could afford a little time to finally hear an apology overdue for old wrongs.

Only now did another part of her brain kick into action and remember why the name Blair had reawakened old memories. Because of Lord Blair in the newspapers. "Lord

Blair is trying to save the whisperwoods. That's why you are in Drake's Bend."

"Yes." Mrs Garrick delicately sipped tea with her pinkie finger extended.

"And now I believe you were going to tell me why I should help you, and why I am to blame for you marrying a horrid man." Fern had left her saucer on the table so she could curl two hands around the cup with its purple spray of violets.

Mrs Garrick lowered her cup to the saucer balanced in her other hand. "After what happened in that ballroom, your uncle was swift in his condemnation of your behaviour."

Fern snorted. That was hardly news. Lord Ashwood declared her dead to his family before she had even slipped out the back door. She doubted Madame Guillotine could act any faster.

"As he had to be—to protect his reputation and that of his family," Mrs Garrick continued. "The earl proclaimed he had no knowledge of your activities. The implication in his state-ment was clear—that others had known of them and either condoned your actions or had been complicit in aiding them."

"Others?" Millie asked, and she glanced at Fern.

"Obviously, Lord Ashwood meant Miss Oakby's circle of acquaintances." Mrs Garrick answered before her gaze turned back to Fern. "You returned here and were beyond the reach of society. We were not. Nor did most of us have a father as supportive as yours." Sliding her cup and saucer onto the table, she picked up the plate to nibble a piece of cake crammed with currants.

Fern's fingers curled tighter around her cup. At the time,

she had drowned in the despair of a broken heart and how callously her lover had cast her aside. Only now did she admit she had not fully considered what might have happened to the others. "I understand that none of you could have stepped forwards that night without being pulled down with me. But I admit it never occurred to me that you would suffer any consequences once I had removed myself from London. I thought, like plucking a thorn from your hand, once I was gone, everything would settle down. I am truly sorry that you had to marry Mr Garrick, but I am also grateful you did not meet the same fate as his previous wives."

She had thought to extract an apology from the other woman, and here she was giving one. Whether they had been true friends or not, it still tugged at an old scar to think she had caused any of the other women pain. No one deserved to suffer because another person had broken one of the many rules society imposed on their kind.

Mrs Garrick huffed. "He was an unpleasant man, but my situation could have been worse."

"How so?" Fern took a bite of the delicious and moist cake. Alice was doing an exceptional job running Millie's little household.

"He died rather early in our marriage. I have been a widow for some eight years now." There was no sadness in her voice, but if she had been forced to marry a violent man, death would have been a relief. And luckily, the death had not been hers.

"Did he really do away with his other wives, and how many of them were there?" Millie snatched at the more interesting details in the story.

"There were three previous Mrs Garricks before me. The first wife died in childbirth. As for the other two..." She let the sentence hang as she drank her tea and seemed to consider what to say. "The staff were too terrified to tell me anything beyond that both had suffered fatal accidents. Coincidentally, just like the one that took the life of Mr Garrick."

"What befell the others from our group?" Fern couldn't recall reading of any marriages among the other women she had known. But if they were all tainted by her scandal, they might never have received an offer of matrimony. Guilt formed a large knot in her throat, and it took several swallows of tea to push it down.

"Lady Ensor was most fortunate to possess that rarest of things—a suitor who loved and protected her. Her young man married her straight away in a quiet ceremony, and they retreated to his country estate. They are most happy with an inordinate number of children running around them," Mrs Garrick said.

Fern remembered the woman who, like the Moray sisters, had the ability to see motes and mould magic. She had been much in love with her beau, and at least she had a happy ending. There had been five in their little group. Fern, Lady Blair, Lady Ensor, and the Misses Foley, Hambley, and Morecambe.

Next, Mrs Garrick told Fern about the woman who had been the quintessential English rose with her pale complexion and blonde hair. "Miss Morecambe waited nearly five years before her father found a match. While not noble, he is a decent man who owns a mill. She is comfortable, but no longer in society."

That left two women, and from the tight set of Mrs Garrick's lips, Fern suspected they had not been as fortunate. "Miss Foley became a governess and, I believe, keeps her charges in order by regularly placing large spiders down the back of their clothing."

Fern snorted in laughter and then explained to Millie. "Miss Foley had a particular fondness for spiders. Naughty boys would not be able to scare her with them. I hope she has some measure of contentment in her situation."

"She has more than Miss Hambley. With no prospects, she is little more than an unpaid servant in her own home. She lives on charity and is a sad figure indeed. I tried to employ her as a companion, but her father insists that she cannot leave the house." Mrs Garrick narrowed her gaze and placed the burden of the others entirely on Fern's shoulders.

Fern stared at the dregs of her tea, the leaves swooping up one side as though they had tried to escape. "I am sorry. I never meant to hurt any of you. At the time, love made me blind to so much. Never again will I be so foolish."

She looked up and locked gazes with Mrs Garrick. After a long minute, the other woman nodded.

"There was fault on both sides. Let us call it done and leave the matter in the past." Putting her teacup down on the table, she held out her right hand.

Without hesitation, Fern reached out and shook it. Now they were both older and wiser, Mrs Garrick would be a formidable friend. Not to mention, she had the connections to stop Sir Luxton's activities at Sibylcrest.

Fern hadn't woken that morning intending to air old wrongs and wounds, but circumstances gave her a chance to apply a soothing balm. The scar from that long-ago season could now fade to a faint line. "That brings us back to present events. The whisperwoods and the scandals that spread in London. What help do you need from me?"

"My younger brother, who trained as a lawyer, is now the viscount and Lord Blair. He opposes the idea of felling these talkative trees. I am tasked to speak to the owner of the land where they stand, to ensure their property is not destroyed without adequate compensation." Having finished both tea and cake, she dabbed at her lips with the napkin.

"You will not be able to do that, unfortunately. Mrs Rawdon, who owned the plot of land where the grove is located, died some years ago. My uncles have been trying to track down her heir ever since. Apparently, she has a surviving great-grandson who has inherited her estate, but he is off having an adventure somewhere in America." Fern couldn't keep the envy from her voice. Men enjoyed an enviable degree of freedom to explore the world. Many abused that privilege by plundering the cultures they encountered. What shape would their world have if women had led expeditions to new and unexplored corners? Although empires weren't built by sharing and reinforcing communities.

"That is an obstacle, but not an insurmountable one. We don't need the owner to appear in London. We can say they relayed instructions via an intermediary, such as myself and Lord Blair." Mrs Garrick sat back in her chair as she considered their options.

"I am surprised the grove has never been fenced off. If it were on my brother's estate, he would have a tall stone wall built around it and be charging an outrageous fee to visitors," Millie said.

Fern suspected the whisperwoods would never survive if they had taken root at Warrington Manor. As soon as Lord Warrington heard any whiff of gossip about himself, he would have told his staff to take an axe to them. "From what the Moray sisters say, the Rawdon family has been guardians of the grove for centuries. That strip of land was never under the control of Sibylcrest, so anyone has been able to walk among the trees and unburden themselves."

She kept the old fairytale to herself. Mrs Garrick didn't seem the sort to believe a tale about the Fae living atop the hill and their magic trickling down to the saplings.

"Do they truly speak? It is not some boy hidden in the branches causing mischief?" Mrs Garrick asked.

"Yes, they speak. No botanist has yet been able to determine how. But the blight affecting their leaves makes them utter cruel distortions of the confidences entrusted to them. No longer do they give sage counsel." Even once she healed the trees and the slumbering spirit entwined in their roots, would people trust them again?

"They say in London that it is a secret taken and a secret given." Mrs Garrick tugged the soft leather gloves onto her hands and smoothed the fingers.

"While there may be a grain of truth in their words, most of it is little more than malicious gossip." However, when one whispered the word *treason*, it had an impact similar to a lightning strike in a forest during a long, hot summer. People would burn if they stood too close to the flames.

"If your brother has any influence in London, could he

stop whatever Sir Luxton is doing?" While Fern wanted to protect the ancient stand of trees, the health and wellbeing of the villagers were a more pressing concern.

Mrs Garrick tilted her head and stared up at the sky outside as she considered the name. "I am not familiar with that name. Who is he, and why must he be stopped?"

Fern sat on the edge of the chair and hoped the other woman could do something to aid their cause. "He owns Sibylcrest Abbey. Apparently, he is making paper in the grand hall, but whatever they burn in the fireplaces is poisoning the whisperwoods. And our crops. Three lads have fallen ill after eating apples with smoke residue on them, and we worry about our grain, which is grown nearby."

"Smoke can poison people?" Mrs Garrick's dark eyebrows shot up.

"Have you walked the London streets at night during winter? I swear I used to feel the coal smoke going down my throat like cold soup." Millie grimaced.

"There is something in the smoke affecting the trees and plants it touches. Do you think your brother could make Sir Luxton douse the fires at Sibylcrest?" Fern could only hope Lord Blair could apply a little pressure to the baron and get him to relocate his *papermaking* to somewhere else. What were they doing if it wasn't making paper? That mystery was well down on Fern's list of things to solve, but it would scratch at her mind until she did.

"I will ask. People need to know that whatever affects the whisperwoods is making the residents of Drake's Bend ill. Although gossip will probably take precedence over the health of…" Mrs Garrick's sure voice faltered over the right word to describe the villagers.

"Peasants?" Fern supplied the missing word.

Mrs Garrick pursed her lips. "It is difficult to galvanise anyone into action to benefit someone outside their own sphere."

Fern wanted to argue, but it would have been in vain and hypocritical of her. Londoners gave no more thought to them than she had to those she left behind in London. "We can only try."

"I shall be on my way. On the way to London, I shall visit these woods for myself. Then I will discuss with my brother what can be done." Mrs Garrick stood.

Fern followed her back along the stacks to the front door. "In a way, I am glad that circumstances brought you here. You opened my eyes to something I had not considered. Once we have stopped Sir Luxton from poisoning the trees and crops, I would like to write to you, if I may? There was a time I thought we might have been close friends." Those were hard words for Fern to say, but the other woman was right when she said that they had always been open with one another.

Mrs Garrick nodded. "Yes, I would like that. I think the others would also like to hear from you. It has been ten years, and society has so many other scandals to titter about these days."

"Even Miss Hambley?" Fern mentioned the one woman whose fate gnawed at her the most.

"Ah. That is more problematic. I believe her father opens all her mail. Perhaps Mrs Carlisle could write in your stead? I don't think old Mr Hambley would object to an innocuous-looking correspondence from a bookseller. I shall write to her also and tell her of my charming visit here and that I spied many...*educational* tomes on your shelves."

"Oh," Millie breathed out the syllable, and her eyes were wide. "A secret correspondence with clues hidden within the text that only she can interpret. Oh, yes. Do let me help, Fern? Perhaps we can bring a little relief to her existence, somehow?"

"I was planning on more than a few letters," Fern murmured. Already she was plotting how to aid Miss Hambley in escaping from her father's clutches. Rescuing the lost or trapped did seem to be a theme in Fern's work these days.

"I will ensure people in London know it is the smoke from Sibylcrest behind events in Drake's Bend. Once we douse that fire, we shall move to the next one." Mrs Garrick winked, and her gaze seemed lighter as she left the bookstore.

Fern closed the front door and leaned against it. "We have found an ally in an unexpected place." With Mrs Garrick doing what she could to bring pressure against Sir Luxton Davies, Fern could concentrate on what she could do. "It's time for me to take the poisoned apple to Lord Drakeman."

Millie's eyes glinted, and she clapped her hands together. "I so wish I could meet him. Then I could more accurately portray his character in my story."

"If he bites the apple and falls into an enchanted slumber, I will return and get you immediately so you can study him." Fern waved and slipped out the door.

CHAPTER 21

Fern left the bookshop and glanced back towards the Drake's Rest on the other side of the river. Mrs Garrick's figure entered the smaller door reserved for those staying in the accommodation upstairs. As Fern stepped onto the road with thoughts of Wyndham Hall, a voice called her name.

"Miss Oakby! Miss Oakby!" An older woman rushed over the bridge, waving her hand. Dark hair laced with silver escaped the knot at her nape, and a bright-red shawl fluttered with her movement.

"Hello, Mrs Kilby." Fern walked to the bridge as the other woman caught up with her. She rummaged deep inside to find a smile. Mrs Agatha Kilby was usually as sharp-tongued as her mother and quick to snap at anyone who looked at her sideways. But now her lower lip trembled as she caught her breath, and the worry on her brow made her appear younger than she did with her usual frown.

"It's my parents. They are both sick. Just like them boys."

Her hands twisted in her apron. "No one will help. They all say they are busy."

Fern bit back a sigh. Agatha's parents, the Herberts, had done little to endear themselves to the village over the years. Just last month, Mrs Herbert had reduced young Sally Putnam to tears, declaring the girl would never find a husband with ankles as thick as tree trunks. And there was the business with Widow Jones's prize roses—Agatha's mother swore a savage wind had snapped every bloom off, but the whole village knew better.

But if they had fallen ill like the lads and the tainted smoke was responsible, Fern had to do something.

"Do you know when they became sick?" she asked, already planning in her head an altered course of action for the day.

"Over a week ago. It started with Ma coughing, then Da went quiet. He's never quiet, Miss Oakby. Always humming or whistling, even when Ma tells him to hush." Agatha herself fell silent, a plea in her dark eyes for Fern to help her elderly parents.

Fern always knew when Mr Arthur Herbert passed by with his sheep, he whistled a happy tune that was at odds with his wife's sour nature.

"I'll get some tonic for them from the Moray sisters and then go out and visit," Fern said.

She may as well go prepared on the chance it was the same sickness as the one that struck down the boys. That would save time riding back to fetch the soothing syrup. The Herberts had a farm at the edge of the village not far from

Sibylcrest, where they kept sheep. It wouldn't take her long to ride out and then double back to Wyndham Hall.

Agatha's relief was palpable. "Thank you. I know what folks say about Mother, but..." Tight lines pulled at her mouth.

Fern wondered what sort of childhood Agatha had, with a mother who tore apart every single thing she did and who constantly belittled her. Perhaps she lashed out because of all the scars she bore on the inside. Fern reached out and squeezed her arm. "We look after each other here, and no one will be left to suffer because of the blight puffing from the abbey chimneys."

They said goodbye, and Agatha hurried back to her cottage. Fern called on the Moray sisters and left with two bottles of syrup to ease a chesty cough. Sadly, the old women were no further along in brewing a cure from the perfect-looking apple. The fruit holding tight to its secrets.

Eurydice was sunning herself in the walled garden when Fern returned to Nemython House. The dragon waddled to the kitchen door as Fern darted inside for her satchel and the poisoned fruit.

"You can't come today, sorry, Riddy. I need to visit the Herberts, and I doubt old Mrs Herbert likes dragons. Then I have to take the apple to Lord Drakeman." She scratched the dragon's head. It had been a few days since she last worked in the conservatory, and it seemed they both missed the neglected space. "Once we have cured the lads, stopped the smoke, and healed the grove, then we will spend days in the conservatory. I promise."

The dragon trilled, but it had a questioning note as though she didn't quite believe Fern.

After saddling her mare, they cantered south along the shady, tree-lined road. At a fork in the road, they took the eastern path, and the forest on one side gave way to gently rolling fields. The road wound past grazing sheep, their newly shorn backs pale in the morning light.

Fern slowed the mare to a walk as they approached the Herberts' cottage. The paddock next to them was fenced to contain their sheep. The roadside boundary was edged in drystone walls so old that lichen acted as a mortar on the north side. Common privet, with its small white flowers, created an overgrown hedge on two other sides.

The sheep bleated as Fern drew near and dismounted. A tingle ran down her spine as she glanced at the front yard while tying her horse to a rail by the gate. The vegetable garden showed signs of neglect, and no smoke curled from the chimney. Her unease grew as she walked up the path. Across the neighbouring field, pale smoke from Sibylcrest drifted on the breeze and seemed to settle in the hollow where the Herbert farm sat, clinging like morning mist.

Before she reached out to knock, a rattling cough came from inside. She lifted the latch and peered inside.

"Mr Herbert? Mrs Herbert? It's Fern Oakby," she said as she walked inside and closed the door behind her.

"Hello...Fern," a faltering male voice answered.

The cottage was dim and stuffy, and Fern waited in the hall for her eyes to adjust. Glancing to the right at the kitchen overlooking the fields, unwashed dishes cluttered the bench that ran under the window. From the sitting room on her left came the sound of laboured breathing.

She found the old couple within, both of them slumped in armchairs before the cold fireplace. Rugs were tucked around them, and it appeared they had been sleeping in the chairs during the day. The silence unnerved Fern. Mrs Herbert, whose sharp tongue usually dominated any room she occupied, sat silent and still. Her skin had a grey pallor, and her eyes were eerily vacant as she stared at her beloved spinning wheel before the window.

"Agatha told me you were both ill, and I've brought some medicine that will ease the cough." Fern pulled the bottle from her satchel.

"Kind...of you," Mr Herbert rasped, and he pushed down the blanket as he tried to rise.

"You stay right there." Fern waved a finger at him. "First, you are both going to drink this. Then I will bring in some firewood and get a fire going so you can both keep warm."

When she passed through the village, she would ensure someone delivered soup to the old couple at least once a day to ease the burden on Mrs Kilby. The Herberts' daughter had her own family to look after and was probably running herself ragged trying to find time to visit her sick parents. The village could rally around them, whether they liked the old woman or not.

In the kitchen, Fern found two clean mugs and measured out the golden tonic. Mrs Herbert didn't even protest or utter a word as she held the tin cup to her lips. The old woman swallowed and remained silent. Her hands were over the top of the blanket and rested limply in her lap. The palms of both hands were stained a deep blue that had worked its way into every crease and line.

"Can I see your hands, please, Mr Herbert?" Fern asked.

When he held them up, the same faint blue covered his palms.

"It's from the smoke," she murmured and glanced around the room. She doubted old Mr Herbert had been out climbing trees and picking enticing apples. So how had the old couple fallen ill?

"Can you remember when you first felt unwell?" Fern asked as she cleaned out the hearth and scooped ashes into the nearby scuttle.

The tonic had eased their breathing a little, and the hacking cough from Mrs Herbert subsided as her husband closed his eyes in thought. His voice came a little steadier when he answered. "A week back. Just after I finished the spring shear. It took me longer this year. But I'm not as young as I used to be."

As he spoke, Fern swept the hearth and found tinder in a nearby box.

"We cleaned the fleece...during that fine spell. Left it out to dry. Then Margaret got to carding. And spinning. We both noticed the blue stain. At first, it scrubbed off. But now..." He held up his hands and stared at the weathered skin and creases that had soaked up the stain like ink on cotton.

Fern sat on her heels and stared at the spinning wheel. A basket of raw fleece was nearby. Rough spun wool lay in another basket. Getting up, she picked up a piece of wool with its aroma of lanolin. Rubbing the wool over her hand, she then held it up to the light. Nothing. Perhaps they were both struck down by handling the fleece. That was good news in some way, as it meant washing had removed the poisonous taint from the smoke.

"She fell silent first. Like the cat had her tongue. Then the cough started. Doctor said it was pneumonia. I made hot lemon and honey drinks. But it did nothing. Not long after...I came down with it." Mr Herbert shifted in the chair, tucking the blanket in around his outstretched legs.

"Both the Moray sisters and Lord Drakeman are working on a cure. We will have you back out in the vegetable patch before long," Fern reassured him.

She'd been so focused on crops and apples that she hadn't thought about what else the smoke might taint. When she saw Lord Drakeman, she would tell him of the new development. Crossing to the spinning wheel, Fern selected a hunk of fleece and tucked it into her satchel.

Next, she fetched an armload of firewood from outside and soon had a cheerful fire crackling in the hearth. As she moved around the cottage to ensure the older couple were comfortable, Mrs Herbert's empty gaze seemed to follow her. But the expected stream of criticism remained locked behind silent lips.

The woman who had cut down half the village with her sharp tongue couldn't speak at all, while the usually silent whisperwoods spread cruel gossip. It was an odd sort of balance. The more she thought about it, Fern recalled how Daniel and his friends often got into trouble for spreading lies and made-up stories.

In the kitchen, Fern found cold soup in a pot and carried

it through to hang on a hook over the fire to warm. Mr Herbert spoke in snatches.

"I think it's judgement. For her cruel words," he said softly.

Once the soup had warmed, Fern poured it into two bowls. "What do you mean?"

He took the bowl and glanced at his silent wife. "All those years. Cutting folk down to size. Our poor Agatha. Beaten down with words. And I never spoke up for her. I think it made her cruel too."

Mrs Herbert's hands tightened on the blanket, the only sign she heard her husband.

"It's never too late to change, Mr Herbert," Fern said as she spooned soup into Mrs Herbert's open mouth. "This could be your chance to stand up for Agatha, and perhaps Mrs Herbert might turn over a new leaf too. That might help Agatha find some peace."

If the cursed smoke from the abbey made some people kinder, then a little good would be salvaged from the damage it spread.

"She wasn't always this bitter, you know." Mr Herbert's expression softened as he gazed at the woman who had shared nearly fifty years at his side. "Life dealt her some hard blows. Somewhere along the way...she decided it was safer to strike first."

Mrs Herbert's eyes glistened with what might have been tears, but she remained frozen in her silence. Only her throat moved as she swallowed the soup.

"The smoke has sought out secrets and gossips." Fern took the empty bowls back to the kitchen. What if Daniel, his friends, and the Herberts weren't poisoned by chance? What if some ancient justice wafted free of the dragon's blood in the cauldrons, targeting those who used words as weapons?

Before she left, Fern promised that someone would call in every day to ensure they had sufficient firewood and a nourishing meal.

After a quick stop in the village to organise the care of the Herberts, Fern carried on to Wyndham Hall. She stared at the house's façade and considered where she might find Lord Drakeman. She could leave her horse in the stables and roam the house, or try to rouse Quint. She decided on the latter course of action. Her banging on the door was answered after just a few minutes.

Quint didn't say a word, his face just crumpled in a scowl. She wondered if the poisoned smoke touched him, would he turn into a gossip?

"Seeing you is always a burst of sunshine in my day." Fern grinned and imagined he was a puppy running towards her through a flower-filled meadow. Her joy-laden gaze worked. The butler's left eye developed a twitch.

"Where might I find his lordship, please?" she asked, not sure how long she could keep smiling in the face of such a stony reception.

Quint gestured with his head towards the laboratory and then slammed the door.

Taking hold of her horse's reins, equine and human walked across the field to the squat building. This door was opened quicker when Fern knocked, although the occupant wore a similar grouchy expression.

"I have the apple." She held up the satchel and hoped this door wasn't slammed in her face.

Lord Drakeman grunted and stood aside to allow her entry.

She glanced around but didn't see the dragon skeleton. "What happened to the dragon's remains?"

"They are elsewhere. Where is the apple?" He leaned both hands on the table's surface, one long finger tapping the wood.

Fern chewed the inside of her mouth to stop herself from demanding to know what he had done with the skeleton. Elsewhere could mean a multitude of things. Buried. Another laboratory. The kitchen. An image of Daniel's young body wracked with coughs passed behind her eyes, and she reminded herself of her priorities.

Dipping into the satchel, Fern removed the cloth-wrapped bundle and set it on the table. "There is also this." Beside the apple, she set out the piece of fleece.

"Wool?" Lord Drakeman tugged leather gloves on his hands before approaching the samples.

Fern should probably have done the same. Only now did she wipe her palms down the sides of her trousers and remind herself not to lick her fingers.

"The Herberts have fallen ill. They have sheep on the northeastern side of the hill to where Sibylcrest sits. I think residue from the smoke settled on the sheep and got into the fibres of the wool." If fleece carried the taint, it had to have also drifted to the wheat in the neighbouring field. How long before more of the village was struck down? "It will keep spreading as long as those chimneys produce tainted smoke."

Lord Drakeman grunted, his attention focused on the cloth-wrapped piece of fruit.

Fern curled her nails into her palms at his lack of concern. Did he care about anything beyond his gate except if he could use it in one of his experiments?

Peeling aside the fabric, he picked up the apple. Its skin was a glossy red like bright blood. He held the apple before his face, turning it slowly. His silver dragon eye caught the light, the slit pupil contracting to a thin black line as he focused on the fruit's surface. His brown eye remained half-closed, shuttering its ordinary vision to allow the magical sight full reign.

"Fascinating," he murmured.

"It might be to you. But it is poisoning our village. Someone could die! Will you still find it fascinating when Drake's Bend is populated entirely by corpses?" Fern couldn't rein in her anger for much longer. He had it within his hands to help the Moray sisters brew a cure, but he saw those who suffered as little more than curiosities under his microscope.

Lord Drakeman's silver eye rolled to one side and passed over Fern before he turned back to the glossy fruit. "No one has died yet, and anger will not cure anyone. This calls for the application of calm, rational thought, not..." He didn't finish the sentence.

If he dared to call her behaviour *hysterical*, Fern would upend his experiments and show him how emotional and out of control she could be when people's lives were at stake.

"No one has died *yet*," she hissed the last word. Her skin itched, and she paced back and forth to give herself something to do.

The position of peer came with a responsibility to the people and land surrounding a grand estate. Sadly, many nobles simply closed their front gates and lived in luxurious comfort while those less fortunate than themselves suffered. For some odd reason, Fern had hoped Lord Drakeman might be different. His family rose through the ranks because of how they cared for dragons, yet that devotion to other living creatures was lacking in the current earl.

"I have not forgotten our promise, Miss Oakby," he said as though the dragon eye could discern her noisy thoughts. "Once I have completed my analysis of the samples you brought, I will know how to approach distilling the antidote." He carried the apple to a narrow bench and placed the fruit in the middle of a silver tray, which was being held aloft by a small plinth etched with runes that spiralled along the edges. From a drawer, he selected a magnifying glass with an odd purple hue to it. He leaned over the fruit to examine the surface. At times, he spun it on the tray to see more of its sides.

"Can you see the residue?" Fern asked, curiosity overriding her anger. Her eyes couldn't detect anything when she inspected both the apple and the fleece. It was only when she touched the fruit or ran her hand over the wool that the faint blue smudge appeared.

"Yes. A faint pattern is laced over the surface, like veins or a spider web. It will be interesting to see if the smoke affects fleece in a similar manner." He tilted his head, his silver eye gleaming.

With his free hand, he dragged over an open book and began making notes without looking at the paper. His writing scrawled across the page in an elegant but barely legible script as he concentrated on the specimen before him.

"Can you make a cure for the lads and the Herberts?" Standing around while he stared at samples was terribly boring, and she had other things to do. But she felt unable to move until she knew he was busy making a cure for the sick villagers.

He made a noise somewhere between a huff and a grunt.

"Is that a yes or a no?" Fern wasn't fluent in monosyllabic answers.

"Yes." He prowled the laboratory like a caged beast, moving from workbench to cabinet to shelf, gathering ingredients and muttering to himself. His dragon eye glowed in the dim light as he selected vials and pouches. "But it will take time. Two to three days, possibly. The process would be quicker if I had a sample of what Luxton is brewing that creates this smoke. There may be something in the ingredients or method used that is twisting the inherent magic of dragon's blood."

"We need to gain access to Sibylcrest and stop them," Fern said more to herself than the alchemist.

"Whatever I brew will treat the symptoms, not the underlying cause. How do you feel about a bit of late-night wall climbing?" A spark of humour lit both eyes when she glanced at him.

"Wall climbing?" she repeated the words, not entirely sure why he was encouraging her to clamber over things she probably shouldn't.

"I sent Quint to obtain a sample. He was unsuccessful. The steward refused to even let him through the portcullis." His lips twitched as he told her of the butler's failure.

Fern snorted. "Did he take any ginger loaf?"

Lord Drakeman stared at her, possibly wondering the same thing. "Quint did, however, inspect the exterior walls. He found a segment that appears damaged by a storm and some of the stones have fallen outwards. He says it wouldn't be too difficult to climb over and into the abbey." Lord Drakeman picked up a mortar and pestle and deposited them in a wooden crate on the floor. Fern wondered if they were sent to the kitchen to be washed and returned.

She took her time considering what Lord Drakeman had told her. Part of her was looking for the trap. Had Quint found some oubliette to push her into or a nun's cell with a door that only opened from the outside?

"You want me to climb over an unstable wall in the dark to fetch your sample?" She wasn't paid enough for all he expected her to do. When she did his monthly invoice, there would be an additional amount for work performed outside the scope of the initial agreement.

"Us," he uttered the syllable and then fell silent.

Us? Odd how it took her brain long seconds to decipher the meaning of that one little word. "You mean...*you* would accompany me?"

He placed both hands on the table and leaned towards her. "I rather thought that, unlike other young women of your breeding, you might be interested in a late-night adventure."

Her blood ran cold. Did he know about another *larcenous* adventure she had engaged in with a lord ten years ago? Impossible. No one knew except her and Lord Talbot. Remembering how that evening had ended made heat rise through her torso.

"We cannot stop Luxton if we don't know exactly what he is up to." Lord Drakeman pushed off the table and crossed his arms.

A new idea sparked in Fern's mind. She most definitely

could stop whatever was brewing at Sibylcrest without understanding anything of the larger enterprise. She didn't have to know what was in a cauldron to destroy one. All she needed was the help of the three witches.

While she had no objections to sneaking into the abbey at night so she could douse the fires, she didn't want to appear too keen on the idea. "I would appreciate your assistance in collecting the samples. Two people means one can act as a lookout."

"Three."

She opened her mouth to question his counting ability, but he carried on before she could speak.

"Quint will be leading the expedition this evening." His eyes glinted in amusement.

A shiver raced down her spine. Was it prompted by the idea of creeping about in the dark with the alchemist, or the thought of Quint leading her into danger?

"This evening, then." Fern grabbed her satchel before she could refuse.

Lord Drakeman told her where in the forest to meet them under the northeast wall that had been damaged by a storm. They settled on just after midnight when the workers and steward should all be asleep.

After she left Wyndham Hall, Fern headed directly for the Moray sisters. There was something in particular she needed from them, and they didn't have much time if they could assist. The three of them cackled when Fern outlined her plan and set to work immediately.

There was one other thing she wanted to try. Being nice.

Fern rode out to the abbey. When she passed by, smoke curled from the chimney of the Rawdon cottage, as the villagers George set up to watch the grove used the empty home. Along the lane were crammed two carriages, while a number of horses and another carriage sat on the main road. A few of those waiting to elicit gossip talked among themselves. Curtains were drawn in the carriages, and the riders pulled their hats low, tucking chins into the collars on their coats.

"Fools," Fern muttered as she carried on up the hill.

She dismounted before the walkway and tied her mare to a nearby tree. Her gaze fixed on the chimneys as she crossed the stone bridge. The wind had shifted, blowing the pale smoke directly to the north, where it settled in the hollows around the Herberts' cottage and draped across the trees and crops.

She needed to visit the miller and the baker to ensure the light-blue poison wasn't being baked into their bread. Grabbing hold of the iron bars that formed the portcullis, she pressed her face to the cool metal. Like before, there were no visible signs of life. Only a few sparrows picked between the cobbles, looking for insects.

Selecting a rock from near the wall, she climbed up and banged on the brass bell. Before too long, the door at the bottom of the abbey swung open, and Mr Sainsbury appeared.

"Oh, Mr Sainsbury! I am ever so glad to see you." Fern jumped back to the ground. "I have a very important matter to discuss with you."

She waited as he crossed the courtyard. His gait was

slower than usual, and he kept wiping his hands on his trousers as though trying to clean them.

"Miss Oakby. The lads and I enjoyed the baking you delivered for us." He stopped a few feet away from the gate as though he feared she would lunge through the bars.

"I am glad you liked it. I did promise a regular delivery, but I have been somewhat distracted of late." She tried very hard to sound pleasant and a little bit scatterbrained, as that tended to lull men into an indulgent mood.

"Well, if you don't have a basket for me, we are rather busy here." He waved to a stack of kegs that appeared the same as the ones she saw inside. Placed three high and seven long, she estimated it would be a full cartload.

Given he told her they were making paper, why did they appear to be shipping out the sludge simmered in the cauldrons and not crates with fresh sheets of paper? It struck her as odd that the process would be spread over different locations. One didn't do that to make paper. Those seemed the actions of a slightly paranoid businessman who didn't want others to know what he was doing.

The steward touched the brim of his cap and turned.

"People are falling sick," Fern called out. "Whatever Sir Luxton uses to make paper, the smoke is poisoning the trees and crops around here."

He shifted his weight and didn't meet her eyes. "I don't know what you're talking about. It's just wood pulp. It must be something else affecting your crops. Probably mould, or insects."

Fern wrapped her fingers around the bars. "Three boys

have fallen ill after eating tainted apples that grow just at the base of the hill. An elderly couple called the Herberts can barely breathe after the smoke contaminated the wool of their sheep."

He shook his head and rubbed one hand over his nape. "It's not possible," he muttered.

"The smoke leaves a taint. It's not visible until it is touched, and then it leaves a faint blue stain. On fruit, leaves, wool...hands."

He glanced down at his hands with the blue stains on his fingertips. Another question struck Fern. Why hadn't Mr Sainsbury and she fallen ill after touching the smoke? Was it because they didn't ingest it? But neither did the Herberts. Perhaps it was close contact with the smoke or prolonged exposure? Or it could be as simple as both the Herberts licked their fingers. She would ask when she checked on them.

"You have to stop. The illness is spreading through Drake's Bend, and it's because of what you are doing." She had tried asking nicely, and that hadn't got her anywhere.

His gaze darted around the courtyard, but he still couldn't meet her eyes. "I'm sorry, miss, but I have my orders."

"From Sir Luxton, I presume. Is he here today? I shall speak to him about it. Surely he would be concerned about the health of the people who live here." Fern couldn't see any horses or a fancy carriage in the courtyard, but she wasn't sure where the stables were at Sibylcrest.

"He's not here, but he sent instructions. We need to prepare for an order dispatching in a couple of days, so we can't stop now." Mr Sainsbury rubbed his hands harder on his trousers.

Fern gritted her teeth. How to get through to the man that whatever they were producing harmed people? When did money become more important than the lives of ordinary folk? "Someone might die."

Something flickered across his face—guilt, perhaps, or fear. He tucked his blue-stained fingers under his armpits. "I can't help you, Miss Oakby."

"Mr Sainsbury..." Fern didn't get to finish as he quickly strode back across the courtyard. "Ugh!" She let out a frustrated yell and slammed a fist against the unyielding metal.

"Coward," she muttered and rubbed her now-bruised skin. While the steward wouldn't listen to her, she did learn an interesting snippet. They had an order due to be dispatched. What a shame if the kegs of *paper* never made it to their next destination.

On her return trip to Drake's Bend, she called on the Herberts. The old couple seemed unchanged, although the horrid, wracking cough was eased by the Moray sisters' tonic. The Herberts had ample firewood, and someone had dropped off a pot of soup.

"Is there anything else that might have been tainted, apart from the wool?" Fern asked Mr Herbert, his wife still silent. "Something you might have eaten? The lads became sick because they ingested the tainted residue."

Mr Herbert's torso shook with a rattly laugh. "I always think I breathe in wool when I shear. Fluff gets everywhere. Margaret does lick her fingers, sometimes, when she's twisting the yarn as she spins."

Fern wondered if that might have done it. She would have to ask Lord Drakeman. There was little more she could do that day. While she tried to snatch a few hours of sleep, she found herself lying awake and staring at her ceiling. When she judged that the hour edged towards midnight, she dressed and slung her satchel over her shoulder before shrugging on a dark-brown coat.

By lantern, she saddled her mare and relied on her local knowledge and what little moonlight penetrated the clouds to guide their way. Fern found the spot to enter the forest not far from Putnam's field and the blighted apple tree. She dismounted and left her horse just under the tree line. The moon soon disappeared behind the dense foliage of the trees as she walked towards Sibylcrest.

Fern narrowed her eyes, but that didn't improve her night-time vision. The world swam in shadows and dark shapes.

"Where are you?" she whispered to the stand of trees beside her. Possibly, this wasn't the best idea, and they should have met somewhere out in the open and then moved into the forest.

Or had the tough-looking butler baulked at the idea of actually doing a spot of late-night burglary? As Fern stepped away from the shelter of the trees to continue up the hill on her own, a hand dropped on her shoulder. Almost simultaneously, another covered her mouth, and she was yanked backwards.

Panic surged up her spine and lit her brain. On instinct, thanks to years of practice with George, she reached for the knife in her pocket. The hand that had been on her shoulder slid down and pressed the bones in her wrist before she could flick the knife open.

Her heart hammered so loud she feared it would burst when a low, gravelly voice whispered in her ear. "Gotcha."

She nearly wept in relief as she recognised who had grabbed her.

"Quint, release Miss Oakby," came a low murmur from nearby.

Sniggering accompanied her being given a slight push away from the solid butler.

"That was not funny," she spat out, trying to calm her galloping heart.

That only made him snort. "Yeah. It was. I was a bit worried there you might have soiled yourself and got it on my boots."

Fern glared at him, or as best as she could in the dark. So this was to be the basis for their relationship—near-death-inducing pranks. Very well, then. She would enjoy plotting her revenge.

"Are we here to chat, or discover what is happening inside the abbey?" Lord Drakeman said in a low tone as he emerged from behind a tree. His dragon eye reflecting unseen moonlight.

"I was not going to soil myself." Fern tried hard not to sound petulant as she followed the outline of the earl.

Her only reply was a chortle that startled roosting birds.

CHAPTER 23

Lord Drakeman led them through the trees and up the hill.

"Can you see where we are going?" Fern had to ask as she kept her hands outstretched so she didn't walk straight into a tree. Why couldn't he have brought a lantern? Surely, no one on the parapet above would have noticed one small light weaving through the forest?

"I can see perfectly fine...from one eye," the alchemist replied.

Well, that was handy. As long as nothing jumped out at him from the left side.

They continued up the slope until they emerged from the tree line. The moon came to their aid and peeked from behind a cloud. The weathered stone of the abbey glinted like silver. Before Fern loomed the damaged section of wall. Part of it had been pushed outwards and offered a slightly easier way in. She wondered what had caused the stones to tumble to the ground as though a giant child had pushed over his toys. Opportunistic ivy and grass crept over the fallen stones that littered the base of the wall.

Before them rose a rough ladder of unstable handholds. They would need to be careful. No one wanted to get their foot trapped in a crevice and be stuck. Or fall and hit the haphazard stones at the bottom.

"Ladies first," Quint murmured from beside Fern. Then he glanced around. "Oh, wait, I can't see any."

Lord Drakeman's dragon eye gleamed as he gave his butler a quelling look. "I'll go first. Then Miss Oakby. You bring up the rear."

The alchemist moved with surprising grace for such a large man, finding purchase in the damaged wall and ascending swiftly. Fern followed behind at a more cautious pace. Quint, at the rear, had the laboured breathing of one unused to much climbing. That made her wonder if he never went up and down the stairs at the Hall.

When Lord Drakeman reached the top and climbed onto the parapet, he turned and offered a hand to Fern. She ignored him, needing to prove she was more than capable of scrambling over the wall on her own.

Quint slipped over the edge, now as silent as an annoyed cat.

"Where to?" Lord Drakeman asked Fern.

She knew very little of the internal layout of the abbey, having only been inside it once. "Mr Sainsbury took me through from the door in the courtyard." She gestured to the southern face of the abbey with its causeway and portcullis.

They set off, crouching low in case anyone below looked up. They were three shadows sliding along the ancient stone.

The walkway along the parapet ran straight until the corner. There, a narrow set of stairs wound down to the ground. With care, they descended the steep stairs worn smooth by centuries of feet. At the bottom, Lord Drakeman pressed himself to the wall so Fern could glance across the courtyard. His warm breath feathered over her neck as she looked around him.

"There." She pointed to the silvered oak door tucked beside an open stairway. Without looking back, she trotted across the cobbles. Two shadows swept behind her. At the door, Fern paused as she lifted the latch, straining her ears to catch any noise from within.

Opening the old wood a fraction, she peered through the gap. A single candle burned in a sconce, giving a clear view of the hall beyond. They crept along the dark corridor, their footsteps echoing softly on the flagstones despite their care.

At last, they crossed the entrance hall, with its multitude of doorways, and Fern gestured to the prominent tall and wide doors. As they approached, Lord Drakeman held a finger to his lips for silence. Or more silence, since none of them had said a word.

Voices drifted from within. Fern's heart raced. She had thought everyone would be tucked up asleep. Quint now took the lead and opened one door a mere fraction of an inch. A quick look and he held up two fingers. Then he eased the door open enough to allow his solid body through, closely followed by Lord Drakeman.

Fern took only a heartbeat to consider what to do. If there was going to be a fight, she wanted to see what sort of combatants the alchemist and his butler were. That might confirm her speculation that Lord Drakeman was really some criminal mastermind and Quint his bodyguard or assassin.

Slipping inside, at one end of the long table and farthest from the door, two men sat playing cards by lantern light. This was going to be awkward. The men would spot them long before they made it down the table that could seat most of Henry VIII's court for dinner.

Lord Drakeman caught Fern's eye and gestured to one side. It appeared the men had been moving the kegs, and instead of being neatly stacked against the wall, they were now arrayed beside the table. It appeared the men had stopped for a break in moving them outside.

Fortunately, the men were engrossed in their game. That and the low light and deep shadows worked to their advantage as they crept from the doorway to the kegs. Fern couldn't resist giving one a gentle push. The weight suggested they had been filled with the pulpy concoction.

We need to prepare for an order dispatching in a couple of days, Mr Sainsbury had said. That gave Fern an idea.

Lord Drakeman and Quint undertook some sort of silent communication involving hand gestures and narrowed eyes, then both men sprang from behind the wooden barrels with the fluid grace of predators.

Fern was a little impressed. She didn't think Quint had it in him.

"Oy! You can't be here!" the man facing them said. He leapt to his feet, his chair crashing to the ground as he gestured at the approaching interlopers.

The other man looked up from his cards, wondering what was happening. Surprise registered in his eyes seconds before

Quint's fist connected with his jaw. Cards scattered to the floor as he flung his hands out.

The first man, the finger pointer, glanced around for a weapon. His gaze settled on the oar-like paddle used to stir the cauldrons. Lunging for it, he brandished it like a stave as Lord Drakeman flowed like water towards him.

The paddle whistled through the air, but the alchemist swirled around the strike. His right hand shot out, catching the man's wrist and twisting. The makeshift weapon clattered to the floor.

The man patted his chest, searching for something in a pocket.

"I wouldn't," the alchemist said softly as the man drew a knife at his belt. There was something in that quiet tone that made even Fern's skin prickle.

Keeping hold of the man with one hand, Lord Drakeman drew the knife and levelled it at the man's eye.

Meanwhile, Quint's opponent had recovered from the first blow and launched himself at the butler. They crashed into the table, sending the lantern careening over the side. The glass broke, and the wick flickered along the ground. Quint took another hit to the jaw but didn't seem to notice. He moved with the economic precision of someone who'd spent considerable time in back-alley brawls, each strike calculated and brutal.

Lord Drakeman's adversary tried to wrench free, but the alchemist's grip was inexorable, and in the low light, a faint outline of scales appeared against the skin of his hand as he forced the man's arm behind his back. "You work for Luxton. What exactly are you making here?"

"Nothing! Just paper, like the steward told the miss over there!" he screeched as his arm was wrenched higher. His wide eyes pleaded with Fern to verify the contents of the cauldrons.

"Wrong answer." There was a quiet pop, and the man yelped as his shoulder dislocated.

Quint had his opponent in a chokehold, though the guard managed to land one solid blow before the butler wrapped an arm around his throat. They grappled in silence, boots scraping on stone, until the man finally went limp.

"Getting slow in your old age, Quint," Lord Drakeman commented as he watched his butler carefully lower the unconscious guard to the floor. "There was a time you wouldn't have let him land that hit."

"Still faster than you." Quint rubbed his jaw where the guard's fist had connected. "And you dodged that paddle like a drowning rat."

Lord Drakeman huffed. "I moved like smoke."

"You moved like an old, rich snob with gout," Quint retorted.

The man in Lord Drakeman's grip whimpered, seemingly more disturbed by their casual banter than the pain of his dislocated shoulder.

As amusing as Fern found the exchange, she had a pressing need to get out of the abbey as soon as possible. "Where did you learn to fight like that?"

The alchemist's human eye held a glint of humour as he pushed the man back onto a chair. "Best not to ask. Quint, find something to secure them with while I take my samples."

He retrieved his satchel, which had been left on the floor

before the altercation. Placing it on the table, he drew out two flasks and what appeared to be a soup ladle. His dragon eye gleamed as he approached the nearest cauldron, and Fern could have sworn she saw flames reflected in its silver depths.

While Lord Drakeman collected his samples, carefully filling glass vials with the viscous mixture, Fern had her own task to complete. She slipped her hand into her pocket, fingers closing around the last two acorns from the dozen that the Moray sisters had given her. They hummed against her skin, warm with contained magic. While the men fought, Fern had been busy stuffing ten other acorns between the wooden kegs.

"For when you need to unmake what was wrongly made," Nona had said, pressing them into her hands.

As Lord Drakeman finished with one cauldron and strode across the hall to the opposite one, Fern approached it, the acorn practically vibrating in her grip.

She dropped the acorn into the simmering mixture, careful not to inhale the eerie smoke. The hard nut disappeared below the surface, and she hoped the old sisters had managed to fuse enough magic to the objects to make their plan work.

Fern ran across the hall to the other cauldron and tossed the last acorn in while Lord Drakeman ladled the porridge-like sludge into a flask.

"What are you doing? You'll contaminate the contents." He scowled at her.

"I'm going to do more than contaminate it." She would destroy whatever Sir Luxton was doing. He might think hiding in his fancy Mayfair townhouse and refusing to answer letters would stymy her and let his noxious enterprise continue. He obviously hadn't dealt with a determined woman before. "I would suggest you hurry up. The Moray sisters said we would only have a matter of minutes."

Fern glanced at the kegs. They should have done whatever they were supposed to do by now. Although the sisters did mention that they would take longer than the acorns dropped directly into the sinister mixture.

Lord Drakeman stared at her, both eyes glowering with a growing rage.

Fern clapped her hands together as though she were dealing with a stubborn child. "Move. Now."

As she walked away, the acorn in the farthest away cauldron exploded and created a sludgy geyser. Fern ducked involuntarily with the thunder crack that momentarily deafened her and pushed her body with a blast.

Her hands scrabbled for the tabletop to keep herself upright as Quint lunged for Lord Drakeman's satchel and his laid-out samples. The alchemist had sealed the flask and jumped back from the cauldron as liquid shot upwards with explosive force, striking the chimney above.

As the wood pulp coated the stone, it crystallised into a hard, blue-tinged mass that sealed the opening completely. The cauldron groaned, its iron sides bulging outwards before shattering like glass. The simmering porridge flowed over the floor, swallowing up the slates and pushing its way between cracks.

"What have you done?" Lord Drakeman roared at Fern.

"Saved the village!" she yelled back.

Any further witty conversation was halted as the kegs

cracked. The sound reminded her of ice breaking up on a river—sharp reports followed by deeper groans as the wood gave way. The contaminated mixture within flowed across the flagstones.

"Let's get out of here!" Quint shouted, dragging the bound guards clear as more kegs burst apart.

The second acorn produced an even more spectacular reaction in the other cauldron. This time, the liquid didn't just shoot upwards—it seemed to dance in the air, twisting like a living thing before slamming into the chimney. Then the cooling metal exploded outwards in a shower of razor-sharp fragments.

Lord Drakeman barrelled into Fern, grabbing her around the waist and throwing them both behind a fallen table as iron shards embedded themselves in the wood like arrows.

"Witches' work," Lord Drakeman hissed over the cracks and pops coming from the congealing mess.

"Yes. I find the trio delightfully helpful and supportive of the village. Unlike certain other people." Fern tilted her chin and met his fury with her own.

Pushing him away, she cautiously stood and glanced around. Both chimneys were completely sealed, the crystallised mixture gleaming a dull grey in the lantern light. The coal fires were extinguished, and the cauldrons were destroyed. What remained of the kegs' contents was rapidly hardening on the floor, trapping broken staves and iron fragments on its surface like insects in amber.

"Do you have any idea what you have done?" Lord Drakeman grabbed Fern's arm, spinning her around to face his blazing dragon eye. "How can I take more samples to analyse now?"

"Analyse?" Fern wrenched free of his grip. "While you tinker in your laboratory, more villagers fall ill. Mrs Herbert can't speak, Daniel can barely breathe—"

"Do you have any idea what you've destroyed?" He gestured at the crystallised wreckage. "Months of work, possibly years, to understand—"

"To understand what? How it kills? Or were you hoping to recreate it in that laboratory of yours?" The words spilt out before she could stop them. "I suppose an alchemist who hordes dragon bones might—"

"You know nothing about—"

"Oy! Save the love talk for later. Right now, get your arses out of here!" Quint hollered at them and, with a shove, pushed them both to the doors.

Shouts echoed from deeper in the abbey, followed by running footsteps.

"Unless you'd both like to stay here and explain to Luxton's lackeys what you've done?" Quint thumped Lord Drakeman's shoulder to steer him in the right direction while he used a modicum less force to practically drag Fern by the coat collar to the door.

Fury still radiated from Lord Drakeman in almost palpable waves, but he stalked through the door. Fern kept her silence, though her hands shook with anger. Counting in her head and taking deep breaths were doing nothing to abate her outrage that Lord Drakeman cared more about the wood pulp than the villagers and their environment.

As they fled back through the dark corridors, she couldn't

deny a small spark of satisfaction at the destruction she'd caused. Let the alchemist rage about his lost samples. She'd done what needed to be done.

Even if she'd just made an enemy of the most dangerous man in Drake's Bend.

When they ran across the courtyard, she glanced at the waiting rows of kegs. Blast. She had run out of acorns and time. But at least the chimneys would no longer pollute the village.

She needed no incentive to run up the winding stairs as more voices came from the main building and lanterns flared in the windows. They hurtled along the parapet, only slowing as they made the tricky descent down the tumble of old stones.

They pushed through the trees, wrapped so thickly in a palpable silence that it kept out the usual forest sounds. Only when Fern reached her horse and untied the reins of the slumbering equine, did she find her voice. The anger had bubbled like the mix in the cauldrons, and her skin became too tight to contain it all.

She exploded.

"You told me I overreach, but you do not reach far enough!" She jabbed her free hand at his face.

Lord Drakeman crossed his arms and ground his jaw.

"This is your community. Your people. They need your help, and you simply turn your back on them." His inactivity and determination to shut himself away fuelled her rage.

"And you destroyed a magical potion that contained dragon blood!" he yelled back.

Still, he cared only for his experiments. What would it

take to get through his thick skull? "People are falling ill. What if someone dies? You, you simply...don't...care."

He flung out his arms and gestured at the fort on the hilltop. "Do you know how potentially valuable that sludge was for my work?"

"Work? What work? Grinding a dragon's bones to dust to make your bread, free of the sickness? When your family was gifted this land and a title by Henry VIII, it came with a responsibility to these people. You are supposed to offer us your protection. But I care. I have taken a stand and done something to ensure the wellbeing of our community. You hide away because of whatever happened in London years ago, yet you still have your wealth and title to comfort you. I can assure you, however bad your season was, it would pale in comparison to mine."

Her temper had almost run its course. Each angry word eased a little of her internal pressure. Fern expected many different reactions from Lord Drakeman at her outburst. She didn't expect what happened next.

He laughed.

CHAPTER 24

Lord Drakeman let out a deep, throaty laugh that had a slight rasp to it as though his body was unused to making such a noise.

That, as it transpired, was the final straw for Fern. She threw up her hands. "Men!"

Quint leaned against a tree, the faint moonlight revealing the amused look on his face. Before he could join his employer in mocking her, she stormed off. Without even bothering to climb onto her horse in her current mood, she strode across the paddock and back to the road, cursing the pair of them the entire way. The mare kept in step with her, perhaps agreeing that the male of any species wasn't worth the bother.

Once the blood had stopped pounding in her ears, Fern balanced on a fallen tree to climb into the saddle.

"Let's go home, girl." She patted the stoic mare on the neck.

Back at Nemython House, she quickly stripped the tack

from the horse and put everything away. She stood in the dim barn aisle lit by a single lantern and hoped the peace and silence would wash away the remnants of her anger. Instead, everything crashed over her. The wall of emotion became too much to bear and broke through the thick armour Fern had built around herself.

Leaning against the stall wall, Fern slid down it to the cold cobbles. Eurydice scrabbled over her stall wall and waddled across to her, the creature's wings outspread to keep balance as she tried to run. The dragon butted her head against Fern, and she wrapped her arms around her scaled companion. And cried.

George found her not long after. Fern didn't care what had roused him from bed in the middle of the night. She was grateful for his calm and solid presence as he sat on the cold stone beside her.

"Midnight adventure didn't go well?" He handed her a clean handkerchief to blow her nose.

"No! They never do. When will I learn?" Fern wailed.

"What was this one?" George had brought a blanket with him, and he draped it over her shoulders.

Fern plucked at the fringed edge of the blanket. "Sneaking into Sibylcrest so Lord Drakeman could collect samples. I took the opportunity to stop the smoke for some time."

"Good," George grunted the word. "So what went wrong?"

"Lord Drakeman got rather upset at how well I destroyed everything in the hall," Fern muttered.

There was a brief moment of silence, then George uttered a low chuckle.

"Don't you laugh at me. It was bad enough that Lord Drakeman burst into laughter at my outburst." Fern's tears had run down Eurydice's side. Luckily, the dragon's scales repelled water.

The creature leaned into Fern protectively and made a low-pitched trill.

George reached out to pat Eurydice and calm the dragon. "What did you say that made him laugh?"

"That my disastrous season in London was worse than his." She dared a look at George.

It was hard to tell with his beard, but she was fairly certain he bit his lip to stop himself from laughing again. Fern let out a sigh. "Yes, well, in hindsight I can see that possibly could be construed as funny. I also berated him for failing our community and his duty of care towards us."

"Feel better having got that off your chest?" George nudged her shoulder gently with his.

"Yes." She did feel lighter.

She'd let go of all her feelings of resentment towards the alchemist. If he wanted to take all the advantages life had offered him and simply waste them, then that was his choice. Fern walked a different path. She would fight to protect those she cared about. There would be a way to find a cure for the boys and heal the nemeton.

"I didn't get everything, though," she whispered the confession.

George met her worried gaze and arched an eyebrow.

"I destroyed the cauldrons, sealed the chimneys, and took

care of the kegs in the great hall. But there were about twenty stacked in the courtyard, waiting to be dispatched. What if they spread more poison or Sir Luxton uses them to set up somewhere else?" Curiosity itched at her to know what the baron was making, since it obviously wasn't paper.

George squeezed her knee and stood. "I'll expand the watch. The lads can keep an eye out for when the cart with them leaves Sibylcrest."

"Then what?" Fern asked. What good was knowing the kegs had left when they needed action?

"Then we take care of it." George's features pulled into a stern look, and he stroked his beard. "You need some sleep."

"I'll be in shortly. I need a few more minutes to cuddle Riddy first." She brushed her cheek against the dragon's warm hide and let love sink into her skin.

THE NEXT MORNING, after she managed a few hours' sleep, Fern crossed the driveway to visit Daniel. William showed her upstairs, and she sat beside the lad's bed, watching his laboured breathing. His skin had a grey tinge as though the life was being drained from his young form. The Moray sisters' tonic eased his cough but couldn't halt the slow spread of whatever poison worked its way through his young body.

The small victory at Sibylcrest felt hollow. Yes, the chimneys now stood cold and silent. No more tainted smoke would drift over the village or their crops. But those already affected grew worse with each passing day.

With little more she could do to aid the lad or his friends, she fetched her horse to check on the Herberts. Their condition had also worsened. Mr Herbert could barely rise from his chair, and his wife...Fern shuddered when she glanced at the old woman. Mrs Herbert's eyes followed her movements, but there was something wrong with them. Like looking into deep water and seeing something move in the depths—something that shouldn't be there.

She returned home in a glum mood. Ambrose poured tea and squeezed her shoulder.

"It's not just here," he said as he sat across the table from here. "The situation grows worse in London. The accusation of treason is being said in a louder voice and aimed at two peers in particular. It seems those who spread the gossip can't decide on which is the more likely culprit."

"Vultures," Fern muttered into her teacup. Every day brought more carriages filled with nobles hungry for the scandal-laced words of the whisperwoods. Even as their villagers fell silent one by one.

She'd heard of others who might have fallen ill that morning—Peter Sutton had lost his voice, and the widow Thackeray hadn't been seen in days. Both were notorious for telling tales, although Peter's were more entertaining than malicious. It gnawed at her that the poison seemed to seek out those who spread stories as though some ancient justice was being meted out through tainted smoke and poisoned fruit. But what justice was there in the villagers' suffering? In the hollow look in Agatha's eyes as she tended to her parents? In the young lives being pushed off the mortal coil before they had a chance to learn some common sense?

Millie! Her friend's name burst into her mind. She had to

check that the writer hadn't fallen ill with the same malaise. Although she had just seen her the previous day and she appeared fine, which mitigated her concern a little. Fern would call at the bookstore as soon as she finished her tea. She had to tell Millie all about the midnight trip to Sibylcrest anyway.

That thought led her to recollect the disastrous end to the evening.

"I thought stopping the smoke would help," she whispered, more to herself than to Ambrose.

But yet again, she hadn't fully thought through her actions.

In her rage at Lord Drakeman's lack of response, she had taken matters into her own hands and destroyed as much as she possibly could with the magical exploding acorns. She imagined the alchemist locked in his laboratory, the window barred as he fawned over his samples. Her plea for a cure for the ill villagers forgotten. Or denied.

Meanwhile, the whisperwoods continued their cruel work, spreading secrets like poison through the roots of their community. And somewhere in London, nobles gathered in drawing rooms to whisper about treason, unaware, or more likely uncaring, of the price being paid in a small village for their entertainment.

"Bollocks," she said. That was the only word that summed up her frustration at herself and her inability to fix things.

"Quite," Ambrose agreed. "But I think the three witches might come through yet. They might be old, but they were powerful in their day."

"I hope so. For everyone's sake." It seemed there was little Fern could do, except hope the old women had enough magical motes stored in glass jars to craft a cure.

"And Lord Blair is vocal in his opposition to those advocating the destruction of private property." Ambrose tapped an article in the newspaper about the latest debate in Parliament.

"His sister was here recently and promised that she would spread the word about what is happening here. But I fear we will have to solve this problem on our own. How do we make Londoners care that our crops and air are tainted by the smoke when they are breathing coal dust?" Fern rapped her nails against the worn table as she tried to figure out ways to galvanise the public to help those beyond their immediate field of vision.

"Things will change, Fern. You have struck the first blow. Stopping the smoke means the village has a chance to heal." Ambrose reached across the table to squeeze her hand and still her frantic tapping.

She blew out a long exhale and mustered up a smile for her uncle. Then she drained the last of her tea. "There's no sense moping around here. I need something to do. I shall call on Millie and then the Moray sisters to see if they have had any success yet." At the very least, she could distribute more of the cough suppressant to those who needed it.

Since the little dragon had not had an outing for a few days, Fern took Eurydice with her for a walk through the village. Their slow pace gave everyone time to call out a greeting, and children walked alongside them, offering encouragement when Eurydice began to flag.

The front door to Scribbles was locked, so Fern and Eurydice walked around the side to the kitchen. The dragon flopped on the grass. Worry etched itself deeper into Fern. Why didn't she try to fly? It was like watching a bird being earthbound instead of taking to the sky.

If she hadn't made such a mess of things with Lord Drakeman, she could have studied the journals in his library. Drakemans of old must have written about hatchlings attempting to fly.

Inside the cottage, Alice worked in the kitchen, kneading and shaping dough on the bench.

"Hello, Alice. What are you making?" Fern couldn't discern what sort of baking magic the young woman performed.

"Sweet bread. I'm trying something new for Mrs Carlisle to sell to customers this afternoon." She wiped her hands on her apron and moved to fill the kettle. "Tea won't be long."

"Thank you," Fern called out as she walked through to the main room.

Squib announced Fern's arrival with an excited trill, gliding down from his perch atop a bookshelf to land on her shoulder. The pixie dragon nuzzled her cheek, then pulled back with an indignant huff, apparently detecting traces of smoke and magic from her midnight activities.

"Nearly done," Millie called out from her tall desk. The raven quill scratched over the paper, and a shaft of light caught the deep green and purple within the black plumage.

"Eurydice is sunning herself outside, Squib," Fern whispered to the tiny dragon.

He bumped his head against her cheek, then took flight to

find his friend by the river. Fern browsed the shelf closest to the desk until Millie made a satisfied noise and placed the quill back in its holder.

As she rounded the desk, she held out her arms to hug Fern. A flash of blue caught Fern's eye, and she grabbed her friend by the forearms and turned her palms upwards. Faint blue stains marred several fingertips. "Millie. Your hands. How do you feel? Do you have a cough?"

Millie laughed and pulled her hands free. "It's just ink." Then she licked a fingertip and stuck out her tongue, to show a faint blue splotch on its tip. "The story I am writing just won't let go of me."

Fern sagged with relief. "Promise me you will be careful. Whatever poison is in the smoke seems to be targeting those who spread stories. Mrs Herbert, who cut everyone down with her sharp tongue. Daniel and his friends, who were always spinning yarns. Peter Sutton and old Mrs Thackeray." Although she had to verify the last two were suffering from the same blue malaise.

Millie's eyes widened. "You think it's seeking out storytellers? But why then is it making the whisperwoods spread nasty tales?"

Fern didn't have an answer to that. "The Moray sisters think words are at the heart of this...curse. The effect on the grove has been the opposite of what it has done to others. Or perhaps the cruel stories of others have been absorbed by the trees...somehow." Did anyone understand how magical transformations happened? Apart from alchemists. "You are a writer, and I don't want you to be next."

Stopping the smoke didn't stop the lingering effects.

They would need to be careful with their crops and even clothing in case it had seeped into the fibres. Nature needed time to heal after the polluting activity had been halted.

"I tell stories that are clearly fiction," Millie said as they settled in the sunny conservatory. "There's a difference between spinning tales for entertainment and spreading harmful gossip."

Out the window, Squib had curled up atop Eurydice's stomach, and the two dragons dozed in the late spring warmth.

"If you notice any change in your health, you will tell me?" Fern would continue to worry until the illness had passed into the village's collective memory.

"I promise. Though I doubt even magical poison could stop me from telling stories." Millie smiled her thanks to Alice for the tea tray.

Once she was settled with a cup of tea in her hands, a slice of refreshing lemon floating on top, Fern recounted her adventures of the previous night.

Millie gasped in all the right places, particularly at the description of Lord Drakeman and Quint's efficient handling of the men in the great hall. "I knew it! Our plot twist will be that he's some sort of criminal mastermind. And Quint his devoted henchman. Oh, this is all simply wonderful material."

"You cannot put this in a story." Fern sipped her tea to moisten her throat after telling her tale.

Millie frowned. "Of course I am. Though I'll change the names, naturally. The readers of the *Midnight Chronicle* are going to love this." She put her cup down to pull a small notebook and pencil from her skirt pocket and began scribbling. "Now, tell me about the explosion. Were there flames? Strange lights? Odd noises?"

Since Fern could see that resistance was futile, she carried on to describe the acorns' devastating effect. "The liquid just...shot upwards, like a geyser of molten metal. When it hit the chimney, it crystallised instantly. Then the cauldrons shattered—"

"And Lord Drakeman swept you into his arms, shielding you with his body?" Millie's eyes gleamed.

Fern nearly choked on a mouthful of her drink. Why did Millie have to remind her of the way he had wrapped his arms around her waist and pulled her against him? "He yanked me behind a table because I was about to be impaled by flying iron fragments," Fern corrected. "Then he started yelling at me."

"Ah." Millie's pencil paused. "The climatic quarrel between the lovers."

Fern spat tea across the conservatory and wiped dribbles off her chin with one hand. "No! He was furious that I'd destroyed all the contents of the kegs and cauldrons. He called me reckless, short-sighted..." She could still see the fury in his mismatched eyes and hear the cutting edge in his voice. "His scientific curiosity is more important than people's lives."

"And what did you say?" Millie's fingers tightened on the pencil.

Fern's cheeks heated. "I may have implied he was the sort of person who would recreate the poison for his own purposes and that he'd do something nefarious with dragon bones."

"Oh, dear. No wonder he's angry. You have besmirched his honour, and men get ever so funny about that." Millie put her pencil and notebook aside to pick up her teacup.

"Wait. What?" Fern wondered what had just happened. "It's all his fault, not mine!"

"Is it?" Millie asked softly. "From what you've told me, he's been helping since the beginning. He is studying both the apple and the wool to find a cure as he promised. He broke into Sibylcrest with you, which allowed you to block the chimneys and end the pollution. That doesn't sound like someone who puts experiments above lives."

"Oh..." Not finding a witty retort, Fern blew a raspberry at her friend instead. "He did all of that to further his experiments. Not to help," she grumbled into her refilled teacup.

Whatever Lord Drakeman's motives, it was all moot now. The villagers would solve their problems, just as they had been doing for years. They didn't need him at all!

So why then was there just a teeny, tiny bit of regret swirling through Fern that she had made such a pig's ear of things with the alchemist?

CHAPTER 25

Millie cradled her teacup and followed the line of a rosebud with her thumb. "Obviously, the priority here is to make the sick people better and stop the incessant nattering of the whisperwoods, but aren't you just a tiny bit curious about what Sir Luxton is making up on that hilltop?"

Yes. Of course Fern wondered what they had been brewing in the ancient cauldrons. But for some reason, her mind baulked when she tried to figure out what he might be producing. A shadow skittered in the dark recesses of Fern's thoughts, and a warning rippled over her skin. She rubbed at her arms to dispel it.

"Dragon blood and kelmsgale, Fern!" Excitement practically oozed from Millie. "Why would you mix such two rare and magical ingredients together?" Then her eyebrows shot up. "Oh! Do you think it is enchanted paper? The Moray sisters did tell you that words have power. You thought it was how the sick people are falling silent while the trees have become chatty. But what if the paper makes whatever is written upon it real? A bit like the Stormborne Serum created Squib."

Fern let out a groan and leaned over her knees as a nightmare was unleashed in her mind. Horrible creatures popped up around the countryside like dandelions, due to the random thoughts written on Sir Luxton's *special* paper.

"No, no, no, no," she chanted while shaking her head to dispel the seeds Millie's idea had planted. Blast it. Now she had to know. At least she had destroyed much of the brew. That only left the kegs waiting in the courtyard and whatever else they had shipped off over the previous months.

Leaning back in her chair, Fern drew a deep, steadying breath. "I'm going to have to go and ask him," she grumbled.

"And possibly apologise." Millie placed her empty cup on the tray and made one last note before placing the little book and pencil back into her pocket.

By the time Fern left Millie, Eurydice had revived enough for the walk back to Nemython House. Although she promptly curled up in the sun before George's workshop and was fast asleep within minutes. Gentle snores drifted from the dragon as Fern worked in the garden.

Talking to Millie had aired a different viewpoint that Fern hadn't considered. Had she judged Lord Drakeman too harshly? He had promised to brew a cure in return for her showing him the dragon bones. She had kept her end of the bargain. Surely honour required him to do the same? And he had ventured beyond his laboratory and the confines of Wyndham Hall to sneak into Sibylcrest with her. Even if his motive was to obtain a sample of the wood pulp and dragon blood mixture, his actions made it possible for her to extinguish the fires.

"Strange things happen when a dragon returns to the Hall," she said to a soft lemon-coloured aquilegia. She couldn't shake the feeling that Eurydice had broken the spell cast over the estate that had once sheltered her kind.

Sleeping Beauty was kissed by a prince to wake her from an enchanted slumber. Perhaps Fern should get Eurydice to spit at Lord Drakeman and see if that made him polite and smile more. Although magic did have its limits.

As the day wore on, worries multiplied like rabbits in her head. Could Sir Luxton be creating a magical type of paper from the two rare ingredients? She had to ask the sisters. There was no point taking a large slice of humble pie and knocking on the door at Wyndham Hall if the sisters said it was an impossibility.

"I may as well get this over with." Fern pulled off her gloves and left them, along with her tools, in the alcove by the back door.

After washing her hands and face, she set off to see the old witches. No one answered her rap on the door, so Fern went around the cottage to the rear garden. There, a cauldron was set over an outdoor fire in a sheltered corner surrounded by a stone wall on two sides. The women stood around it, and Nona stirred the pungent mix. The sharp tang of peppermint and eucalyptus filled the air.

"More tonic?" Fern asked as she approached.

Morda held out a hand, and Fern took it. Standing at the woman's side as she peered into the pot. Part of her expected to see frogs' legs sticking out. Or perhaps the wings of a bat.

"Yes. Once completed, this will chase away the corruption that has fouled bodies." Decima turned to a stone bench that nestled into the wall and picked up what appeared to be an empty jar. With care, she levered free the piece of cork stopping the end. Keeping one hand over the glass mouth as she eased her fingers in and seized something.

"Motes." Fern guessed at the invisible contents. How she wished she could see the dancing golden specks of magic.

With the seed of magic in one hand, Decima replaced the lid with her other. Then she approached the cauldron, whispering to her cupped hands as she walked. The old woman dropped her fist so close to the simmering contents that Fern worried she would scald her skin. Then she uncurled her fingers and pushed her palm to the very surface.

Fern couldn't see the actual mote, but she could see the results. A blue swirl ran in the opposite direction to the forest-green mix. The two colours mingled at the edges, and their pace increased as Nona continued to stir. The blue spread like an ink stain, and soon the green surrendered and the contents of the pot turned the rich blue of a deep ocean, with just spots of mossy green.

"I have a question," Fern asked, mesmerised by the ocean contained in the cauldron. "Could Sir Luxton make enchanted paper by combining dragon blood and kelmsgale shavings?"

Nona sucked in a breath, and her hands stilled on the wooden paddle. Decima stared at her wide-eyed, while Morda made an alarmed snort.

"Anything is possible if one has sufficient magic and knowledge." Nona picked her words with care.

That didn't reassure Fern. "Is there a way to tell?"

"We only have traces of smoke. To discern any spell in the mixture, we would require some of it," Decima said the one thing Fern really didn't want to hear.

The chill change in the atmosphere broke as Morda cackled. "You will have to seek him out if you want answers."

Fern glared at the seer. Her face was a mass of wrinkles topped with a confection of almost pure-white hair. Delight radiated from her as she laughed at Fern's predicament. "If you weren't so adorable, I don't think I would like you nearly as much, given your interference in my life."

Even stern Nona had a sly smile on her lips. "We have not interfered, Fern. I give you my oath on that. You are strong-willed, and even the Fates can only shine a guiding light. How could three old women force you to do anything against your will?"

As much as Fern wanted to blame someone or *something* else for the bumps in the path before her, she had to take responsibility for her actions. She destroyed the cauldrons at Sibylcrest and the kegs. Although none of the sisters had suggested another approach when she sought their help.

"Could I have two more bottles of cough suppressant, please, Decima?" Fern decided to ignore the whole event, especially the moment when Lord Drakeman grabbed her and tossed her behind an upturned table. If she tried hard enough, she might be able to forget their argument out in the meadow.

A few minutes later, with two bottles wrapped and stored in her satchel, Fern called on Peter Sutton. He had the now familiar grey tinge to his skin and a wracking cough. Mr

Sutton was being cared for by his family, none of whom seemed afflicted. The man himself didn't speak, but his wife said he had eaten what he claimed was the *perfect apple*. The taint had poisoned him the same way as Daniel and his friends.

Mrs Thackeray lived in a cottage on the eastern side of the village. Fern found her in bed, being tended to by her neighbour, Mrs Emley. Much to Fern's relief, the elderly widow's condition was the result of old age and confusion, not the blue smoke.

"Poor old dear wandered off," Mrs Emley explained. "My Bob found her cold and confused down by the river. A few days in bed, and she'll be right as rain."

"Perhaps she might be better living in the village?" Fern suggested. The old woman had no family, and her husband had passed at least ten years ago, leaving her entirely on her own in the world. Since her cottage butted up against the forest, she could slip among the trees like a sprite, and no one would notice. "I'll ask George. He will know of somewhere safer for her."

The shops along their main street were sprinkled with smaller cottages, often used by the store owners or let out to others. One might suit the widow. Given the bustling nature of the village, there would be more eyes to keep a watch on Mrs Thackeray for when she next wandered off.

Fern returned to Nemython House, having convinced herself that the hour had grown too close to suppertime to visit Wyndham Hall and enquire of the alchemist what he had learned about the samples he had taken. After her dinner, Fern enjoyed the quiet of descending twilight in the garden. The soothing work among the plants settled the turmoil stirred up by Lord Drakeman. The sweetness of stocks and roses eased her sense of helplessness at not being able to cure the sick villagers with anything from her garden.

As she stood on the path, she scanned the darkening sky for the first star. She thought she spotted a shooting one that streaked across the golden grey. Then she realised two things. It ascended from the ground rather than falling from the clouds. And it was purple with a tinge of green. Suddenly, an ear-splitting shriek, like an indignant peacock, assaulted her ears.

"The alarm!" she shouted to no one in particular since there was no one around.

The display in the sky meant only one thing—someone was destroying the whisperwoods.

Fern ran for the stables. Not bothering with a saddle or bridle, she grabbed a lead rope, clicked it onto her mare's halter, and urged her from the stall. Stopping at the mounting block, Fern flung herself onto the mare's warm back and wriggled into a comfortable spot. She curled one hand into a fistful of mane to steady herself as George and Ambrose raced from the house, roused by the screech of the alarm.

Fern paused for a moment, but George waved her on with a shout of, "*Go!*"

Trusting that her uncles would bring what she needed (like a warm coat and possibly a bridle), Fern urged the mare forwards. Bareback riding was different to using a saddle. It sent her back to memories of riding a pony as a child, when she pretended she was a creature at one with an equine. Without leather in the way, she sat closer than a mounted rider could achieve as skin pressed against a warm pelt. Since she didn't have a bridle either, Fern guided the horse with her knees and upper body as they cantered along the road towards the whisperwoods.

A faint acrid scent of smoke wafted in the air as they drew closer. When she glanced up, an orange glow pulsed in the southern sky, painting the underbelly of clouds with hellish light.

"Oh, no." She could only hope the villager watching over the grove had raised the alarm in time.

Twilight eased into night as Fern directed the mare down the lane. More horses waited at the end, tied to the rail and trees. Men dismounted or climbed out of carts carrying buckets and blankets. The Moray sisters' magical alarm had done its work and alerted everyone nearby.

Fern slid from the mare and looped the rope around a branch loose enough that the mare could pull free if the fire swung towards the lane. Then she ran down the narrow path.

The closer they got to the grove, the thicker the smoke became. It coiled through the trees like a malevolent serpent, carrying the acrid stench of burning leaves and wood. Fern halted so quickly that the man behind collided with her. Flames licked at the undergrowth around the whisperwoods, the fire creeping towards the ancient trees like grasping fingers.

"Grab a cloth for your face and form a line!" a voice boomed over the chaos.

Fern recognised the speaker as Ben, the village black-smith, but with his dark skin amid the shadows, his form was invisible.

Someone had placed a bucket full of water and lengths of cloth nearby. Fern grabbed one, dunked it in the water, and then tied it around her mouth and nose. The Rawdon cottage had a well in the front yard, which would be closer than the winding creek that meandered through the woods and out to the fields.

More voices called out as order was wrought from the chaos by the commanding blacksmith with his calm and steady nature. Some of the carts were piled with buckets, and soon villagers spread out, forming a chain from the cottage's well to the grove. Fern stood close to the grove and grabbed the bucket shoved in her hands. She hurled water at the burning branches, sending up a hiss of steam. Again and again, she doused the flames while around her, the villagers fought to contain the fire's spread. The whisperwoods shuddered, dropping burning leaves that scattered like fallen stars.

Buckets were passed from hand to hand, full one way, empty the other. Others used spades and hoes to cut firebreaks in the soil, working by the light of hastily grabbed lanterns.

George and Ambrose arrived at some point with a cart loaded with woollen blankets. They were doused in the well, and more people used the wet fabric to beat back the flames where the fire threatened to spread.

Smoke burned Fern's eyes, and, at times, she worked through tears using the back of her hand to wipe her vision clear. When the cloth dried out, she dropped it into a bucket before tying it back in place and continuing. Fear for the old grove ate at her like the flames.

Needing to do something more, she gave up her place in

the line to another. Then she grabbed a damp blanket from the pile and thumped at smouldering embers nibbling at the base of the whisperwoods. Screeches surrounded them, adding to the horror assaulting their senses. The piercing sound like that of a rabbit caught in a trap jammed itself into Fern's ears as smoke tried to force its way down her nose and mouth. Heat prickled at her face and arms as she used the blanket as a weapon. When it dried out, she tossed it to the ground, and quick hands replaced it with another.

No matter how many flames curled around the trunks of the whisperwoods, the sentinels seemed untouched. The screams of the leaves were replaced by a heavy hum. Magic pulsed around them. Old magic, deep and strong, that fought back against the flames that tried to consume the woods.

Fern extinguished the flames at the base of the smallest whisperwood and placed her hand on the bark. It was blackened, but intact. She didn't have time to be fascinated by the discovery. Fire could spread to the entire forest if they didn't stamp it all out.

"The whisperwoods are resistant to the flames. Focus on stopping it from spreading!" she shouted.

Amid the screeches and hum, the leaves whispered and groaned above her. Words distorted by smoke and fear. Fragments of secrets leaked out like sap from wounded bark. "...betrayed...silenced...burn the truth..."

"Look!" Someone pointed to the base of the largest tree. Smouldering wood was piled up like a pyre to burn a witch. On the ground nearby, they found a tin of oil and a discarded tinder box with the dull glint of worn silver. This was no accident. A malicious hand had tried to ensure the grove would burn.

"The coward who did this has scarpered." George appeared through the haze and held up the tin and box.

Hours passed in a blur of smoke and steam as the village united to save the grove and forest. The ancient trees might have some ability to fend off the flames, but no one wanted to see if they survived an inferno that would devastate the entire area.

Finally, as false dawn began to lighten the sky, the last flames spluttered out. The first caress of faint light revealed that the grove was scorched but unbowed. The magical hardwood of their trunks had refused to burn, though the surrounding vegetation was charred and smoking.

Fern placed her hand against the largest tree's bark. A single pulse of life beat against her fingertips, an acknowledgement of what the villagers had done to save them.

The whisperwoods rustled their remaining singed leaves, "...protected... endure... truth..."

Around her, villagers slumped in exhaustion, faces streaked with soot. Ben took a few men and wet blankets to spread out and find any lingering flames. George organised others into watches to keep an eye on the area, while others headed home to tend to their families or wash before they had to start their work for the day. They had saved the grove.

For now.

CHAPTER 26

Fern returned home to wash and snatch a few hours' sleep. Worries compounded inside her. Someone had tried to silence the whisperwoods permanently. Would one unsuccessful attempt be followed by another that worked? There had to be a way to ensure no one tried again. Fire was obvious, but a man could sneak in with an axe and ring bark the trees before the alarm was ever raised.

As she scrubbed at her skin with cool water, it lifted her spirits that the village had responded to save the old trees. Even amidst the smoke and dark, there had been two faces notably absent from the night's work to save the forest—Lord Drakeman and Quint. Neither had bothered to pitch in alongside the villagers, and the alarm would have been visible and audible at Wyndham Hall.

Closer to the grove, the men at Sibylcrest would have been roused and seen the flames from the ramparts. Those safe behind thick stone walls had ignored the rally to help.

But that shouldn't have surprised her. If people weren't

roused to save their fellow human beings, why would they care about trees and shrubs?

THE NEXT MORNING, a subdued mood settled over the kitchen. Fern stared at her bowl of porridge and created eddies of cream with her spoon.

George and Ambrose joined her. Both men had weariness tugging at their eyes.

"I shall have to sleep for a week to recover from last night," Ambrose declared as he took a seat opposite Fern.

George huffed and pulled the coffee pot closer to his spot.

"They will try again. Then what do we do?" Fern slid her bowl to one side. Her stomach couldn't take food while worry had it tied in knots.

"We can't have a guard stationed day and night, unfortunately. We all have lives to lead." Ambrose snapped open the newspaper and turned to the scandal pages.

"They won't try again. The trees burned," George said over the rim of his mug.

Ambrose frowned at his partner. "I know you are sleep-deprived, but no, they didn't. We put out the fire, and while the old things are charred, they are intact."

"We know that. They don't." George used the mug to gesture to the newspaper.

Ambrose stared at the sheets of paper in his hands.

Fern's tired brain couldn't grasp what George meant.

"What's the quickest way to stop anyone coming to

Drake's Bend to hear gossip?" Delight sparkled in Ambrose's eyes as he figured it out before Fern.

"Tell them there's nothing to hear," Fern said each word slowly, still not entirely sure she had got the answer right.

"Exactly!" Ambrose dropped the newspaper on the table for a polite clap of his hands. "We put it about that the arsonist was successful. Job well done, and he gets a pat on the head from his master." Her uncle held his teacup by the gold-edged handle and took a sip while he considered their next step. "I have contacts at several newspapers, not to mention in all the best parlours. We will have the tale of the tragic destruction of the ancient grove circulating within a day or two."

Fern could only see one problem with that idea. "What happens when someone comes out to see, though? They will realise the whisperwoods stand intact."

George refilled his mug with coffee and took a long drink. "Go see the witches. Ask them for an illusion."

"There's a lot of charring around the area, and we lost a few old beech and birch. People will see what they expect. Charred stumps and ashes. Londoners won't know which trees were the whisperwoods." Fern warmed to the idea, or it might have been the coffee reviving her mind.

"Oh!" An idea emerged from the smoky haze clinging to the inside of her head. "Millie could write it! She could craft a perfectly tragic tale. Something that would make Londoners weep for the lost trees." She ate a mouthful of cooling porridge as another thought rapidly followed the first one. "There's still all those kegs sitting in the courtyard at Sibylcrest. I didn't have time to explode those."

"Leave that to me. The lads watching for any flare ups from the embers will see when the cart takes them away." George turned chatty when his veins were flush with hot coffee.

Fern didn't see how watching the shipment leave would stop the unknown sludge from possibly poisoning another community. "But…"

George met her gaze. Both his bushy grey eyebrows shot up, and a knowing twinkle lit his eyes.

"Right. I shall leave it to you." A little more of the hopelessness cleared now that Fern had a plan. She was able to finish her breakfast before heading out to the stables. Eurydice was awake and swayed from foot to foot, as though agitated, and made short, clipped noises.

"I'm sorry, Riddy. I know you have been a bit ignored with everything else happening in the village. If you are up to a walk, I need to visit Millie and Squib." Fern knelt down to scratch Eurydice's itchy spots and reminded herself that she needed to give the dragon a good scrub and oil.

Only when Fern had eased sufficient itchy bits did they set off for the bookstore. The dragon's walk had become steadier, and she could now go longer distances. But still, she didn't stretch her wings any more than needed to keep her balance.

The kitchen door to the cottage was closed, and Fern pulled the latch open. All was quiet within, although the warmth inside suggested someone had been up to light the range and set a kettle to boil. A faint waft of steam came from the spout.

"I'll find Squib to keep you company." Fern let the dragon in, and she settled on the slate floor before the stove.

Creeping into the main part of the cottage, which felt more like a cosy library than a store, Fern found Millie slumped at the desk. She jerked awake when Squib squawked.

"Sorry, I didn't mean to startle you. Where is Alice?" Fern held out her arm for Squib, who gave his customary heated puff of a welcome.

"Asleep. She was helping last night, and I told her not to wake early this morning. She has done an admirable job of teaching me how to light a fire and boil water." Millie sat taller and pointed to her cup of tea.

"Well done, you. It was an exhausting night. Riddy is in the kitchen." Fern launched the pixie dragon in the direction of his larger friend.

"Are the whisperwoods truly saved? Alice said so, but I couldn't go out myself. All that shouting and chaos." Millie tugged a bright-green shawl around her arms with a shudder.

"They are scorched and lost a few leaves, but they will survive." It had been frightening, but Ben had marshalled the villagers like a battle-hardened general at war, and they emerged victorious against the fiery opponent. "I need your help to ensure we protect them from other such attempts."

"Oh. Of course. If I can. But I don't know much about trees." A frown marred the writer's forehead as she imagined how she could offer assistance.

"I need you to write a story, entirely fictional, about the horrible destruction of the woods last night and the depth of our despair at losing them. Then Ambrose will spread your tale far and wide." Fern leaned her elbows on the desk. It was built high so a person could stand while using the surface, making it the perfect leaning height.

"Yes. I can see it now. A tragic tale of ancient wisdom lost forever. The centuries-old guardians of secrets, reduced to ash in a single night of senseless violence..." Millie's eyes misted over as a story danced before them. She shuffled pages covered in tight script to one side as she searched for a blank sheet.

"Don't forget to add that the smoke will be visible for days. And how the entire village heard the death screams of the spirit bound to the trees as they all burned." Fern thought that would add a suitably horrifying touch to the story.

"That is brilliant and gives the tale a gothic element. People love a frisson of horror from the safety of their parlours." Dipping her quill in the open pot, Millie gently tapped the excess off before starting her piece.

"But don't make it too dramatic." Only now did it occur to Fern that the story might veer a little too far into being fictional. "We want it to be believable, so it stops people from coming out here to seek gossip."

"Have a little faith, my friend." Millie wagged the raven feather at Fern. "By the time I'm done, all of London will be mourning the whisperwoods. No one will dare come looking for gossip in a grove of ashes in case the vengeful spirit of the slain ancients seeks revenge. They'll probably commission a plaque instead and put it somewhere on a street corner a safe distance away."

Fern watched Millie work, amazed at how she spun truth and fiction together into something powerful. While someone would probably still venture to the grove out of curiosity, using words against those in London would give the stand of trees time to heal and for them to find a way to better protect them.

Squib returned from the kitchen and a curious Eurydice waddled into the store (only just fitting through the doorway) to sit at Fern's feet. The pixie dragon perched on Millie's shoulder and emitted encouraging chirps as her quill danced across the page, creating the perfect lie to protect an ancient truth.

As soon as the tale was finished and blotted, Fern waved goodbye to hurry home. Ambrose would send a rider to speed to London with the account. As she walked up the driveway, an unfamiliar bay horse was tied to the rail by the stables. She recognised the man talking to William. Denis Fawcett.

"Hello, Denis," she called out as she approached. Had he escaped the tyranny of Lord Drakeman and sought a safe place to hide?

"Good morning to you, Miss Oakby. And Miss Eurydice. My, how you have grown in just the few days since I last saw you." The stablehand crouched down to scratch under the dragon's chin, and she trilled happily. Then he picked something up from the ground behind him. "I have a delivery for you, miss. Lord Drakeman said I was to only hand it to you. No one else."

Fern hesitated. It was probably some form of explosive device. Although she was intrigued by the wooden box with iron handles. A circular metal disc on the top was etched with the image of a dragon in flight, its claws extended.

"His lordship says to handle it carefully." Denis took a step towards her, and Fern took one back.

If the box couldn't be shaken, then it most definitely contained something that would blow up in her face.

Denis halted and frowned at her retreat. "He also said that if you drop it, he can make some more, but it will take a few days."

She couldn't decide if that meant it was something unpleasant or not. Were his words a threat that if she threw the thing away, he would simply send another? Blast the man. Now she had to know what was in it.

"Thank you, Denis." Fern plastered a gracious smile on her face.

He tugged his cap. "I'll be on my way, then."

She watched him ride down the driveway before carrying the container through the arch in the stone wall surrounding the garden. As a precaution, she opened it outside on the path. She lifted the latch; within the box and nestled in straw were eight glass vials. Their contents glowed with a pearlescent light that seemed to shift between blue and silver.

A folded note lay on top, written in an elegant but barely legible hand:

> *Miss Oakby,*
> *Despite your dramatic interference at Sibylcrest,*
> *I have kept my word.*
> *My analysis of the pulp has resulted in a potion*
> *that will counter the effect of the corrupted dragon*
> *blood. This must be combined with whatever hedge*

magic the Moray sisters have concocted—their intuitive understanding of natural forces will bolster my cure.

One vial is sufficient for one person.

Try not to explode anything this time.

- Lord Drakeman

Fern read through the note twice more as she carried the box into the kitchen and sat heavily on a chair. She had been certain he would withdraw his help after their argument and leave the village to suffer for her actions. Yet here was the proof that he'd worked through his anger—eight vials of glowing hope.

"Oh, bollocks!" She threw the note to the table.

She really would have to apologise to him now.

She lifted one vial free and held it to the light, watching the colours swirl within. The opalescent shimmer reminded her of the way sunlight caressed Eurydice's scales. Had he used dragon scales to counter the blood that tainted the blue smoke?

"You are a surprise," she murmured to the absent alchemist. Then she carefully packed the tiny glass containers back into their straw nest. It was time to visit the Moray sisters and heal some very sick villagers.

With the box tucked under her arm, Fern and Eurydice walked the road to the elderly sisters. At times, the dragon headed off into the long grass as she chased an insect or caught the scent of something in the air. Her scales gleamed in the sun, and her ribs were no longer as visible underneath.

The old women sat outside. Morda on a bench under the tree and Decima beside her. Nona paced the short path between the tree and the front gate.

"There you are!" she called on seeing Fern and her dragon companion.

Eurydice walked up the path and announced herself to Morda before sitting at the seer's side and leaning into her outstretched hand.

Nona stopped before Fern, worry pulling her brows close together. "I don't think we can do it, Fern. Not on our own. Our hands no longer contain sufficient magic to combat dragon blood and kelmsgale combined."

Fern took one of Nona's age-gnarled hands in hers and laid it on the box. "You don't have to do it alone. I have brought you a bit of extra help from a moody alchemist."

Her fingers caressed the wood before sliding down to lift the catch. "Oh, this contains a powerful brew."

Decima joined them and peered over her sister's shoulder as Nona took a vial and held it to the light. "That looks like the distilled essence of dragons' scales."

"Set the beast to defeat the beast," Morda sang from under the tree.

Fern wasn't sure what that meant but figured it was something like *fight fire with fire* and that the scales plucked from a dragon would, in some way, counteract the blood.

"I don't care what it is, so long as it works," she said.

Nona placed the vial back in the straw with care and tucked it in.

"Lord Drakeman says one vial for one person and that it is to be combined with what you have brewed. Not that he enquired about what cure you had created." Fern suspected he had a low opinion of the magic crafted by the three old women. He probably thought they brewed little more than honeyed water, and their concoction would sweeten the taste of his foul potion.

"He thinks we are three mad, old women with no power." Decima returned to her younger sibling and helped Morda to her feet.

"Magic is writ on his face, and yet he still tries to deny that it is all around us." Nona led the way around the side of the cottage to the sheltered nook with their outdoor fire.

"He and George would get along swimmingly, then. They can both deny the magic happening right in front of them and waste their time on scientific explanations." Fern snorted as she imagined the two men with their *rational minds* trying to argue away the magic in their world.

CHAPTER 27

Decima poked the glowing embers with a stick before tossing it into the fire. "Alchemy is nothing more than magic practised by men."

Fern thought that was a good way of putting it. Lord Drakeman used many unusual and magic-infused ingredients in his experiments and brews, and yet he stared down his nose at the sisters with their natural gift to wield power. "So long as we cure the sick villagers, I don't care if we use magic, alchemy, or pond water."

Eurydice snuffled at the edges of the fire pit and found herself a spot to sit where she could watch the women. Nona peered under the stone bench and fetched the cauldron. Fern helped her hang it on the hook that dangled from a blackened beam. The chain had been placed so the pot hovered a mere inch above the embers.

Morda took her place by the fire. The three old women stood an equal distance from the brew as it slowly heated. Steam curled as it rose and cast a hazy mist around them.

Fern placed the wooden box on the flat stones and wondered how they would combine the two different potions. She opened the lid and stared at the softly glowing contents. If one vial was for one person, they probably shouldn't just tip the lot into the cauldron.

"Now what do we do?" she asked the sisters.

"Wait," Nona said. Stretching out her hands, she took hold of her sisters on either side, then Morda and Decima joined hands.

The women chanted a soft, lyrical tune that soared like a bird skimming the countryside. Fern thought she recognised the occasional word in Gaelic, the old tongue spoken by Celts, long before the Romans stepped foot on English soil. When the song reached a poignant end, the women fell silent. From within the pot, a large bubble welled up, straining against the potion until it burst with a dull plop like an appreciative belch at the end of a delicious meal. A light trace of purple swirled through the steam and released the delicate scent of lavender.

"It's ready." Nona broke the circle.

"Give me a hand, Fern," Decima said, gesturing to the cottage.

Inside, they gathered up empty bottles, a funnel, a stone pitcher, and a clean soup pot. Back outside, they set the items on the stone bench.

"Hold this, dear." Decima thrust the soup pot at Fern and then selected the pitcher for herself.

Approaching the simmering cauldron, Decima pushed the sleeve of her dress up past her elbow. Then she dipped the pitcher into the brew. When Fern peered within, the purple steam had gone, and the previous soup appearance had clarified to something resembling tea with a zesty tang to it.

The old woman poured the mixture into the pot, all the while muttering under her breath.

"Not too much!" Nona called out.

"I know, I know," Decima muttered. "After seventy years, she still thinks I don't know how much is one measure." She glanced at Fern and winked.

Fern carried the pot to the bench, while Nona helped Morda to a wooden stool set beside it. Decima set out three of the bottles, while Nona selected one of the vials from the box.

Using the funnel, Decima poured a measure into each glass container. The witches' brew reaching to about two-thirds in each bottle.

"One drop for each," Morda said, her blind eyes fixed on the vials as though she could see them perfectly. "Wild magic and tame, earth and air, natural and..."

"Scientific." Nona finished for her sibling as she uncorked the first vial. The pearlescent liquid caught the firelight, shifting between blue and silver.

Decima held the first bottle steady as her sister added the alchemist's potion one precise drop at a time. The liquid seemed almost alive, the colour shifting as it rolled down the glass neck. With each drop, the sisters murmured words that made the air thick with magic.

The mixture hissed and sparked, tiny motes of light dancing upwards like fireflies. When she had emptied the tiny glass cylinder, Nona placed a stopper in the larger bottle and gently swirled the contents around. The potion within glowed a sparkling gold that slowly disappeared until it appeared to contain nothing more than cold tea.

"That's it?" Fern asked, wanting to make sure they hadn't missed a step.

"Mostly," Nona answered.

When they had tipped the additive into the other two bottles, Decima fetched three more. Soon, only two full vials remained in the wooden box, and six full bottles formed a line on the cool stone.

"Now we finish the ceremony," Nona said.

The three witches joined hands once more. The chant this time was different—deeper, older—like the sound of roots growing beneath the earth. The bottles began to glow, their contents swirling of their own accord.

Eurydice crept closer, drawn by the magic. She sniffed at the bottles and sneezed, sending up a shower of sparks that danced with the magical motes still floating in the air.

"Dragon magic," Morda said with satisfaction.

Fern glanced at her friend. "She has magic?"

Nona reached down to pat Eurydice on the head. "Of course, her body feels the pull of the scales used by the alchemist. Her blessing is a special final touch."

The mixture in each bottle settled into a clear liquid that seemed to hold starlight in its depths. When Fern held one up to examine it, she caught the faint scent of summer rain and morning dew with an underlying tang of Lord Drakeman's more clinical brew.

"Wild magic and tame. Working together," she murmured, understanding at last.

Nona handed the closest bottle to Fern. "Start with the

children. They are to have a spoonful three times a day—morning, noon, and night. The young ones will heal fast. The adults will take longer to recover."

Fern fetched her satchel and nestled the bottles in the soft folds of a woollen scarf.

"What of Mrs Herbert?" Fern asked, thinking of the old woman's unnatural silence.

"Her path is the most difficult. The poison worked deep roots through her body. Wool and words have bound together to create a net that holds her tongue silent," Decima said.

"But she will recover?" Fern had been on the receiving end of a tongue-lashing from the cruel, old woman and had no desire to repeat the experience. At the same time, Mrs Herbert didn't deserve to suffer when Fern could simply avoid her once she was better.

Nona squeezed Fern's hand. "The alchemist's potion will heal the physical, ours retrieves lost voices. But each person is different and must choose their path back to health. Some of the affected will find their lessons more difficult to understand than others."

If the old woman had to learn to blunt her sharpest words to get her voice back, that didn't seem a bad outcome to Fern. More than one person needed to realise that some words were better left unspoken.

"Be back at twilight!" Decima called out to Fern as she turned to leave. "There is still the nemeton to heal now the smoke has stopped, and we need your green fingers!"

"I'll be here," Fern called out as she left with Eurydice at her side. First, they delivered a bottle and instructions to the friends of Daniel. After leaving the dragon in George's care in the garden, she knocked on the door to the Bentley family's cottage.

Lucy opened the door and followed Fern up to the boys' bedroom. Daniel's skin had a grey tone, and sweat beaded his forehead. Heartache speared through her at what the smoke had done to the lads.

"This will make you better, Daniel. Nona says it will take a few days, but it will drive the poison out of your body." Fern poured the mixture onto a spoon while Lucy helped her brother sit up.

Resting the tip of the metal on the boy's lower teeth, Fern let it dribble over his tongue. The lad swallowed, but never opened his eyes.

"One spoonful three times a day, Lucy." Fern squeezed the young girl's hand. Her fine features were tight with worry for her sibling. "He'll soon be better and annoying you."

By the time Fern had called on the older villagers who were suffering from the effects of Sir Luxton's *papermaking*, the day was almost over. She managed a quick bite to appease her empty stomach and then changed into an aqua silk gown that had once belonged to her mother. While trousers were terribly practical, they weren't particularly...magical.

For the ceremony at the grove, Fern wanted a dress that flowed around her and made her feel like some ethereal creature that belonged in the ancient forest. The silk trailed behind her, and she imagined herself the heroine in one of Millie's tales. For once, she wished she had long hair that she could let tumble down her back and move with the breeze. But with Fern's luck, she'd just get strands tangled in a branch. Which was why she had shorn it off in the first place.

For warmth, she wrapped a woollen cloak around her shoulders.

She chatted to William out in the stables as he harnessed the solid little horse to the cart.

"Dan's cough has eased already, miss," he told her as he did up the buckles on the harness. "And he doesn't look so grey."

"I'm so relieved to hear that." Fern squeezed his arm.

The people would recover. Now it was time to restore the whisperwoods. After a snooze in the garden, Eurydice refused to be left behind. The dragon sat in the back of the cart with Decima and Morda. Nona sat on the seat beside Fern as the horse took them all to the secluded lane.

The sharp tang of smoke still hung in the air, and charred trees encircled the grove. Lights shone in the Rawdon cottage as people took turns guarding the ancient trees.

"We will soothe the spirit and create a veil of illusion," Nona had told Fern when they loaded what appeared to be a sack of stones into the cart.

"The time between times. When veils are thinnest," Morda said as Fern helped her from the cart. The seer's wrinkled face turned to the sky as twilight washed the countryside in a deep golden light.

While the women walked to the grove, Fern took the sack of stones and dropped them around the perimeter as Nona had instructed. Each was nestled in the scorched earth a few paces from the next in a circle. When the sack was empty, she tossed it into the cart and joined the sisters.

The forest seemed to hold its breath after its brush with disaster. No birds sang; no leaves rustled. Even the ever-present whispers had fallen silent. Fern's heart ached for the destruction the arsonist had wrought. Smaller shrubs and ferns were reduced to charcoal fragments. Trees were twisted skeletons with blackened limbs. Soot crunched under her boots.

Thankfully, the whisperwoods were largely untouched by the flames. Their bark was scorched and blackened. Silvered knot-hole eyes appeared to weep from where rain-drops pooled and ran through the soot. Their branches were almost stripped bare for winter, but the season had been one of fire.

Fern laid a hand on the smallest tree at the end. "We fight those who set fires, not those they would burn. You will endure," she told it.

In the centre of the grove, the sisters formed a triangle around the oldest tree. Its trunk bore scorch marks from its brush with the flames, but beneath the char was healthy wood—waiting, healing, hoping.

"The spirit is restless. Poisoned by smoke. Twisted by pain," Nona said, raising her hands to join with the golden light of the gloaming.

For once, Fern could see the sparks that flowed around them darting like fireflies.

"We will rouse it from its nightmare," Decima added, her own magic forming intricate patterns in the air as though an invisible spider spun a web with golden thread.

Morda held out a hand to Fern. "Take your place, child."

Nona had told her what to do on the ride to the whisper-woods. From her pocket, Fern pulled a round and flat container that fitted in her hand. Unscrewing the lid, she swiped two fingers through the thick concoction and smeared it over her palms. It tingled, not unpleasantly as though she had grabbed a stinging nettle, but enough of a ripple over her skin that she had a moment of panic at what she had just done.

Stepping under the outstretched arms of the sisters, Fern knelt before the oldest whisperwood with her palms facing up on her thighs so she didn't ruin the silk gown. Eurydice settled beside her, the young dragon's presence somehow right and necessary.

The sisters began to chant in a language that wasn't quite Latin or Gaelic, but something older than both. Each word rippled through Fern's bones, and her palms tingled until she expected to see sparks dancing in her hands.

"Now!" Morda commanded.

Fern reached out and laid her hands on the scorched bark. A sharp jolt ran through her body like those that sparked from a Galvanism machine when the handle was cranked. Fern gasped and gritted her teeth against the cry from her brain to pull back in case she was burned. Instead, she leaned more weight into her hands, and the pulse washed over her, leaving behind the thrum of life beneath her palms. Eurydice pressed close, adding her own magic—young and bright and pure.

And suddenly, Fern could...see. Her mind was pulled through the connection and into the tree. The whisperwood wrapped her in its embrace as the tree showed her the heart of the nemeton.

The ancient spirit wasn't just bound to the roots—it *was* the roots, spreading out beneath the soil in patterns both primordial and perfect. It had slumbered for centuries, gathering whispered words and holding them safe. Using the confessed secrets, they tailored their gentle advice. Then the poisoned smoke seeped down like a black stain and turned wisdom into bitterness.

The sisters' chant grew louder. Their magic sinking into the earth. Tears rolled down Fern's cheeks as the spirit's pain washed through her. Its thousands of secrets were twisted into weapons, and the benign entity had been unable to stop the harm it caused.

"It's alright. We have stopped the poison," she whispered to the ancient consciousness that brushed against her mind. "You can rest now and heal."

Eurydice threw back her head and keened—a note of despair that tapered into hope. Conjuring the new growth that pushes free of the ground in the wake of fire. Dragon magic, old as the earth itself, flowed from her into the spirit beneath their feet.

The sisters' chant reached a crescendo. Magic surged through Fern like lightning through water. The spirit stirred as the poison in its roots shattered, and the pieces broke apart to return to the earth. Wisdom and mercy flowed back into the whisperwoods like spring rain.

At the same time, around them shimmered a watery veil. Rising from the ground, it created a translucent curtain that encircled the grove. On the inside was a silver, reflective mirror. The outside was painted with the burned and charred remains of the destroyed forest.

Their work done, the chanting faded away. The magic retreated from Fern's body and returned to the spirit. Darkness closed around her mind as the old tree gently pushed her consciousness back into her body. Disorientated for a moment, Fern pressed her cheek to the bark as one last pulse reverberated through her palms. Dropping her hands to her lap, the silence and emptiness overwhelmed her.

Eurydice nudged her head under Fern's elbow. Hugging the warmth of the young dragon, her senses returned along with a sound she hadn't heard for a long time. The gentle whisper of leaves stirring in a breeze that wasn't there. But now the whispers held no malice, no twisted secrets. They sounded like lullabies. Like comfort and peace.

Fern stroked Eurydice's head as the last echoes of magic faded from her skin. Above them, stars pierced the darkening sky. The whisperwoods creaked and settled like an old house at night.

Or like an ancient guardian, finally able to rest.

"That was beautiful. I became part of the whisperwoods and the spirit. But how was that possible? I can't cast magic." Fern climbed to her feet and sought answers for what she just experienced from the old women. Nona had told her that she had a pivotal role to play in the ceremony and, at the right moment, had to apply a healing salve. "What was in the pot?"

Only now did she sniff her hands. As a botanist, she knew of many plants that could induce visions. What had the old women dosed her with? If it was datura, they could have killed her with an incorrect dosage. Or had they used a Psilocybin mushroom?

"Nothing," Nona said as she linked arms with Morda to guide her sister out.

Fern picked up a lantern to guide their way as night

settled around them. "But I was the tree. That's not possible without some form of hallucinogenic."

Morda cackled. "Not for one with dryad blood."

Dryad? "Wait. What?"

Decima took the lantern from Fern's limp hand and left her in the dark. Her mouth opened and closed, but her brain couldn't decide what question to voice first, and the words jammed in her throat.

Only when Eurydice bumped against her side did Fern move. "They might be old, but they are a trio of pranksters," she told the dragon as they returned to the cart.

While she and her father often joked that botany ran in their blood, she was no dryad. It simply wasn't possible. If she could turn into a tree, she would know.

Wouldn't she?

CHAPTER 28

When Fern asked the old women what they meant about dryad blood, Nona patted her arm and replied, "You have an affinity for the natural world and green fingers."

Which was exactly what she thought they meant. Until Morda added with a chuckle, "You carry the soul of the forest."

When she returned home, the lights burned in the parlour, where Ambrose and George sat in comfortable silence with their evening glass of port. Fern unlaced her boots in the kitchen and carried them in her hands, dropping them at the parlour door. She sat cross-legged on the sofa, her feet tucked under her skirt.

At first, she wanted to blurt out that she touched minds with the spirit slumbering deep under the whisperwoods. But the experience had been so private, she kept it to herself. Instead, she held out her hands and stared at her palms. "The Moray sisters said I have dryad in my blood. They were having a jest, weren't they?"

Ambrose put a tasselled bookmark in his novel and placed it on the table. "If you did, that would explain much about you and Rowan."

George snorted. "Dryads are only found in books. Not wandering the streets."

"Well, of course not. Dryads are forest and garden creatures. I imagine they would avoid busy streets laid with cobbles." Ambrose sipped the deep-red wine, and a pleased expression softened his ageing features.

His life partner stared at him. "You know what I mean."

"George has a point, Uncle Ambrose. There are no dryads. Or gargoyles, or werewolves, or any such creatures. They are fairytales." Fern usually sided with Ambrose over such matters, but how could she be descended from a creature that didn't exist?

"You mean like dragons? Or the Fae? Both are part of our world. Or were, since the Fae went back to their own realm." Ambrose swirled the tiny glass, and droplets of port turned the clear crystal into a soft gold.

No answer came from George, only a heavy silence. Fern had the distinct impression he was choosing his words carefully. "It's a hypothetical question at best. Even if there is some botanical...affinity..." George couldn't bring himself to say the word dryad, "in your blood, there's no one left to ask."

George was right. As usual. Her father was dead, as were her paternal grandparents. There was only one person who might know, but who would never answer any questions from her. "Except my *other* uncle."

She wouldn't dwell on it. Although the mere idea

brought her comfort, so she would tuck the possibility away inside her.

"The whisperwoods are on the path to recovery, as are the sick villagers. The Moray sisters had me place rocks around the grove, and they tied an illusion spell to them. Any strangers approaching will only see the burned forest." By rallying together, the people of Drake's Bend had made a difference. They would need to be vigilant for some time to ensure the leftover residue from the smoke didn't end up in their food. Given time, both trees and people would heal. She still worried about the kegs she had seen in the courtyard at Sibylcrest. "I wonder where the kegs of pulp went."

"Down a hole." George huffed a quiet laugh.

Fern dropped her feet to the ground. "Really?"

Ambrose grinned. "Did you know that George and I make a rather dashing pair of highwaymen?"

Fern stared at the two men she loved most in the world. "Actually, yes, I can believe it. But what did you do?"

"One of our men saw the cart arrive. We rode out with a few others, diverted it, and dropped the kegs down an old mine shaft." George went back to studying the chessboard. He often played with a friend via letter and was considering his move before writing it down for his correspondent.

"Then we returned the empty cart to the driver and sent him on his way." Ambrose winked, and Fern suspected he enjoyed every minute of their adventure.

"Sir Luxton might come looking for them." Given the ingredients, the pulp was valuable. Even more so if it could be turned into enchanted paper to grant a writer's wishes.

"Not from us, he won't." George made a move and leaned back in his chair.

Fern turned to her uncle for a further explanation of why the baron wouldn't seek reparation from the village.

"Remember after the fire, we found that little tinder box? It had a crest on the bottom. We made sure that was carelessly left in the back of the cart." Ambrose mimed the object being tossed into the back with a cavalier throw.

"I wonder whose it was." Someone in London had sent the arsonist to silence the trees. Fern's best guess was that it was the peer trying to hide their treacherous activities from the king.

"Lord Perry." George wrote his chess move on a piece of paper and folded the sheet.

Fern laughed. That was too perfect. He was the noble who had advocated for the whisperwoods to be burned down.

With the crisis behind them, Fern could concentrate on other things. Like her work restoring the conservatory at Wyndham Hall. "Oh, blast," she muttered.

Ambrose arched an enquiring eyebrow.

"There's something I need to do," Fern muttered. "But it can wait."

When Fern climbed into bed that night, she held tight to a sense of satisfaction at what they had achieved. As she waited for sleep, she let her mind recall every detail of the marvellous moments when she had touched the ancient spirit that was the whisperwoods.

As it transpired, Millie was right about a number of things. When her article about the wanton destruction of the whisperwoods was printed in the daily newspapers, Londoners wept for their loss. Lord Perry was soundly castigated for encouraging the arsonist and cut off from all good society. A group of ladies raised funds to commission a brass plaque to commemorate the ancient grove. Which they intended to place at the base of a tree in Hyde Park—a safe distance from any vengeful spirit that the fire might have released.

A few days later, William approached Fern in the walled garden, where she oiled Eurydice in the warmth of the sun.

"Could you spare me a moment, Miss Oakby?" He knelt down and scratched the dragon's head.

"Of course. It's not Daniel, is it? I thought everyone was better?" A tendril of worry curled around her.

"Oh, no. He is fine and helping Da today. There's something growing in the compost heap, and I don't recognise it." He pointed off behind the stables, where the manure and hay were turned into rich compost for the garden.

"I am finished here. Let's have a look at what has sprouted." Usually, mushrooms grew in the mix. Or grain that made it through the horse's gut undigested. Sometimes, it was seeds dropped by birds.

They had four composting areas that were used in rotation. William led her to the one second from the end, where bright-green tendrils poked through the heated soil.

"What are you?" Fern murmured as she leaned closer. Certainly no sprouting fungi. Nor was it wheat or barley with its distinctive arrow-straight appearance. This was no grass or grain but a different sort of plant with a tiny, serrated leaf unfurling on the largest seedling.

With her trowel, Fern brushed aside the decomposing hay to reveal more. Some of the dung still kept its form, and the rounded balls differed from the larger deposits from the horses. Whatever grew did so from Eurydice's manure. What had the dragon eaten with such a distinctive leaf…?

"Oh! These are kelmsgale seedlings." Fern's brain burst with excitement, and her eyes burned with tears. "It's the seeds she ate. Oh, Father, they had to pass through a dragon's digestive system to germinate." Goosebumps erupted along her arms, and, at long last, one mystery was solved. "This is marvellous, William. There are enough seedlings here to replant the grove on the village green."

She needed to tell her father. She also needed to apologise to Lord Drakeman and thank him for his part in the potion that healed the sick villagers. By busying herself with other tasks, she had managed to avoid that visit for a few days.

"Let's leave them to grow a little bigger, then I will pot them up," she told William and thanked him for alerting her to the marvellous discovery. Then she decided to go for a walk. Which would give her time to rehearse what to say to Lord Drakeman.

The stroll through the village in the sun helped soothe nerves that had erupted inside her. By the time she rapped on the door at the Hall, she had decided on a forthright approach. Apologise, thank him, and get back to her work in the conservatory. That would keep everything on a friendly footing, and they could forget their yelling match under the moon.

Quint opened the door, crossed his arms, and glared at her.

"I do not have time for you today. Where is he?" Given the generous size of the doorway, she had an opportunity to dart in and around him if required.

"His study," the butler huffed out. Then he walked away, leaving Fern to shut the door.

She remembered how to find the smaller and more intimate study. The door was open a sliver, and peering inside first, she found Lord Drakeman at the desk, his concentration on a letter before him. Fern gave a gentle tap.

"Enter," he called without looking up.

Pushing the door aside, she walked in and stopped a few feet before the desk. Placing her hands behind her back to stop herself from fidgeting with them, she felt like a soldier reporting to a superior officer for a dressing down.

"Lord Drakeman, I wanted to apologise for my outburst the other night. And also to thank you for the formula you sent. When combined with the brew the Moray sisters concocted, all the sick villagers have been healed." There. She had said her piece, and now she could escape.

He stared at her, his eerie silver eye peeling open her soul.

"Well. Thank you for your time," Fern said when he remained silent, and she turned to leave.

"After some consideration, I believe I also owe you an apology, Miss Oakby." His softly spoken admission stopped her in her tracks.

Fern turned to regard him but remained silent, not

wanting to miss his apology. She suspected he didn't make them very often.

"You were correct. In the pursuit of my studies, I have ignored the world beyond Wyndham's gate and neglected my obligations to Drake's Bend. It is a situation I intend to remedy." He rose from behind the desk. "I would show you something, if I may." Gesturing to the door, he walked across the rug.

Fern paused, wondering what it could be. There were a number of possible things he might want to show her. The door. Her severance letter. His dungeon.

"Contrary to what you accused me of, I did not use the dragon skeleton to make my bread. I wanted to determine how it died and if its blood was indeed used in Luxton's concoction." He crooked a finger for her to join him.

She hesitated for a mere second before curiosity won out, and she followed his broad form. Lord Drakeman turned left and headed along the corridor away from the main entrance. Not too far along, he stopped and reached out to the panelling. His nails slipped under the edge, and he pulled to reveal a dark opening behind.

He held the door wide for her. "After you."

Fern glanced at the shadows. With the only light being that from the hall, there was little to see except a narrow stairwell. He was definitely showing her the dungeon. Light flared behind her as he lit a lantern.

George and Ambrose will mount a rescue if I'm not home for dinner, she reassured herself, and then she began the descent.

The tread was narrow and steep, requiring her to carefully place her foot sideways on each small stair. Fern kept one hand on the wall for balance. They twisted to the right and wound deeper into the earth. She counted to sixty in her head before the stairs opened out into a larger space. Or at least it felt larger. The temperature dropped, and her unsteady breaths echoed.

Lord Drakeman moved around her, lighting wall sconces until more of the room was revealed. The glint of metal bars came from one side.

I knew it was the dungeon. The apology was bait in his trap. Would he shove her into a cell and lock the door?

Her eyes adjusted as the light grew steadier from the many lanterns. Fern let out a gasp when she turned a slow circle. She stood in some sort of laboratory combined with a mausoleum. Two mounted dragon skeletons stood before the wall opposite the cells. Their wings folded against their sides, the dragons much bigger and older than Eurydice. She walked towards them, one hand extended. They were taller than a horse but still not fully grown.

Against the end wall sat an enormous skull with jaws large enough that Fern could have curled up inside them. That had to have come from an adult dragon. More bones were laid out on shelves in some sort of order, given various piles all appeared to be of similar size and shape. Behind the skeletons was a painting that extended the entire length of the wall. A dragon was stripped of its skin and bones, and tendons were named in a curly script with more notes in a tiny font she couldn't read.

Only then did she turn to the table in the middle of the room, where another dragon skeleton was laid out.

"Oh," she breathed out the syllable as she approached. Scanning the creature, it appeared to be intact. So he truly hadn't ground it to dust to use in his experiments. Or baking. Instead, he had added it to the gruesome collection in his dragon ossuary.

The creature was arrayed like the drawing on the wall. Its wings were spread to show every delicate bone. The tail hung in a curl below its pelvis. Fern's heart ached for the life not lived.

"I believe this specimen had been starving to death. Like the other one you found," Lord Drakeman said.

"How can you tell?" Fern's hand hovered over the skull, and she imagined petting Eurydice.

"I have been studying the decline in dragon numbers for the last few years. There is evidence in the bones of their affliction. Starvation affects their growth and development, but I can also tell by the lack of bone mineral density. I took a small sample from a rib to examine more closely." He stood at the end of the table but appeared to be watching her and not the bones.

He had been studying the decline in dragon numbers?

She thought he didn't care for the creatures at all. Her world tilted, and Fern rested a hand against the cool marble top of the table to steady herself. "Is that how this poor thing died?" What a horrible, slow way to perish.

"No. But I believe it would have starved before too long. As to what ended its life...I found a notch on a vertebrae." He mimed drawing a hand across his neck.

Fern swallowed, and the lump stuck in her throat. "That was how they got the blood."

He grunted in agreement. "There was a circular depression in the soil under the creature's head. I suspect someone placed a bucket there."

"They killed you and chopped down the kelmsgale. All for enchanted paper." She rested one hand on the skull and hoped the soul of the dragonet was at peace.

"Enchanted paper? Who told you that?" His silver eye took on a bright, metallic shine in the low light.

"Mrs Carlisle suggested it, given how the smoke affected the whisperwoods and the villagers. Words were twisted, or voices silenced. The Moray sisters said *words have power* when I asked them about it. Do you think it is possible the mixture is magic paper?"

He rubbed one hand against his chin, and Fern found herself staring at his jawline. "Anything is possible. But given my analysis of the pulp, I don't believe that is what Luxton is brewing. I think we uncovered one part of the process, not the final result. I made enquiries, and Luxton has no interest in either the manufacturing or sale of paper. But he has recently invested in a mill used to spin cotton."

Yet again, he surprised her that he cared enough to find out. "Well, thank you for telling me. I hope that recent events have not affected my working here."

"Your presence has been missed," the words whispered from him as though he had meant to say them to himself, not aloud.

Fern swallowed, unsure for once what to say. He had facets to him that she had not expected to find. Originally, she thought him cold and uncaring. Yet he had been quietly working to discover what caused dragons to die young, and had helped heal the villagers.

As she stared in fascination at his dragon eye, she found that, like him, it wasn't what it first appeared. Up close, there were slivers of different shades within its depths. Inky blue and royal purple were speckled on either side of the elongated pupil that reflected the lamp light.

"What do you see?" she asked as she reached out a hand. She had to know what the scales felt like. Her fingertips grazed the side of his face. Warm.

"You," he rasped.

"You don't have to tell me." With her thumb, she traced the edge of a scale by his ear.

He held her gaze. "I see you. The true you. The face most people hide from the world and even themselves. I see the lies people tell. The deceptions, betrayals, and petty jealousies they hoard. I see the bone-weary tiredness, loneliness, and sadness that we all keep inside."

"The true me? What does she look like?" What did she hide deep inside? Not terribly much. Grief at those she had lost. The pangs of emptiness were eased by Millie, Squib, and Eurydice.

"Remarkably close to what you see in the mirror. It appears you have no qualms in letting the world know what you feel." Humour glinted in his eyes.

"What of others?" The cool dimness of the dungeon wrapped them in intimacy, and she dared to ask the questions that had flared inside her since the day they first met.

"It is as though they wear a mask. On some, it fits better over their features than on others. When I went to London..."

He drew a ragged breath. "I saw the rotten core of those called beauties. As you surmised, I was not rejected. I rejected them. There was no face among them that I could tolerate to look upon." He gestured to the dragon eye. "What I saw with this, turned all their words to lies."

Now she understood something else. "That's why I'm tolerable. Quint is the same, I suspect. Surly on the outside and inside."

His full lips pulled into an uneven smile. "Yes."

She tried to imagine what it would be like. To see a person's soul and their true self exposed. To know everything, but have to pretend not to know. It would be exhausting. "You must have hated the House of Lords."

He huffed a quiet laugh in keeping with the sombre setting. "It was like being seated at a table of the dead, watched over by Death himself. Most of them are like carrion to me."

"Is this how Riddy sees the world?" she wondered.

He leaned closer. "Yes. Which is why the dragon has given you her loyalty. It is more than you saving her from being trapped under the fountain. She has bonded with your true self. Your soul."

The solemn atmosphere wove them closer. With her hand still on the side of his face, Fern closed the small gap between them.

And kissed him.

ABOUT THE AUTHOR

Tilly drinks entirely too much coffee and is obsessed with hats. In her spare time she writes whimsical historical fantasy novels, set in a bygone time where magic is real. If you love found family and comfort reads, come and escape reality in her tales.

Email: tilly@tillywallace.com
Web: https://www.tillywallace.com
STORE: https://www.tillywallacebooks.com

If you would like to support Tilly for as little as a coffee a month, her *Caffeination Crew* read early chapters of her current work, vote on story ideas, and read exclusive short stories and novellas. You can find more information at: https://www.patreon.com/TillyWallace

 patreon.com/TillyWallace

 facebook.com/tillywallaceauthor

 instagram.com/tillywallaceauthor

www.ingramcontent.com/pod-product-compliance
Lightning Source LLC
Chambersburg PA
CBHW030938120726
47906CB00002B/625